GATES' BOOKSTORE

JAMILA A. STONE

BLACK GLORY
PUBLISHING HOUSE

Gates' Bookstore

Published by Black Glory Publishing House

Washington, DC

Cover designed by Chandima Madura

Editor: Dimitra Manda

Black Glory Publishing House

www.blackglorypublishinghouse.com

Printed in the United States of America

ISBN: 978-1-7339717-7-5

Library of Congress Control Number: 2020916272

CONTENTS

Chapter One

The constant blaring noise from the nightstand echoed around the room, disrupting her slumber. The alarm had gone off some minutes ago and she managed to hit the snooze button fairly quickly, granting her the opportunity to sleep some more, but once again, it sprang to life, making her turn on her other side in the hopes that it would somehow stop, and nothing but silence would greet her ears.

That incessant ringing alerted her to the unquestionable fact that it was morning. The day was already weighing on her, considering she'd slipped into bed a few minutes past four in the morning. She'd spent the better part of yesterday at the police station, as a consultant in an investigation related to an old case, she'd helped close three years earlier.

Once more, she'd offered her assistance and helped identify a copycat rather than a serial killer. Unfortunately, despite the happy ending, the paperwork and reports that ensued took her until four in the morning to finish. She thought that she had left that career behind, but never managed to shake off her need to bring down the bad guy.

"For God's sake," she seethed when her ringtone blared, accompanying the alarm.

Now wide awake, but still refusing to open her eyes, she blindly reached on her right and hammered her hand down on the alarm clock, successfully putting it out of its misery, even though she still had her cellphone to deal with.

"You can ignore it," she reasoned. "Whoever is calling can wait until you wake up properly."

It might not have been in her nature to leave things unattended, but her body protested with tiredness. Her eyelids refused to open even when she tried to force them apart. Her bed felt like a warm and relaxing sea, ready to cover her in its embrace and give her abode and shelter. She stretched her slender frame, spreading her long legs to the sides of the queen size mattress and sighs. She would have caught at least one more hour of sleep if it wasn't for the persistent caller.

Like a wife set in her ways and delivering her husband an earful, her cellphone rang once again, granting her a total of only two additional minutes of rest. She frowned as she blindly attempted to reach her cellphone and cringed when all she managed was to knock the alarm clock to the ground.

"Hello?" she demanded as she held the phone to her ear, her voice still gruff from a heavy sleep.

She rolled on her belly and felt ready to drift into a lulling slumber as she waited for the caller to speak.

"Am I speaking to Miss Gates?" an elderly male voice inquired.

Short and formal. Obviously, someone she wasn't acquainted with or hadn't met in quite some time. Something about his voice prompted her to sit up, still without opening her eyes, and rest her back against the headboard.

"Yes." she responded softly. "Good morning, who am I speaking with?"

The caller on the other end of the line cleared his throat, and after a long pause, he finally responded. "I don't think you know me. I'm Ted Willow and live next to the house enlisted to this phone number. I might have some information of importance."

Something about the way he chose his words struck a nerve in her and she slowly forced her eyelids open. The first ray of light hit her directly into the eyes, and she flinched from the sudden onslaught onto her senses. Having chosen to slip under her sheet naked, the morning sun slowly warmed her lightly tanned skin. Absently she glanced in a far corner where she saw last night's clothes exactly where she'd kicked and tossed them.

"I am all ears."

"Last night, my wife heard some weird noises as if someone was breaking into the property, and we don't think Coleen and the kids are around," the man who had introduced himself as Ted explained. "I didn't want her to call the police for nothing as I didn't see any movement or heard anything myself. Could you come and check it out to be sure their things are safe?"

She bobbed her head gently before resting it into her hand, closing her eyes once again.

"Thanks for letting me know, Ted," she graciously replied. "I will make the appropriate inquiries and I'll check things out for myself."

Ted thanked her and, after a loud cough, ended the call. She held the cellphone tightly and signed into her phone's cloud in search of the property information file, all the while wishing that her renters would have a perfectly logical explanation for everything, sparing her from having to visit the home. When she found the phone number on the file, she immediately dialed Coleen's cell phone. The line rang and rang before the mechanic voice of an operator informed her that the phone number she'd dialed was no longer in service.

Sighing softly, wondering what would happen if she didn't investigate the possible break-in Ted had reported, she scrawled back into a sleeping position while her heart began to race. For some time, she tossed and turned in the hopes of dispelling the need to go over to the property, but with every passing second, it only felt harder to do.

How long has it been now? She wondered, thinking of her childhood home that was left to her in her father's will. The same house she rented out to Coleen not willing to sell it, but also unwilling to live within its walls.

It was ages, no doubt, and she had lost count.

"Oh, screw it,' she mumbled and slid out of bed.

As she stretched, she was assaulted by the cold morning breeze. Looking over her shoulder, she realized that she'd cracked her bedroom window open last night, and a cloud blocked the warm sun. Promptly she walked to the window and made quick work with locking it shut.

Gliding graciously across the floor, she headed for the bathroom for a much-needed shower. As she passed in front of the full-length mirror, she stopped just before her reflection disappeared from the glass and smiled as she checked out her tall perfectly streamlined shape.

"Still got it," she mumbled proudly as a faint smile graced her lips.

Still tired from last night's events, and somewhat unsure as to why she had to head to the property, especially since she could easily call the police and ask them to handle it, she hurried and with an exhausted sigh, she slammed the bathroom door behind her.

The roaring sound from her black luxury car came to a halt as she turned off the engine and rested her head on the headrest with her eyes staring blankly at the property she was about to examine. Oddly enough, the entire street was eerily silent, resembling a ghost town, and she had a hard time comparing it with how it was when she lived there.

Back then there were kids running around the streets, and families gossiping with their neighbors. In a way, the neighborhood resembled a family and quite often they would all go out camping and have weekend barbeques. Thoughts of the past slowly crept into her mind, bringing a smile in the corners of her lips, the same time her eyes widened with the realization of how much she had left behind and grown apart from. The once lively neighborhood was no more.

She took a deep breath, as her hands clenched nervously into fists. "It's just a routine check. You'll be out of there in no time."

Her childhood home brought too many memories.

She stabbed the engine on/off button turning off the ignition and stepped out of the car. A storm door creaked open in the distance, almost as though an alarm had been set off the moment she stepped out of her car and onto the ghost street.

Soon enough, another followed, and before she had taken a step further, she could count at least four houses with their storm doors partly open and people peering out to see who had driven into their cul-de-sac.

She smiled to herself, as she reached into her purse for her sunglasses. "Just like old times," she muttered and absently shook her head.

Certain of the fact she was the object of intense gawking from those inside the houses flanking her on both sides, she graced the walkway leading to her rental property like a glamour queen would take on the runway. Whispers sounded from the house on her left and two more people hurried to its window to take a peek at the woman they had not seen in years.

"It *is* her!" She heard someone whisper-yelling. "It *is* Diane Gates!"

Those words brought a forced smile to her lips, as her footsteps slowly oozed enough grace and poise to make her the subject of constant reminisce even after she had gone. She refused to let anyone see her weak. Growing up she was always successful, a leader, glamorous, and a bit of a troublemaker. No doubt many of those people would still have lasting memories of her. Her dark figure-hugging dress, the red lipstick, and the certainty in her gait gave the impression that confidence oozed from every pore of her body when in truth, she was worried those who knew her would swarm her with idle chat about things that should be left in the past. Sickening pity and sympathy about her father's murder.

Diane finally stopped a few feet from the rental property she owned and looked to her right where a white three-story stood, just as she remembered it from her childhood days.

"Here goes nothing," she muttered as she headed for the neighbors' house and climbed the porch steps, standing before the windowpane.

Diane's knuckles banged on the door three times. She heard the locks turning and took a step back as the rusty old door opened, revealing an old man.

"Ted?" Diane asked with a smile on her face.

The elderly man, with his disheveled gray hair and a few missing teeth, nodded gently while he held the door for support, and he continued to stare at Diane, his expressionless face giving away nothing.

"I am Diane Gates," she tended her hand to him. "You called me earlier about my rental property next door and a possible break-in?"

Ted finally smiled and shook Diane's hand, stepping out of the house in his white shirt and shorts.

"Yes! Yes," he replied, pointing at the property next door. "My wife, Abel, has been listening to some ruckus going on in the house for some days now, and we know that the people living in there are out of town."

Diane glanced at the house and wished that she didn't have to go inside her house, hoping that meeting with the neighbors could somehow solve the problem or assuage their worries.

"Did you see anyone park anywhere near it or even step out of the house at any point recently?"

Ted shook his head. "I don't hear much these days, but Abel was pretty certain she heard something in one of the rooms."

Diane nodded, and after shaking Ted's hand once again, she hurried down the stairs to get to her childhood home. She had almost gotten to the final step when she heard Ted coughing, no doubt to get her attention.

"I am so sorry about your father," he spoke in a rather emotional tone. "We all loved your family and I still don't know how such a tragedy could have struck our neighborhood."

Donning a brave face, less than willing to let herself drawn in whatever streams of past events Ted had recalled, Diane smiled at him. "It's in the past now, Ted, but thanks again for everything."

He waved at her and turned around to return to his house. Diane felt oddly relieved as she walked away from Ted's house, but not before overhearing what appeared to be a ruckus, coming from the old man's house.

"I wasn't checking her out, Abel!" Ted yelled as loud as his croaky old voice could permit him.

"The hell you weren't," an equally elderly female voice yelled back. "You'd need a million pills and God to make you less wrinkly and handsome to land a lady like her!"

Diane held herself from laughing.

"I could have gotten her back in my days," Ted assured his wife. "I landed *you*, didn't I?"

Diane heard Abel laugh hard. "You'd better not turn around again to look at her ass, you wrinkled old pervert!"

Diane shook her head, smiling wildly as she climbed up the porch of her childhood home. The world suddenly felt different and the air around her grew colder. She bit her lower lip as she tugged at the door handle to examine for any obvious signs of a break-in. The door did not open which meant that the lock wasn't forced.

"They didn't come through here," she muttered, immediately leaving the front porch.

Diane took a moment to circle the house and every possible point of entry. The dynamics of how criminals worked weren't foreign to her and in fact, being able to think like them or even predict their moves was almost as easy as breathing.

"For a house this centered, and with such an easy view from the other houses, they couldn't possibly enter this way without being seen," she mused.

Walking along the side, she closely examined the fence to ascertain if there was any damage to the demarcations, but nothing seemed out of place. The backdoor had not been disturbed and all the kitchen and bedroom windows were closed, with no signs of people having recently crawled through them or having even tried to tamper with them.

Diane wondered if the elderly folks next door had been hearing things. In their age, they might have heard noises from another home or an animal. As she returned to the front door, she took a good look around to make sure she wasn't being watched. Thankfully, those peering through their windows had lost interest at the sight of *The* Diane Gates and returned to their activities, leaving her alone to carry out her business.

Diane crouched gently and took a good look at the lock. With a smile she took out a pin from her hair, and bent it into shape, glancing around her once more. "Let's see if I still have it."

She twisted the contorted pin, clicking the sweet spot inside the old lock, and feeling the door obey her command within seconds, as it slowly creaked open and grated her entrance into the living room. She cautiously took note of her surroundings before walking into the house.

The entrance into the room was laden with a bunch of mail. She leaned down noticing that the mail didn't look disturbed, and one of the envelopes appeared to be a check of some sort, further proof that nobody had entered unless they arrived and didn't care about going through the mail which was not normal. A thief would have noticed the check just as Diane had. More so, thick barbs of cobwebs lined the right corner of the door and looked undisturbed as Diane began to seriously doubt whether there had been an actual break-in.

Diane gently closed the door behind her, and an overwhelming feeling of nausea threatened to consume her, as it swirled from the pit of her stomach the moment, she caught sight of the living room. The painting on the wall was no different from the one in there twenty years ago when she last lived in the house.

The room felt somewhat smaller, too, and the new occupants had filled the place with items Diane struggled to connect with. She tore her gaze away from the items for a moment, and observed the windows from the inside, hoping all the locks were secured.

She turned and headed for the large-sized kitchen where a marble center table was situated, and felt her heart begin to rump and thump just upon getting to the entryway. The kitchen felt cold and the air felt even colder as she struggled to breathe. Her eyes swept its gaze across the room, falling oddly on a crack in the kitchen cabinet where her father had once had to come rushing to pick her up from after a nasty fall that meant she needed stitches on her forehead.

"You were always there to lift me up," she thought to herself.

She could feel his essence traipsing around the room and making sure she had everything she needed before heading off for school in the morning. The euphoric aroma from his famous blueberry pancakes teased her nostrils as she struggled to keep her knees from feeling wobbly, and her heart from tearing through her chest as it began to hammer louder and harder into her ribcage.

"*Diane*!" She still could hear his voice in her mind, and –like always—she parted her lips to reply but halted.

Diane closed her eyes and turned around. She felt torn between wanting back the lost time and being able to live with the fact that she could never have what she wished for. The years with her father were the best of her life, but being in the house, staring at the kitchen, and reminiscing brought nothing but painful stings.

Diane hurried back out with a loud exhale. She raced down the porch and marched to her car, panting, and hyperventilating as she struggled to breathe.

Breathe Diane! Breathe, the voice in her head encouraged her as she approached her car.

Ted had just walked out of his house and was waving at her, but she ignored him, and good thing, too, especially since a few moments later his wife stormed out of the house, no doubt to give him a piece of her mind for ogling at the young woman's figure. Diane felt the floor beneath her feet move and urged herself to keep it a bit longer until she got into her car and closed the door.

Leaning her head into the steering wheel, she tried to regulate her breathing.

"It was a mistake coming here," she admitted before starting her car and speeding away as fast as she could.

Chapter Two

Some minutes past nine in the morning, Diane walked into her favorite coffee shop. She was immediately greeted by the smell of freshly brewed coffee, doughnuts, and her favorite of all, relaxation. With a small smile on her face, Diane headed for her usual seat in the corner of the room, overlooking the road and her bookstore.

She slipped into her seat and opened her newspaper. The front page reported some violent incidents in New York and how things had been spiraling out of control for the past few months. Something about the news brought a tinge of excitement, but before it grew any higher, she gently laid the newspaper to rest on the table and looked up at the slender-framed waitress, approaching her table.

Diane smiled and placed her right hand on the table happy to see her friend after so many days, being busy with the police investigation. “Good morning, Catherine.”

Catherine smiled as she always did, wearing her usual blend of blue striped uniform and tiredness. Bags had been formed under her eyes despite the cheap makeup she'd applied so generously.

Diane arched a brow. “Rough night?”

Catherine ran her fingers through her hair and said nothing before slamming three books onto the table. Diane looked at the Sydney Sheldon series she had read some time ago and glanced back up at her waitress.

"Okay, I don't understand how it is possible for someone with that low intelligence quota, failing school, to be so smart and elusive over the years as a serial killer," Catherine looked befuddled. "I know you understand."

Diane pressed her fingers to her temple and subtly smiled. Her knowledge about killers was, without a doubt, exceptional, but having learned from previous encounters with Catherine, one book would lead to another, and discussions would go on longer than her coffee time. And that would not include the time Catherine would talk about her poetry and other aspects of her writings which Diane wasn't sure she would be willing to entertain for the morning. After visiting her childhood home all Diane wanted was a quiet day and a cup of coffee if the young waitress ever got it for her.

"How about we discuss those books when I come for lunch? I wouldn't want you to get in trouble for talking to me while at work." Diane suggested.

Catherine suddenly looked gloom, reaching for the underside of her left wrist to run her fingers to a spot Diane had noticed since she began frequenting the coffee store.

She looked back up at Catherine slowly and muttered. "I'll trade you my time, for the knowledge on what caused you that scar on your wrist which you subconsciously keep feeling as if you cannot rid your mind off it."

Catherine immediately dropped down her sleeve to cover the scar, before letting off a wild grin intended to distract Diane from thinking much of it.

"I've told you before, it's just an old wound. Completely superficial," she replied as her grin widened.

Diane laced her fingers together and sat up in her chair with her piercing gaze cast over Catherine as the waitress looked nervously at her feet.

"The scar obviously holds some mental bond over you, which I believe you still haven't gotten over yet," Diane continued. "The rise of the scar tells me the wound was very deep and at the time it needed stitches, but you didn't have any, leaving you with a partially healed wound. Also, you didn't treat it properly afterward at it got infected since the skin around the scar is discolored and wrinkled. That's a bit unusual for a woman of your age."

Diane noticed the skittish look on her friend and knew that once again she had gone too far. She cleared her throat in an attempt to salvage the situation. "Sorry, I'm psychoanalyzing you. A bad habit I need to break. Just know I'm here for you if you ever want to talk."

Catherine immediately turned around and walked away without a single word. Diane rested back into her seat. She had finally attained the peace she craved and at the same time ensured that Catherine wouldn't bother her with Greek myths or ancient facts she wasn't interested in.

She watched the young girl waddling her way through the store, serving orders, and collecting cheques, before bringing her coffee along with a hot doughnut with jam.

"Just as you like it, Diane," Catherine mumbled while she laid down the cup and plate.

Without another word, the young girl turned around no doubt to avoid engaging Diane in another conversation.

"Catherine!" Diane leaned back into her seat and called out to the girl while she still was within earshot.

Catherine halted in her steps without turning around. "Yes?"

Diane took a bite from her doughnut and sipped some bit from her hot coffee, waiting for her to turn around.

"What time do you get off?"

Catherine shrugged as she faced Diane. "I was hoping to work overtime today just to spend some more time outside, if you know what I mean and maybe earn some extra cash too."

Diane had no idea what she was talking about but recognized a workaholic when she saw one. No doubt Catherine intended to spend another full day at work as she had done so many times. Diane could see that the girl pushed herself too hard. It was evident from her rumpled hair, the same socks she had donned for the past two days, as well as the same shoes on her feet. To top it all off, there was the coffee stain at the helm of her right sock from when a clumsy fellow had spilled his drink on her shoe just the day before.

"Don't ask for an extra shift, and make sure to meet me at eight tonight at Baldwin's when your shift ends," Diane instructed in a rather authoritative tone.

Catherine took a few seconds to respond but eventually nodded and turned around to leave. Diane peeled her gaze off her friend, wondering what sort of secrets she was hiding and why she was so vested in reading books and writing poems. She pulled the three books on the table toward her and flipped open the first page to see a note with some poems scribbled into it.

"Dark as always," Diane muttered.

Taking another bite from her doughnut and sipping her coffee, Diane allowed the radical taste from the black and sugarless brew to smack her taste buds, as she topped it off with some nice poetry about the futile search of hope and love. She couldn't help but admire the artistic handwriting and the buoyant words that Catherine had written.

Diane had gone in two events where Catherine read her poems. Literature was what brought them together. At first, Diane didn't want to be bothered by the waitress forcing her company during Diane's breaks. Diane had even gone as far as complain to the shop owner, Alan, once, but that didn't stop Catherine from drawing Diane into a conversation at the coffee shop or while visiting Diane's bookstore.

Little by little, Diane came to look forward to their conversations, and even though she tried to keep things at arm's length, Catherine was like the young irritating sister she never had and it was a pleasure to have someone to talk about literature with.

"8:30 p.m.," Diane murmured before downing a shot of tequila.

She stood from her seat at the bar and made a move to leave when she felt a hand wrapping tightly around her wrist.

"Hello beautiful," a slurred voice greeted her before the stench of liquor hit her face as the figure came to sight.

Diane struggled to get his hand off without using force since the last thing she needed was spending a night in a jail cell for a bar fight. The man's grip tightened even more.

"You need to get your filthy hand off of me," she warned without losing her composure.

Round, pot-bellied, and unable to maintain a stable stance, the drunk man, didn't let go of her wrist as she'd asked him to. Instead, he stood before her with his lips curled into a pout.

"I can give you everything and anything you want for the night." His disgusting words were accompanied by an equally disgusting belch.

Some men in the bar cheered and laughed loudly, but all Diane hoped for was for him to let her go so she could head home and indulge in her favorite documentaries that would be on in a few hours.

"I'm Stanley, but you can call me Stan," the man stepped closer and brought his mouth along with his bad breath to her.

Diane ducked, lowering her center of gravity, before slamming her free hand into the left side of his neck, sending him staggering back.

"You bitch," he yelled, holding his neck where she had chopped him hard with her strong hand.

Diane ignored his words and picked up her purse from the bar, turning around to leave as others made fun of the man. He growled and grumbled as she walked out of the room and continued to curse in words that Diane willfully ignored for the sake of getting home as soon as possible.

Diane's heels clanked on the sidewalk. It was time for her to simply go home. Nothing had gone right that evening and Catherine hadn't called so Diane doubted she'd show up. Scowling, Diane made her way to the streets' edge, feeling her body tense from head to toe.

"Diane!" she heard a voice call out from behind her, but she pretended she didn't hear a sound.

She began to walk faster and with each step clenched her hands into fists so tight her knuckles turned white. Diane was seeing nothing but red, and anyone, or anything, to get in her way would likely meet the business end of her fist. The voice called out again and was quickly followed by a swift and light tap on her left shoulder.

Diane flung herself around in a rage to meet her new assailant face to face. It was Catherine with a bright smile and a waft of cannabis. Despite her inebriation, Catherine was dressed beautifully in a tube top boho dress, ankle boots, and her hair freely down around her shoulders. Diane stopped mid-swing, barely stopping herself from clobbering her friend's face.

"Whoa! Easy there. Rough night?" Catherine asked as she took a slight step back from Diane's range of motion.

"You have no idea."

Diane turned on her heel once more and continued her stampede down the sidewalk. She could hear the almost immediate retort of Catherine's boots like an echo of her own footsteps.

"Night's just begun. What happened?" Diane's jaw clenched as she let out an audible sigh not answering Catherine. "Sorry, I'm late."

Heading for her car, Diane unlocked the door and tossed her purse into the passenger's seat before getting in.

"We said eight and now it's half-past! I had to deal with some prick who wouldn't take no for an answer."

Catherine held out her hands. "I swear to you, the coffee shop was swamped, and I was the only one on the floor."

Catherine shook her head fervently and waved her hands. "Alan needed me… I am sorry for being late. You know that's not usually the case—" It was evident that Catherine wanted to plead her case some more, but she stopped and smiled when she saw the look on Diane's face. "Ok, fine, sometimes I'm late, but by like five minutes tops. It's not like I was as late as *you* were when we went to the Renaissance fair. What was it, an hour?"

Diane nodded with a small smile, remembering that day. "True, but I'm serious. Look I got in a fistfight with some guy and I'm just frustrated and tired. I just don't think the night can be saved. It's fine. It's just better to go home. We can try again another time."

"Come on. I can let you go home...or you could trust me to turn the night around," Catherine said with a wink.

Her side smile coaxed Diane's lips to curl just enough for Catherine to know she was making progress. Diane rolled her eyes finally letting herself smile at her friend's pleading.

Diane started up the car. "Fine, we can still go out."

"So, you beat some guy up? Who would have known you were so scrappy?" Catherine joked, lifting Diane's right arm into the air for examination.

"Trust me. It wasn't my best moment. But maybe you're right the night *can* be salvaged."

Diane opened the glove compartment and took out some paper stacks. She held the papers out to Catherine and motioned for her to take them.

"What are these?" Catherine asked with an arched brow and proceeded to turn on the lights above her.

"Contract papers for you to sign, should you still intend to leave your job with Alan, and work for me at Gates' Bookstore."

Catherine swallowed hard and felt words failing her while Diane stared at her in anticipation.

"You can take your time coming to a decision," Diane offered even though she had expected her friend to eagerly accept the position. They had talked about it in passing when Catherine would volunteer at the bookstore during events. "I have read many of your poems and works and I believe working around the bookstore will enlighten you about things I might find tedious to explain, as well as give you the chance to find out what you want to do with your life."

Diane grew nervous that her approach was too sterile when in truth she had invited Catherine to the bar so they could celebrate the offer. Diane had opened her mouth to inform her of the pay—that by all estimation was better than her waitressing job— when Catherine finally got ready to answer.

"Yes," Catherine responded excitedly and the two of them squealed with excitement, hugging tightly to seal the deal. "Well, now we have to celebrate! It's a must." Catherine started to input an address in the car's GPS. "I know this great club."

Diane put the car into drive and turned to her. "You begin at 8 a.m. sharp. Try not to be late on your first day."

"Yeah, yeah, let's see who's going to be late tomorrow after I get you good and drunk." Catherine laughed.

"Oh, no you're not. We're not staying out too late either."

They peeled out of the parking space and sped down the road. It wasn't long before they arrived at the *Whiskey River* club. They were able to find a parking space just two blocks over and the two of them bounced through the front door almost as if dancing a jig. They each ordered their first drink and sat at a corner table.

Diane chose a strawberry daiquiri that the bartender— at Catherine's request—accompanied with two shots. Catherine took a somewhat harder approach to the night and started with a whiskey on the rocks. They both downed their shots before sipping their drinks, chatting animatedly about daily life, and after a few moments, found themselves using the two plastic swords from Diane's drink to fight.

After the first round, Diane made the rule that the loser of the swordfight had to buy the next round of drinks, and after three rounds, she abolished that rule. The room was flooded with flashing lights of rainbow colors and the loud thud of the music's base pounded in tandem with Diane's heart.

Without warning, Diane found herself running to the dance floor. She spun in circles, moving her arms and hips to the rhythm of the music. Her head rose and fell, and wisps of hair bounced along her jawline, as she danced with wild abandon. Diane looked across the room to her friend and signaled with a draw of her lanky fingers. With feline grace, she found herself slinking slightly towards Catherine with a devious smile.

Catherine downed the remainder of her drink and slammed the glass onto the bar top, but the music drowned the thud of glass to wood. Diane watched as Catherine stood from her stool and bumped her hips with each step toward the dance floor. Her hands were raised above her head, creating a shadow puppet of a bird on the floor.

Diane moved closer to her friend with a sway of her hips and when they were close enough to touch, they bumped hips with a joyful bout of energy. The two women moved and swayed as they allowed their bodies to simply express the feel of the music through motion.

Two songs later, the music came to a slow rhythm and the two of them realized they were exhausted but still giddy with excitement. Diane wiped the sweat off her brow and sat at the bar once more for a drink of water. Her smile was evident. Her heart pounded but she felt exhilarated. She wasn't sure where the night was leading but for the moment she didn't care. Diane laughed as Catherine flirted with the bartender, trying to convince him to dance with them. Diane was grateful for having Catherine as a friend, her personal life had been one of isolation. She tried to keep people at a distance, but Catherine wasn't going to allow that. Diane smiled once again picturing how great working together would be.

Two hours after Diane and Catherine had gone to the club, they found themselves at Diane's house. Catherine announced that her head was spinning so she'd go straight to shower and then to bed. While waiting for her turn in the shower, Diane popped open a bottle of scotch and poured herself a glass before turning on some slow music. Life felt good, albeit without the usual excitement she was used to. Aside from the fact that she had to punch a man in his throat earlier that night, she couldn't quite recall the last time she had to pick locks or even fight with anyone.

Owning Gates' Bookstore had put a damper on things, but it was what she chose, and she had no regrets over it. As she sipped her drink, she was interrupted by the shrilling sound of her home phone. Glancing at her wall clock she saw that it was well past ten, but stood, turned off the music in the background, and went to answer it.

She leaned closer to the ringing phone and touched the receiver, but she never picked it up as it went to voicemail. A sigh of relief escaped her, and she turned around to continue enjoying her moment of tranquility, but the voicemail machine beeped, indicating a message.

Torn between listening to it, or simply going on with her night, Diane opted for the former, and with a heavy gulp, she downed the containments in her glass. She punched the 'play' button on the receiver and took a step back to listen to the message.

"*Hello, Diane*!" She heard a familiar voice greeting her. She frowned almost sure of what the message was about and puzzled as to why the sender had left it in the first place.

"I'm only checking in for the umpteenth time to know if you're available for work because I have some cases piling up my ass here and you are—or were— the best I ever had, working on our team..." The voice paused

again, before clearing her throat to continue. *"We did a lot of great things with you on the field and active... you know where to find me if anything comes up and you change your mind."*

Diane cringed and gently sat on the chair closest to her.

"I am done with that life," she whispered if only to reassure herself.

She had finished dipping her toes back into that life and this time she meant it. She was done.

There was no turning back even if her ex-colleagues kept on badgering her. She shouldn't have helped with the recent copycat case. Diane knew from the start that this case would prompt her old job to rear its ugly head.

After her father's death, she no longer felt the same enjoyment in her career. She had been so traumatized and fixated in finding out what happened to him that Diane started to develop an unhealthy relationship with her job, distancing herself from family and friends. That life drained her, not to mention that it didn't give her a chance to live the life her father thought she deserved. No, she was done with her old job. Even if that meant that she would be bored most the days and never got around to having the kids her father wanted.

Diane understood she needed to make a change and thankfully with her many degrees she had her career options open. Admittedly, a bookstore wasn't even on her list until her last big case made her want to be completely out of any law or medical field. Another serial killer who had been apprehended thanks to Diane and her forensic team, but it was also because of her that five children chained in an underground tunnel died of poisoning. She never managed to decipher the clues on time. It wasn't until a day after police and the forensic team had combed the two-acre property where they'd caught the serial killer when she realized she'd missed something in an autopsy: his victims were kept underground.

Diane had quickly gone over the evidence found the previous day, knowing there were still missing children, and when she put the pieces together and jumped into her car and back to the site, she found a hidden door in the field and the dead bodies of the children. She tried her best to save them until the ambulances arrived, but it was too late.

Diane had failed and the images of those children joined her nightmares of her father. She needed to get away from that job and everything that reminded her of it.

Chapter Three

Diane glanced at her watch, noting the time as she had done so meticulously for the past two weeks, coming up with the same results: it was just a few minutes after 8, and Catherine had already opened her bookstore which was supposed to open an hour later.

Diane approached the front door with the OPEN sign greeting her warmly and stepped into her second favorite place in the world. She wasn't sure she could explain it, but the smell of books and the relaxing feeling it brought her was irreplaceable.

"Good morning, Miss Gates," Catherine greeted from behind the counter.

"We've talked about this, Catherine, you don't have to call me that. I might be your boss now, but we're still friends."

Diane smiled then looked at the well-stacked and cataloged rows and columns of books, before noting that the new arrivals had been properly put away as well. She walked over to the spreadsheet, recording the new deliveries and tracking the sales, and everything seemed in order.

"When did you finish all this?" Diane asked surprised, looking around her.

Catherine smiled and ran her right hand over her left nervously. "I learned from the best."

Diane waved off Catherine's humble words and motioned her to follow her to her office at the back, but she was momentarily distracted by the sight of the trash bin. As Diane approached, Catherine averted her gaze immediately and pretended to be busy with some work behind the counter.

"What is it?" Diane asked with an arched brow.

Catherine tentatively looked up. "What is what?"

Diane sighed, holding out her hand and gave Catherine a look that indicated she was in no mood for lies.

"It is just some stash I got from friends," Catherine replied. "I swear, I haven't touched it."

Diane shook her head and leaned closer to the girl, placing her purse on the counter.

"For starters, I know you've slept here, and judging by the full bin in the corner, I can tell you worked through the night. I imagine that if you'd gone home, you wouldn't have dragged it away from its usual spot by the door. I emptied the trash before I left last night so unless a burglar came in just to fill it with trash, someone else did. And the spreadsheet I just glanced at was saved at five in the morning."

Catherine seemed dumbfounded as she looked from the bin to Diane. The air in the room felt thinner and Catherine's face continued to pale with each passing second.

"Is there something at home you don't want to go back to?" Diane asked with her head lowered so she could meet Catherine's eyes.

She decided to deal with the weed in the bin later. "Is it family or a lover?"

Catherine burst out laughing. "It is none of the sorts. I don't sleep much, and I just find it soothing to work at night. Not to mention that having all these books around me means I get to read as much as I want."

Diane imagined that the young girl probably had done the same while working in the coffee shop across the street. Catherine rushed to her backpack in the corner and returned with a small bag of marijuana, passing it out to Diane.

"I promise it's the last batch and I'm not going to look for anymore."

Diane looked at Catherine's hand, momentarily perplexed by the odd marking on the package's wrapping, before taking the marijuana and tossing it into her bag.

"I am thirty, not ninety and I understand that you sometimes need to blow off steam. You know I don't judge you. Just make sure not to do it around flammable items such as books," Diane warned. "I'll keep the bag though. We can enjoy it the next time you come over."

Catherine nodded.

"And bear in mind that if you feel like spending the night in the store working instead of going home and your warm bed, you can always use the shower in my office bathroom," Diane added, before picking up her bag and heading for her office.

The front door chimed, welcoming a new customer and Diane stopped and looked back.

"Steve," she exclaimed, rushing out to the newcomer with a smile on her face and took his arm to guide him to a nearby stool.

Catherine stared at the blind man as Diane engaged him in a conversation. He was just an average guy with a mustache, long brown coat, and somewhat dirty boots.

"Back for your bi-weekly read for your daughter?" Diane asked with a grin.

"You bet I am. But tell me, what is this new perfume I pick up?" Steve sniffed and tilted his head to the side.

Diane smiled at Catherine. "Oh yes! You haven't met my new assistant!" She waved Catherine over. "Steve, I want you to meet Catherine. Catherine, this is Steve, one of our most loyal customers that comes every two weeks to purchase a book for his daughter."

As soon as the introductions were over, Diane left them to get to know each other, and went in search of Steve's next read.

"How old is your daughter?" Diane heard Catherine asking him.

Diane once again remarked on her new employee's apt communication skills, yet another reason why she'd decided to hire her, besides her vast knowledge of books and her sincere and intriguing fascination with them.

A few minutes later, Diane returned with a stack of books and laid them on the counter for Catherine to process them.

"When do I get to meet your little girl, Steve?" Diane asked.

"I should bring her around sometime soon," Steve replied, taking out his credit card to pay for the books Catherine had neatly packed for him.

Diane was about to speak but was interrupted by her ringing phone. She excused herself and hurried to her office, closing the door behind her to answer the call.

"What!?" she replied without any form of polite greeting.

"What do you mean 'what'?" the voice on the other end of the line asked. "Is that a new way of answering the phone?"

Diane ran her fingers through her hair and started pacing. "I'm telling you, Vivian, the phone calls, the messages and emails, they all have to stop," Diane stated. "I've put that life far behind me."

Diane waited for a response, but all she got was a low chuckle. Vivian might be her best friend, but the woman had been working on her sanity with her constant offers to return to her old profession.

"So, I've heard. Anyway, how about we meet tonight at our regular spot to discuss things further?" Vivian asked.

Diane was sure the badgering wasn't going to stop if her friend didn't read it in her eyes that she actually meant business. Perhaps a face-to-face wasn't a bad idea after all.

"I'm free tonight if that's what it takes for you to stop your nagging."

"Tonight, it is!" Vivian exclaimed. "See you soon, Sherlock." Vivian ended the call and Diane rolled her eyes, pocketing her phone.

Heading out of the office she found Catherine by the door, waving at the blind man as he got into a cab.

When Steve's ride was out of sight the girl turned around and gasped. "Jesus! You scared me," she said and brought her hand to her chest.

Diane shook her head at her overreaction. Eventually, Catherine returned to her post behind the counter while Diane noted some new poems her employee had worked on.

"These are good," Diane stated, as she went to pin them on the readers' board by the front door. "I like the touch of William Blake and some diddle of George Elliot to the notes."

Catherine blushed, but Diane had to elaborate.

"I had some thesis work done for my bachelor's degree in English Literature, and boy was I stumbling for a while before I truly began grasping the essence and methodology of his words," Diane explained as her mind drifted back to those days.

Catherine tucked the logbook away and smiled. "Steven is a pretty decent guy. He told me about how his daughter reads to him. I found it strange though that he kept asking about me."

"Sadly, being blind doesn't allow him many friends, so he enjoys chatting someone's ear off if they'll listen to him," Diane admitted, but knew Steven was a lovely person, perhaps inept to social norms and cues of when to stop talking.

Deep in thought, Diane headed for her office, but Catherine called out to her, disrupting her wandering mind. "Alan called in earlier to ask if the series on Swamp Monsters Mysteries he's ordered will arrive this week."

Closing her eyes, Diane let out a groan. She had forgotten all about his order even after she had promised him, they would come in that week.

"Tell him that he can pick them up next week," Diane replied, before disappearing into her office.

Diane walked over to her desk and collapsed into her chair, absently taking in her well-furnished and spacious office with a small kitchenette to her right. On the left wall was the smiling face of a prized jewel she never wanted or wished to forget every single day for as long as she lived.

With a sad smile and her hands cushioning her head, she swiveled in her chair. "I miss you dad, and I wish you were here."

She wondered what he would make of her decision to use a large chunk of her inheritance to buy a bookstore. The odds that he would love the idea were high, considering he embedded the zeal of reading into her. Growing up, he used to read novels of various genres to her and never hid the fact that he wasn't a great fan of her working as a criminal forensic scientist.

After a rather tiring day at the bookstore, Diane walked into the crowded bar and looked around her in search of Vivian. She smiled when she spotted her redhead friend taking a sip of her martini. It's been a while since she had a night out with her friend.

"Just like old times," Diane murmured as she walked forward, squeezing through the bodies in her path.

She put her hand on the petite lady's shoulder, but her friend took her by surprise at how quickly she sprang to her feet to hug Diane.

"I was beginning to doubt you would come," Vivian admitted hugging Diane tightly. When they settled, Vivian took another sip from her drink. "Sorry, I started without you, but I had a busy day."

Diane sat opposite her longtime friend and decided to tackle the issue at hand. "You cannot tempt me back into that life. Or even try to guilt me into how busy your day has been, trying to take down criminals without my great evidence and testimony. You will just have to find a better team, able to provide you the necessary evidence you need in court."

Vivian remained silent, eying a couple of guys who had just taken a table a few feet from them.

"At least I get to meet with you after hundreds of phone calls and endless messages," Vivian finally responded. "I have a case on my hands which I could use your help and expertise."

Diane rolled her eyes. "I should have known that you brought me here to work on some case." Spotting a bottle of wine on ice and an empty glass, Diane assumed it was for her, so she poured herself a glass of wine. "You need to buy me some amber liquor if you want me to agree to another case. I just helped on that copycat case a few weeks ago and got no sleep."

Vivian giggled as she reached for the bag by her side.

Diane got to her feet. "I cannot get into this, Vivian. You of all people should understand why I left and why I chose the life I am leading right now."

Vivian held her hand up and nodded. She knew the mental scars her best friend carried and felt like shit for pushing her. In all honesty, she thought that after the loss of her father and her rather gruesome last case, she just needed a break from all that violence and death not retiring in her prime. "I'm sorry, Diane. Please, sit down and I promise I'll refrain from mentioning anything work-related."

Diane glared at her friend, uncertain as to whether she should believe her.

"I promise," Vivian brought her hand to her heart.

"So, what are we doing tonight?"

Vivian looked around her and allowed herself to get engrossed in the sight of the handsome men drinking two tables away from them.

"I guess it is just like old times," Diane mumbled with a smile.

"Did you say something? Sorry, I was somewhat distracted."

Diane waved over the waiter and ordered two Rosemary Margaritas, before turning her attention to her friend.

"Since I see you're checking out a list of terrible morning choices for the night, is it safe to assume Adam is out of the picture?" Diane asked about Vivian's husband.

Vivian paused from mid-sip and frowned. "That son-of-a-bitch cheated on me with his fucking assistant! And don't think I didn't hear your order. You know what tequila does to me. I'll really start making bad decisions."

Diane grunted to stifle her laughter. "You were surprised that he cheated on you? I mean, the man had a thing with the freaking coroner while we were working on the Digital killer case."

Vivian's face got red no doubt angry at the memory. "What about you, my friend? I don't see any men waiting to rip your bed to shreds, not while you continue to raise that giant wall up and around you."

The waiter chose that time to bring Diane's order and set it on the table. Diane leaned closer to take a sip of her drink. Vivian's words stung. "You know me too well, honey. The brass and brawns aren't enough to hold me."

Diane decided not to take Vivian's words to heart. Her best friend was just upset, and Diane should have been more supportive instead of judgmental. She never liked her best friend's husband and they usually avoided the subject.

Vivian shook her head and laughed out loud, attracting the attention of the nearby tables. "I wouldn't want to be in your shoes," Vivian whispered.

"Why?"

Vivian stared intently at her friend, who knew exactly what she was talking about. "Get yourself a man to serve you some," Vivian purred. "Being a damn hermit in a freaking store filled with books can't get you laid." Vivian picked up the other Rosemary Margarita and drank from it.

Diane laughed hard and almost spilled her drink on her blouse as more guys glanced at their table. Two very beautiful ladies, drinking alone were bound to be a source of attraction for the night in the lounge.

Diane wondered what could have been, had it been two years back. "To a wonderful night," she toasted, holding her glass up.

The night was young, and despite the allure of a case file in Vivian's bag, Diane was sure that she wasn't ready for any of it for the time being. She would simply enjoy some drinks, enjoy the night, and maybe flirt with a boy or two before heading home.

Chapter Four

Struggling to get to her feet, Diane fell to the ground for the umpteenth time. The pools of blood under her feet continued to bring her down, threatening to break her back. Her eyes swelled with tears, and her hands trembled as she desperately tried to figure out what exactly was going on.

The oddity of the situation baffled her. The room was locked from the inside and had not been tampered with. She recalled falling asleep in his arms in a drunken stupor just the night before and he had promised to remain there until morning dawned on them both. He had failed to keep his promise. Even more disturbing was the presence of a copious amount of blood on the bed and the floor.

"Oh God!" she mumbled, still slumped against the floor unsure of where to go next.

The bedroom door suddenly felt distant, and the blood only continued to stretch into the distance with nothing else in sight. It felt impossible and utterly ridiculous to assume anything had occurred in that house and taken him away without her knowing. She blamed herself for sleeping too soundly, but even that didn't make any sense.

"Where did he go?" she had croaked, wondering, but no one offered some kind of an answer.

Shuddering in fright and utterly consumed with despair, she dragged herself along the floor and headed toward the telephone hanging on the south wall of the room. He had always told her where to call should anything terrible occur within the house. It was the first number she ever memorized as a child and she slowly stood up against the wall and punched the numbers.

"Hello," a feminine voice answered almost immediately. "This is the Metropolitan police department. What is your emergency?"

Diane took another look around the room. "Something… something happened!"

"Hello? What's happened?" the female on the other end of the line asked, just before Diane felt her feet slip once again, and her body hammer into the ground.

Her vision dulled and her breathing slowed as she closed her eyes wondering what had happened to her father…

The table clock blared, dragging a drowsy Diane back into consciousness as the book she had been reading slipped off her chest and fell to the ground.

It was the second night in a row she had dreamed of her father's murder and it was beginning to bother her. The events unfolded in the same fashion. She would dream of the meltdown she had all those years ago after the case she had helped with the bad guy's arrest. But in that instance, she had failed the children he used as sex slaves. They were buried and by the time she and her team had pieced all the evidence together, it was too late. Even now, Diane recalls how she'd dug with her bare hands and helped to bring out the dead bodies of children huddled together. It was too much for her and her father came over and held her, promising that he wouldn't leave her alone.

The dream always ended when her alarm clock decided it was time for her to get up. Sadly, her intention of having a sleep-in Sunday was ruined.

"Bloody clock," she mumbled in disgust but blamed herself for not turning it off the night before.

Diane dragged herself on the edge of the bed and stood up to go to the bathroom when something on the wall caught her eye. It was the telephone belonging to her mother who'd died in a car crash after sustaining a heart attack when Diane was a little girl. She couldn't bring herself to get rid of it as it was one of the little things of her mother, even though it made her cringe on the inside.

She dragged her feet and gently shoved the bathroom door open. Her spine felt stiff and the idea of a shower to help ease off her tiredness felt like a pretty good one. She'd barely made it into the shower when her cellphone rang. Diane turned around with a grunt and marched over to the nightstand.

Checking the Caller ID, she saw Catherine's name flashing on the screen. She never called on a Sunday. Odd, since they had no business on Sundays at the bookstore. Diane swiped right and brought the phone to her ear to take the call.

"Who in God's name would be calling on a Sunday?" she asked in a tired voice, trying not to be overly snarky. For a moment there was no answer, just heavy breathing. "Hello?" The breathing intensified and Diane began to worry about her new employee. "Calm down and speak to me, Catherine... what is going on?"

The girl continued to hyperventilate, each word out of her mouth a real struggle. "You need to get here... there's been a break-in at the store."

The loud screeching from the tires dragged the people's attention near the bookstore. Diane jumped out of her car and rushed toward the crowd. She'd spotted Catherine amidst the crowd of bodies in blue, and Diane felt relieved. Her friend looked distressed, but not injured. When Diane marched up the stairs of the entrance, she gasped at the sight of all the damage in her bookstore.

"Miss Gates," a police officer nodded at her.

Diane momentarily looked away from the officer, before replying. "Good morning, Jake. How is your partner Dennis?"

Officer Jake smiled and shrugged. "Same old... same old. I'm sorry about your store. Your assistant is giving a statement right now."

Catherine stepped away from the two officers and approached Diane, looking disheveled. "Someone broke in last night but didn't seem to take anything other than *my* stuff."

Diane remained silent while she took note of the entire scene. Most of the shelves were intact with the books neatly stacked. There was no way without extreme difficulty or assistance for the thief to have knocked down the massive bookcases. She rushed to the cash register and noticed that it had not been forced open or even tampered with. The front door had been pried open with what appeared to be a tire iron or something similar. The further Diane walked into the store, the less damage she noted. Most of the vandalism had occurred on the window displays in the front of the store and some of the smaller table book displays were upturned. She approached the section where she knew Catherine stayed before and found the whole area ransacked. Catherine's personal items, paintings, and writing station were either broken or gone.

Diane spotted her employee and went to her. "What are you doing around on a Sunday?"

She had talked to Catherine about not overworking herself and thought they'd come to an understanding.

Catherine stuttered, struggling to give a straight answer. "I needed a quiet space and some books to finish some poems for my blog. The front door was ajar, so I called you immediately. I promise I didn't stay over last night, I just kept things here just in case…I mean if I…" her words were cut short as Diane waved her hand in a dismissive gesture.

Her explanation made sense, but the reasons behind her things being taken didn't. Especially since the intruder could have gone for the cash register, cart away expensive books, or even go to her office, but they didn't.

"Any ideas on who could have done this?" Officer Jake turned to Diane. "This seems personal."

She shook her head, admitting that she was equally at a loss. The store was in a secure and safe neighborhood, one of the reasons she decided to buy the bookstore there in the first place.

"If anything else comes up on our end, we will let you know. I *do* suggest getting a security system, though." The officer stated and after writing one more thing on his notebook, he bade them farewell.

Catherine looked uneasy and began to pace around the room, but Diane remained silent as she swept her gaze around in the hopes of finding a clue, but there seemed to be nothing.

"Who would take my things?" Catherine finally stopped pacing.

"I'd assume someone who bears some form of odd fascination with you. Or someone you offended greatly," Diane offered before walking up to the girl and hugging her. "Regardless of the reason, I need to get a new door and we need to clean up the store. We have a long day ahead of us."

"I haven't had any problems with anyone in years and other than men flirting with me while I was a waitress, there hasn't been anyone recently. I'm sorry, Diane, I understand if you want to fire me," Catherine said in a small voice as she began to rub the scar on her wrist.

Diane grabbed Catherine's hand and squeezed it reassuringly. "Catherine, this was not your fault. I want you to know that if you're in any trouble I will *not* fire you for it if you are honest with me. Do you owe anyone money? Is anyone hurting you at home? It seems as if you never want to go home and you never had me over. If it's money, I will give it to you."

Catherine shook her head. "No, I'm telling you the truth. I owe no one money. With what you pay me I've caught up on my credit card debt. And there's no one at home. I told you before, I just have trouble sleeping, so I'm either working or going out with friends. And you've never asked to come over. You can come over anytime."

Diane nodded. "Alright, try not to worry about it. Break-ins happen all the time and you're a pretty girl, some insecure creep too afraid to ask you out might've broken in. I'll feel better if you spend the night. Actually, I'll come over to your place and stay over. For now, let's focus on getting the store back together. Shouldn't take too long."

Diane hadn't spent the night at anyone's house for years, not since she got drunk over her best friend's house Vivian after a long evening of going over a case file. The sheer idea of a planned sleepover hadn't crossed her mind since her teenage years, but she was excited nonetheless. She had packed her overnight bag, a few bottles of alcohol, and a deck of cards. After the day Diane and Catherine had, she was looking forward to some downtime with her friend.

She arrived at Catherine's place a little after seven. Diane tapped on the door and could hear the muffled sound of music playing inside. Diane couldn't hear if someone was coming to the door, so she brought her fist to the door with a little more passion the second time.

The music was turned down and she could hear rustled movements from inside. The door flung open and Catherine greeted her wearing… a swimming suit. "What are you doing?" Diane asked confused.

"Oh. I forgot to tell you to bring your swimming suit, didn't I?" Catherine asked as she lowered her sunglasses to peer over the edge directly at Diane. Diane's jaw hung open at the sight of Catherine holding a coconut shell cup decorated with a slice of lime, orange, and a small cocktail umbrella. "No worries. I have an extra. Come on in."

"You have a pool?" Diane asked as she crossed the threshold of the apartment.

"Yep," Catherine said with a snort as she gestured to the children's pool in the middle of her living room floor. "I figured why not. I felt like I wanted to have a pool party. And since I don't have a pool, I decided to make the best of it. What do you think?"

Diane couldn't help but laugh. Catherine was unlike any friend she ever had. Her cheerful personality was hard to ignore, it just pulled you in. Diane looked at the kiddie pool again knowing Catherine wasn't joking and tried to contain any sarcastic or rude remarks. It wasn't every day she could lounge in a living room with her feet dangling from a kiddie pool.

Diane put her bag down in the entryway and watched Catherine frolic to the pool and plop herself down in the middle of the water. She lifted her massive coconut to her lips, pursed them around the straw, and took a huge gulp of liquid. Then, she leaned her back against the sofa and relaxed her body in the small wading pool.

"Coconuts are on the counter," Catherine offered as she leaned her head back soaking in the rays of her LED lights above.

"I hope you don't mind that I brought some friends with me," Diane confessed as she backtracked to the entryway. Catherine sat up intrigued. "Tequila, vodka, and rum." Catherine let out a hearty laugh as Diane came back with three large bottles.

"Let me get you a swimming suit!" Catherine sprang from her seat and skipped off to her room. Loud thuds of drawers opening, and closing could be heard as well as the tossing of clothes to the floor. Catherine re-emerged from her room with a few options. She held up the first option which Diane quickly denied since it looked more like dental floss than a bikini. The second was a one-piece leopard print and the third was a simple black bikini. "I've never been a wild cat." Diane joked. "I think I'll start now."

Catherine tossed Diane the leopard print one-piece with a claw of her hand and a growl. They giggled at their exchange and Diane quickly walked off to change. As she was off preparing herself for their indoor pool party she could hear the blender in the kitchen. Diane wondered how much of the alcohol she had brought would be mixed into whatever concoction Catherine was currently creating.

Slipping out of the bedroom door and into the cool water unnoticed, Diane watched Catherine dancing in the kitchen while she poured liquids and fruits into the blender. When the concoction was ready, Catherine poured the drink into a large coconut for Diane and sauntered over to the pool.

“Purrfect.” Catherine rolled her tongue to sound like a cat and handed Diane her drink.

The two of them leaned back enjoying their alcoholic drinks. Diane didn’t mind the fact that the concoction was pungent. She was looking for a nice and relaxing time. She swallowed past the burn and allowed leisure to consume her.

After a few moments of quietly sipping their cocktails, Diane was struck by an idea. “I brought cards with me.” Catherine looked perplexed. “It could be fun. I’ll show you.”

Diane sprang up from the pool and rushed to her bag. When she returned, she opened the packet of cards while she sat back in the pool and began dealing them on the sofa.

“Have you ever played war?” she asked. Catherine nodded as a slight look of boredom crossed her eyes. “Whoever loses the round has to tell a secret about themselves.”

The game must have become more interesting because Catherine sat up straight.

Diane picked up her card and threw it down. She had a two, but Catherine laid down a five. “Pay up. What’s your secret?”

Diane hoped she wouldn't have to reveal first because her mind was blank.

"I once lied to my father that I was sleeping over at a friend's house, but I really hopped on a train with some friends and went to an overnight frat party at a college two hours away."

"Well, that is a surprise. Honestly, I never would have thought you were the type."

Each picked up another card. They stared each other down and then slammed the cards to the sofa. Diane laid a ten while Catherine won once again with a Queen.

Catherine chuckled taking another sip of her drink. "Looks like you'll be spilling all your secrets tonight."

"Very funny. My secret. When I was in fifth grade and we had library day, I would always sneak a magazine into the library with me. Usually something with celebrity gossip or something like that. When we were told to grab a book and find a place to read, I would slip my magazine into the book jacket and read that instead."

"Oh my god! You should be locked up, you liar!" Catherine shouted with sarcasm. "Is that the worst you've ever done?"

The two of them laughed heartily as they each drew a new card. This time the pause before the reveal was much more drawn out.

Catherine cracked first and laid down her Jack. "Tell me your secret."

Diane smirked as she flipped over her King. "Not this time. Your turn."

Catherine squealed at her defeat.

"So, when I was seventeen, I used to wait until my parents were asleep and sneak out of my house by climbing out of my bedroom window. I went to the garage where my father had his prized Mustang. This car was crazy souped-up for drag racing, so I drove it off to race it in illegal street races. I won so much money doing that! Until one day I accidentally crashed the car."

Diane couldn't believe the story she was hearing. "So, your Dad found out you were drag racing?"

"No. I was able to leave the scene, luckily without a scratch, and my father just assumed the car had been stolen. So, when the cops found the car all busted up, I didn't even get caught." Catherine shrugged and took another sip of her drink.

Diane shook her head in amazement while staring at Catherine, trying to find out if she was telling her the truth, but her friend didn't falter.

"Sometimes I don't know if I should take you seriously or not," Diane said with a glare, but Catherine shrugged again.

"That's for you to decide," she said as she took another sip of her drink, reaching the bottom and slurping loudly whatever liquid remained at the bottom. "Oh! I need a refill. You?"

Diane looked into her coconut and saw it was still half-full. "No. I'm good."

Catherine stood and threw down her two while Diane then threw down her three. She rolled her eyes and thought about which story she wanted to tell. "When I was sixteen, I used to work at a brothel."

"I know that isn't true. Try again. You are a terrible liar."

"Fine. When I was sixteen, I tried to break up my best friend and her boyfriend because I liked him. I did it by forging love notes to a mystery girl and him. She bought it and thought he was cheating."

"Whoa! That is savage."

Diane nodded in agreement. "It's fine. They got married. I'm pretty sure they eventually figured it out too because neither of them has spoken to me since graduation." Diane cackled.

Catherine returned to the pool, clutching one coconut on each hand. "Double fisting?"

Catherine placed both straws in her mouth and choked at Diane's words. They both laughed before Catherine resumed inhaling her drinks, but she quickly set the coconuts down and framed her temples with her hands.

"Oh! Brain freeze!"

Diane couldn't help but laugh as Catherine tried to shake the burn in her brain. Diane reached for her new card and drew an ace when Catherine laid down an eight.

"Spill," Diane ordered, poking Catherine's arm.

"I haven't had sex in a year," Catherine confessed.

Diane threw her head back with laughter, as Catherine's words were totally unexpected.

"Not much of a secret," Diane admitted, finishing her drink.

"You're one to talk. You're holding back on me."

Next, Catherine drew a king while Diane set down a nine.

Diane took her time thinking about what secret to reveal next. Catherine was right when she mentioned that she was careful about what secrets she gave. Diane found it hard to open up to people but knows she can and should trust Catherine.

"You can't tell anyone. When I was at my last job, I helped cover up a shooting by a detective. The detective shot an unarmed prostitute. He claimed it was self-defense, but evidence showed it wasn't and that he had sexual relations with her. He had put away many sickos, including Jaxon Moore who had a violent history throughout his whole life and we finally landed him behind bars for four murders. There were talks about the detective's cases being re-opened. I couldn't risk letting Jaxon Moore back on the streets. I figured the prostitute would survive the gunshot and not say anything and if she did, she wouldn't be credible. I found out a week later that she died. There was no way to bring the detective down without potential jail time for myself and risking many killers getting out of prison." Diane kept her gaze downward not wishing to see disgust in Catherine's eyes.

Catherine took Diane's hands into hers. "Hey, you thought you were doing the right thing. I know you, you're a good person. Thanks for telling me." Catherine hugged Diane before leaping up. "Alright we need something stronger and to shake our asses. Be ready for a headache tomorrow."

Diane laughed and watched her friend dance away to the kitchen in amazement.

A week passed and things finally seemed to be returning to normal both in Gates' Bookstore and the neighborhood. The break-in at the bookstore barely dampened the sales as people trooped in for their orders, and Diane wondered if she was going to need another pair of hands to assist her in moving things faster. The break-in had done nothing but solidify her relationship with Catherine in the oddest of ways, but at the same time, they managed to maintain a respectful employer-employee relationship.

Diane realized she didn't initiate much in their friendship and started calling her friend more often with suggestions or invitations. It didn't just help their friendship, it helped Diane to stop isolating herself. All she did was work then go home and the next days she had to do it all over again. The only time there was a change was when Catherine dragged her out for fun. Now it was Diane's turn to make an effort and do the dragging.

Diane stepped out of the back carrying a couple of books she needed to inspect before stacking them on the shelves, before setting them on the table in front of Catherine. The ladies stared at one another, smiled oddly in sync, and Catherine took the books to make a note of their labels and names.

"Here I was thinking all those months I pestered you about novels and poems, that you weren't interested in reading them," Catherine giggled motioning at the romance novel Diane had picked among her personal list log.

Diane smirked and picked up the book. "I figured I could spice up my reading a bit."

Catherine nodded and packed the books into their respective cases before passing over the new set of books that Diane had asked to get ready for her.

"Can I ask you something personal?" Catherine asked tentatively. "You can decide whether to answer or not."

Diane sat on a stool and waved her over. "Since when do you need to ask?"

Catherine cleared her throat and looked at the ground momentarily. "Do you feel complete doing this job?"

Diane sat up taken aback by Catherine's question.

"Well, life comes in phases, darling, but the most important aspect is being able to enjoy it at your pace. With this job I can do just that," Diane stated as she got up and extended her hand for her books.

Catherine obliged but still seemed confused.

"Close up early today, and don't forget to turn on the alarm," Diane reminded her before heading out of the bookstore.

Each step Diane took down the stairs and toward her car felt longer and slower than expected. Her heart weighed with thoughts and answers to the question Catherine had asked her. Her life wasn't sad or filled with regrets, but her past held familiarity, challenge, and a sense of purpose in comparison to now. There were times of her old life that she missed, what used to define her, and what used to make her feel like she mattered.

The bookstore was meant to be a safe haven and it had worked well for a while, but her heart thumped and cried for some adventure more often than not. It yearned for the excitement she felt she was missing, that was until the reasons she had stopped doing all these made her heart thump loudly in her chest. Diane reached her car and sighed.

As she unlocked the door and got inside, she chanced another look at Catherine through the glass window display of the bookshop. The young girl worked hard to finish her tasks, but Diane could see that Catherine wasn't planning on going home. Earlier on she'd spotted a change of clothes in her handbag, and it was the same for the past few nights as well. She wished Catherine would take advantage of her guest room more often, but the young woman only did so if she had stayed late or had too much to drink.

"I'll figure her out," she promised, recalling Catherine claiming she preferred working late than go home.

The girl seemed reluctant to go back home, but Diane trusted that Catherine would talk to her in her own time, so she decided not to push for answers. In a way, they weren't all that different. Diane, too, wasn't a fan of going back to her condo at times. She had spent years working odd hours and the only friends she had were those who worked odd hours as well so most days she didn't even see them. Home was a loneliness to contend with time and time and again. Yet, it brought her peace and that counted for something. But Catherine didn't seem to get peace from her home.

Someone waved at her from the other side of the street, and Diane unlocked her door. The lanky framed man in a casual shirt and faded denim jeans was Catherine's old boss, Alan. Diane waved him over immediately.

"Sorry I'm catching you at a bad time," Alan spoke, almost out of breath.

Diane shook her head and leaned against her car. "Not at all, Alan. What can I do for you?"

Alan nodded and turned around when he heard his name from a customer asking for some service, before looking back at Diane.

"Are the books I ordered ready? I know I ought to have come to pick them up, but things have been moving at a rather crazy pace in the coffee shop lately."

Diane had almost forgotten about the man's books. "Ooh! Yes! Yes, and I believe Catherine should have them ready for you already."

Alan beamed at her. "Thank you," was all he said before turning on his heels and jogging toward the bookstore.

"Goodnight," Diane called out before getting into the car and pulling off immediately.

Chapter Five

Diane was drinking her coffee while watching the news on T, enjoying her much-needed time off from work. She planned to go into the bookstore in the late afternoon, though, to help Catherine with the evening events that were planned. Having Catherine around took a big load off of Diane's shoulders.

Suddenly, loud yelling seeped through her walls. Once again, her neighbors were accusing each other of cheating. To her knowledge, they were both guilty, but it wasn't her place to say anything about the husband's sexcapades when his wife was out on business, or about the wife's boyfriends visiting when the husband took the kids camping.

They both lived in a vicious cycle of deceit and love or at least claims of love and had every right to the drama that unfolded in their lives. Until she saw the worst of them both in those shadowy nights they snuck around, she had envied them, wondering what life must be like for the man and woman who showed their love so freely in public.

"Dumb asses," she mumbled as she stretched.

When Diane decided to check her voicemail as she straightened her living room, one stopped her dead on her tracks.

"Hey, Diane, I finally finished painting the room and am taking a break. It'll take me a few more minutes to finish. We need to get together once I'm done. You better have great stories to tell. Call me."

The voicemail ended with a single beep.

Diane smiled. She never knew when she would hear from her best friend, Paul Riley. He was a soldier and it's been a year since she last saw him. Judging by his message he was doing some undercover work since it was definitely not painting that would keep him away for a few more months. They had set codes for each other. Minutes equaled months and hours meant years. Anytime they did secret work they gave fake jobs over the phone to notify each other.

Hearing his voice, she felt relieved he was ok and excited to see him again. In the spur of the moment, Diane decided to text Vivian to see if she had time to go out that evening, wondering if she'd got a call from Paul as well. As she finished texting Vivian her phone rings.

"Hello?"

"Hi, Diane, this is Peaches. Is everything alright? I just drove by the bookstore and noticed it's not open."

Shocked, Diane shot up from her seat on the couch. Peaches owned a clothing store a few doors down from Gates' bookstore. She was in business longer than her and knew everyone in the area.

"I'm alright, my assistant must have gotten sick. Thank you for calling." Diane hung up and immediately called Catherine, but without getting an answer. She tried two more times before rushing to get ready for work.

Once in her car, Diane called Catherine again and to her displeasure, no one answered again either. Pulling out of her driveway, she sped off to the bookstore. Diane cursed at the thought that Catherine might've had too much fun the night before and just overslept.

When she put her car into her usual spot opposite the bookshop, Diane relieved spotted Catherine's car. Her friend must have stayed overnight again at the bookstore and just overslept. Getting out of her car, Diane crossed the street to the coffee shop, but noticed that Alan's car wasn't in sight. That was strange, but she continued until she was close enough to see the doors locked shut.

"Closed!?" she asked dumbfounded, before taking out her cell-phone to call Alan to see what was going on.

Her call went straight to voicemail. She turned around as did some other people who had hoped to grab themselves a coffee or even satisfy their early morning hunger with a bagel or two. Disappointed just as the rest of the strangers, Diane decided to head for her store and make her coffee there or even get Catherine to go on a breakfast run.

Crossing the road once again, she reached into her pocket and took out her bunch of keys. After some fumbling, she finally located the right one and put it to the lock, but the door was not locked. Slowly, she stepped into the dark room with the blinds all rolled down.

"Catherine," she called out. "The CLOSED sign should be flipped over! It is the first thing we do when we open, remember?"

Diane stepped further into the shop, but paused and sniffed the air, instantly realizing that something wasn't right. The bleach-tainted air was not her bookstore's usual aroma. Catherine knew better than to use such a potent cleaner near sensitive materials. The smell was strong, too strong. Her next step came with a crunching sound and she stopped walking and breathing altogether. Her professional instincts were screaming at her and Diane reached into her purse and took out her taser. She moved quickly and turned on the lights.

Once the room was illuminated, her jaw dropped. It appeared that someone once again had broken into and vandalized her bookstore. Some tables were turned over, while some of the displays were completely shattered. Her security system hadn't alerted her.

"Catherine," Diane called out and moved toward the area she knew Catherine liked to spend her nights.

When Diane called her assistant's name for the fifth time and still there was no answer, she thought about going back outside and calling the police, but something pulled her along further back into the store to the reading nook Catherine made her own and slept in many nights. The moment she turned the corner, her heart sank to her chest as a wave of dizziness threatened to consume her.

It wasn't her first time witnessing such a sight, but she felt the words slipping past her lips. "Oh my God!"

The sun rays fell on the red floor, illuminating the atrocity once concealed by darkness. She had the option to either panic or do what she was well-versed to, but not before she took a moment to gather her emotions and thoughts, fully aware that her world was now shattered.

"Catherine," she mumbled, feeling drawn in and out of consciousness. The sight of her friend laid out on the floor bloodied, mutilated, and bruised brought bile into her mouth preventing her from wailing in pain. Diane tore her gaze away from Catherine's empty eye sockets.

It had been quite some time since Diane had come across a dead body, but like always, the Grimm Reaper had left *her* an unwanted gift like a cat bringing its owner a dead mouse. She wasn't sure about where or how to begin. Still trapped in between her old self-assurance and the current shock, she took out her cellphone, dialed the numbers every normal person would, and placed the phone to her ear.

Diane made the dreaded call she never thought she'd be making again. "There has been a murder."

The police arrived within minutes. Diane was standing with her back against the wall, her eyes refusing to look away from the desecrated body of the young girl on the floor. Every ounce of her wanted to start examining the scene and collect evidence, but she knew she couldn't. That wasn't her job anymore and anything she might collect would be inadmissible to the court.

"Ma'am," a police officer called out to Diane, bringing her to the here and now.

Diane arched a brow at the man and cleared her throat. "Her name is Catherine Williams. She's my assistant. My friend. I came in at exactly ten this morning and by the looks of things, I'd say she never left the store to go home. She has a habit of staying late."

The police officer shot her a bewildered look before looking to his colleague who had come over. They both had their notepads in hand and scribbled down while Diane waited for them to finish.

"When does the forensic team arrive?" she asked, trying to sound as calm and collected as possible.

"Sorry, Ma'am, but we will need you to step outside while we secure the crime scene," the police officer to her left motioned for her to get out.

She leaned closer to him to read his name off his tag. "Officer Duke?"

He nodded and straightened his shirt and adjusted his belt in a classic cocky move.

"First of all, don't call me Ma'am! My name is *Doctor* Diane Gates, the ex-forensic scientist who continues to get calls even from the mayor begging me to go back to work. Secondly, I'm not the one contaminating anything, unlike you who have tracked blood all over the crime scene with your shoes! On your way over here, you stepped into some blood splattered by the shelf over there and have now tracked it all the way here. You might have noticed blood splattered on the shelf and books, moving downward, and for anyone with brains that would mean that blood got on the floor as well." Diane finished her hysterical outburst and openly glared at officer Duke, all the while reminding herself to stay calm. "I have to be here," she added in a whisper as tears fell down her face.

The room fell silent as both police officers silently stared at her. She shoved her way through both and marched toward a woman standing feet away from the dead body, yanking at her uniform and asking her to step back. Looking around her she picked up a decorative tray of to-go cups Catherine used as her pencil holder and began placing them at strategic spots throughout the crime scene.

"Lady," the infuriated female officer, who no doubt felt belittled, yanked at Diane's arm, pulling her backward, but she quickly learned that was a huge mistake.

Diane reacted swiftly, toppling the female officer over, and pinning her to the ground with a knee to her side.

Bringing forth the anger she had previously managed to conceal, Diane whispered breathlessly. "I hold a master's degree in Forensic Criminology and a Ph.D. in Psychology, so I'm not your classic amateur working a crime scene. You are only supposed to secure the scene, officer, and wait for the criminal forensic team and district attorney."

Officer Duke stepped in, yanking Diane from his fellow officer and guided her toward the door. "I don't care who you are, you're going to jail."

Diane closed her eyes as she felt the stinging cold metal being clamped around her wrists. Catherine was dead. She had spent half an hour staring at the dead body, wondering about a host of things that just didn't make sense. The murder was strange. Why didn't their new security system go off? The way Catherine's body was left, told her that things were going on for a long time and Catherine had fought hard. Her body showed signs of torture. She was violated and worst of all, there was no sign of her clothes. Diane could imagine what had gone down, the pain Catherine was in before she died, and it ripped at Diane's heart, threatening to take away her sanity.

"Take some time to cool off in the back seat, will you?" Officer Duke sighed heavily before helping Diane into his cruiser.

She rested her back into the car seat deep in thought. Glancing over at Alan's shop, it was still closed.

"What on earth is going on?" she whispered. Alan's absence continued to baffle her, as small crowds of people slowly gathered to find out what the police cars were doing at the bookstore.

"Today cannot get any worse," Diane mumbled with her head bent low.

Officer Duke stepped out from the bookstore as the forensic team arrived. Diane watched them as they marched up the stairs and she couldn't help her small pang of envy as she remained trapped in the backseat of a police car.

"Miss Gates," Officer Duke called out to her, bending low to meet her eyes.

Diane only arched a brow in acknowledgment.

"If you could apologize to the officer you assaulted, I can set you free and we will forget any of this ever happened," he offered.

Diane gave it a brief thought, weighing the pros and cons glancing over at the people who had started gathering. She wasn't sure she was up for answering questions or being the one to break the news to them.

With a condescending smile, she locked gaze with the impatient officer and shook her head. "No, thank you… I don't believe I have anything to apologize for."

He grunted no doubt in shock before straightening up and sighing loud enough for her to hear.

"Women," he exclaimed.

Feeling satisfied, Diane urged herself to relax, trying to decide what she was going to do next. First things first, though, she had to brace herself.

After all, she was going to jail.

Chapter Six

The scent of coffee and doughnuts wafting through the air along with the endless bustling of the police station weren't new to her. What was new for her was being marched into the station with her hands cuffed behind her back and being glared at like a criminal. Most of the officers and detectives knew her and looked either confused or amused by her presence.

Many began to whisper or mumble words she could barely hear, but she could very well guess what they were on about. Just as she had suspected when Officer Duke drove off with her in the backseat of his car, he was new in the precinct and didn't know who she was.

He tugged at her arm gently and smiled to himself before leading her to a small cell.

"You had your opportunity, Ma'am," he informed her as he removed the cuffs.

Diane remained silent and walked right into the cell to come face-to-face with a 'working girl' with little to no clothing on. She was, without a doubt, a red-light district worker they must have caught the night before. Those girls were regular customers to the police station but would often get released a day or two later since the city had no use of them piling up in prison.

She looked at Diane and smiled. "What did they get a well-dressed babe like you in here for?"

Diane smiled and decided to indulge the girl's curiosity. "I kicked a cop's ass and I wouldn't apologize."

The lady stepped closer, reeking of booze and weed, smiling and barely able to stay upright. "You must be a badass," she concluded.

Diane wasn't sure about that, but she knew too well that she had managed to manipulate the police into bringing her to the one place she could get ample information. All she needed to do was wait. She was sure that it was a matter of time before the entire floor would be buzzing with news of the murder. She headed for the metal bench bolted into the wall and sat down, crossing her arms and legs.

Thankfully, she didn't have to wait long, and soon after her jail mate got released, the Captain walked into the room to debrief his men and women. She watched them gather around, wearing long faces as the information of someone being killed riddled their minds.

"Someone murdered a twenty-five-year-old girl, blonde and slender. Some of you might know her as Catherine from the coffee shop opposite *Gates' Bookstore* on 6th Avenue," the Captain paused to let the information sink in.

Alan's coffee shop was on the same route to the police station and it was their preferred spot whenever they wanted to grab a coffee or have a lunch break. Many nodded while others affixed their gaze on their superior, hoping to get some more information.

"We have a killer on the loose and I need every street corner combed, every shop with surveillance tapped for their feeds until we find this bastard," the Captain ordered before dismissing the officers.

Diane felt somewhat disappointed by their disregard of the fact that whoever did the killing seemed to understand the importance of keeping their DNA out of the crime scene. She had smelled the bleach and it only meant that some major cleaning had been done after he had assaulted and killed Catherine. She also wondered why no one mentioned anything about the rape.

"Dummies," she mumbled in disgust before bowing her head.

She wished she hadn't come and had the opportunity to handle things by herself. As tormenting as being back on the field was, she owed it to Catherine to find out who would commit such heinous crime in her store. Standing from her bench, she approached the bars, tapping against it in the hopes of attracting some attention from the officers.

The Captain was going to his office when he turned and looked at her direction with a frown. She returned the frown as the man neared her, tucking his hands into his pocket, and properly bursting into laughter.

"I'll be damned. If it isn't the famous Diane Gates."

Diane held her equilibrium, showing no signs of emotion as he approached.

"You don't remember me, do you?"

She had come across a lot of egotistical, self-absorbed, and cocky police officers over the years, but she didn't have any reasons keeping tabs on them. The police Captain was a different thing, though. She never liked the man and always tried to avoid him if she happened to go to the precinct he worked at.

Thankfully, she didn't have to talk with him while she was a consultant on the copycat serial killer case a few months ago. She had remained either in the lab or with the detectives in their offices. Word had gotten around of who the new Captain was, and her old coworkers were eager to share their opinions about him. The stories were far from favorable to him, but what Diane found difficult to comprehend was how such an idiot managed to become a Captain. Yet, Diane feigned ignorance, curious to gauge his reaction.

"It's Larry Henwick. Larry, from the Riverside case?"

Once again, Diane wondered how he managed to become Captain, considering he was nothing but a bully and a lazy detective when she was forced to work with him all those years ago.

"I wish I remembered you, but on the off chance that I do, can I get out of here?" she asked with a thin smile and the best poker face she could don.

Her words didn't sit right with him and he briefly frowned before wearing a smug look once again. Diane had just found a way to discredit his existence in her life when they had a rather telling episode together. The act had both diminished and angered him, but she didn't care one bit.

Antagonizing people like him was fun.

"I need to get back out there… someone killed my assistant and while you guys here clearly don't seem to possess any clues or relevant information, I can be of more use out of here."

Captain Larry shook his head and laughed at her before turning away and waving at one of the officers. "Keep her there for a few more hours before letting her go."

Diane felt her face turning red, fuming in anger as she returned to her seat. Officer Duke smiled broadly at her, and while the others were amused, Diane's day seemed to be getting worse. She wished she had remained calm to get out quicker.

"Such incompetent bastards," she concluded.

A few minutes past noon, Diane's jail door rattled open as Officer Duke came to set her free.

"You could have made things easier for yourself, had you…," he paused, no doubt noticing that Diane was in no mood for talking.

"I chose to be here," she reminded him. "But I have a favor to ask."

The officer froze and looked over his shoulder nervously, before pointing a finger into his chest. "Me?"

"What have you guys found out about my assistant's murder? Did anything from the crime scene stand out?"

Officer Duke slid his hands into his pocket, shaking his head. "We don't know much right now, other than the fact that whoever did this is a sick bastard."

Trying not to show her disappointment Diane thanked him for his time and walked away slowly. His response generalized what anyone witnessing a crime scene such as this would think. On her way out she kept her ears open for any information she could pick up, but sadly there was none. It felt as though they weren't entirely keen about finding out who had murdered the girl and that angered her even more.

"If you want something done right, you have to do it yourself," she mumbled, before picking up her pace.

She was almost out when the front door opened, and a tall built man walked right in. He held the door open for her, and might have barely acknowledged him, but managed to pick up his lavender cologne.

"What sort of man wears lavender?" she asked herself without looking back.

She flagged down a taxi, got into the backseat and watched the police station grow distant as they veered ahead.

Chapter Seven

Looking around carefully, and ensuring she wasn't being watched, Diane stepped under the cordoning tape and marched her way up the bookstore steps. The forensic team had done a nice job placing the entrance under lock with the yellow tape, but it wasn't going to stop her.

Tearing through the tape with her hand, she slipped into the room and gently closed the door behind her as she fondled the wall for the light switch, opting not to open the blinds for fear of being observed. The smell of bleach had somewhat dissipated and Diane walked to where Catherine's body had been. All that remained were some markings, indicating where Catherine's body lay.

She stepped closer to the white markings on the floor and gently kneeled toward it as a memory flashed into her mind of how the girl's body was when she found it. Diane remembered every visible injury Catherine had on her but what haunted her most was the fact the murderer had taken Catherine's eyes out. She still could not understand why the killer would do that. Many killers, especially professionals, took items from their victims as trophies but never something like that. Diane was sure that Catherine wasn't the killer's first murder.

What happened in here? This seems personal, way too personal, she mused while looking around the room.

She returned to the door and retrieved her keys from her pocket. She locked and unlocked the door several times until she was satisfied that nothing was wrong with the locks. She then turned toward the alarm with a raised brow before climbing on a stool to get a better look.

"Everything seems in order. Then why didn't it—" she never finished her question as she noticed that one of the cords were hanging loose from the back of the alarm box.

Picking the locks would be easier without having to worry about the alarm. Still confused, she returned to the door and examined the locks carefully once again. Her father used to say that only God could pick a lock without leaving a trace, and Diane believed him since before he died, he was one of the best in doing so.

"It wasn't picked. They must have come in while the store was still open, or Catherine knew them and let them in."

She wished she had urged Catherine to open up more about her life and the demons that kept her from sleeping and always staying late to work. The unlocked door, the position of the dead body, and what had been done to it, as well as the disarmed alarm and cameras, all bothered her. She needed answers but being at the precinct hadn't helped her cause in any way.

Maybe the forensics team found something, she thought.

Diane had many connections from her previous job, so she took out her phone and called the lab tech she used to work with before retiring. Ian Gilbert was a good friend and always wanted more, but she didn't.

"Ian, hello. How are you?" Diane asked with feigned excitement and sweetness.

Ian chuckled on the other end of the phone. "Diane, you are so predictable. You haven't spoken to me in months, but no worries my wounded heart can easily be mended if you buy me lunch. I can have the copies of what we found and Dr. Vance's report to you then."

"You know me so well. That's why you were always my favorite, so efficient. But I will need a copy of everything immediately and I will buy you lunch for the rest of the month. Dr. Vance is competent, but I need to see everything with my eyes. Not just a report." Diane leaned against a bookshelf.

"Alright, come down late, around midnight and I'll show you everything."

After hanging up Diane took a step back to look at the entire room again from a different angle. Putting her emotions aside as best as she could manage, she looked from the spot where the dead body was found, to the front desk and cash register. Everything in the room looked to be in place. That was impossible, considering the signs of struggle on Catherine's body. Unless the perpetrator had a working knowledge of the entire bookstore and space.

It might not have begun in here, she mused, but her assumptions were cut short when she heard someone push against the front door. Gasping loudly, she rushed to the back of the bookstore.

Diane paused, holding her breath hoping that whoever was tugging at the door would eventually leave. The moment she heard the telltale sound of the door hinge Diane closed her eyes. A few moments later footsteps sounded on the wooden floor but promptly stopped.

She had remembered to turn the lights off before the intruder came in, and she would have been caught if she hadn't acted fast enough and ducked behind a small desk at the front.

"What do you have for me?" a male voice asked as the lights came back on.

She could hear him breathe, almost as if the entire room had fallen silent and his existence alone was all she could perceive. He moved around slowly, but without touching anything. From the tiny slit in the middle of two stacks of books, she could make out his physique. He wasn't huge, but the man surely had some build, and his shoes were somewhat unusual to belong to a policeman. Those were nice shoes and if her assumption was right and that was leather then they were expensive, too.

It could be the killer coming back to the crime scene, she thought.

She understood killers to a great extent, having spent years studying subjects of intense personality such as Charles Mason, Ted Bundy, and the Alphabet killer. More often than not, those psychologically imbalanced killers sought ways of release or pleasure, which they derived by revisiting their crime scenes.

She heard him rifling through some things before stopping and letting out an audible sigh.

"Those dumbasses messed with the scene," he mumbled in a disgruntled tone.

Diane's body began to go numb and her crouched position didn't help any. Attempting to readjust herself, she moved to the side and heard the vase sitting on top of the desk dropping to the floor. At that moment Diane wished whoever was in the room with her was deaf.

Shit, shit, shit, she heard the voices screaming in her head.

She was sure he had heard. At first, nothing happened, but soon enough the figure turned and silently approached the spot where the vase had fallen. "Who's there?" Diane prepared herself for the worst.

The thought of a killer being in the same room with her terrified her, but she remained as calm as possible. She had been in the room with some on different occasions, but it was either without being certain they were the killers she was hunting, or they were in cuffs.

Regardless, no situation felt as terrifying as the one she was in and her mind buzzed with scenarios to get out safely without becoming his next victim. Her purse wasn't close to her, so she couldn't count on her taser. She chanced a look and saw him kneeling by the broken vase picking up the pieces, before walking away slowly. The heavy footsteps reached the front door and a moment later the lights went out as the doors opened and closed immediately.

Diane sighed in relief and thanked her lucky stars it was all over. It never occurred to her that perhaps she might have thanked her lucky stars too soon. The man had outsmarted her, and she fell right into his trap. In an instant, the desk she was hiding under was lifted clean off the ground and got tossed to the side. Acting on instinct, she rolled to the ground in an attempt to distance herself from him before crouching and slowly rising to her feet.

"Who are you?" the man asked, hiding well in the shadows.

Diane took in steady breaths and clenched her fists, ready for her flight or fight in her to kick in.

I'm the person who's in a room with a killer, she thought, choosing the worst-case scenario over the other possibilities.

She figured being gullible or even assuming she could be safe was the first route to getting killed in situations such as this. With her guards up and her eyes fixated on the figure in the darkness slowly moving toward her, she clenched her teeth.

"Who are you?" she demanded.

He stopped moving and calmly reached for the inner pocket of his jacket, taking out something. "I'm an officer of the law. Now, will you tell me who you are?"

He moved toward the light but promptly stopped as his scruffy chin graced the light.

"Hell no," Diane mumbled, making a run for the door.

Heart pounding, and face drenched in sweat, she had barely gotten to the door when the man grabbed her arm from behind or at least tried to do so. His second attempt was successful, and Diane only missed the doorknob by inches as he yanked her back into the room.

A burst of adrenalin coursed through her veins. Diane swung her arm and managed to catch him in the face before bringing her heel backward, finding his groin and causing him to fall to the ground. The stranger grunted before he was yanking her jacket hard, but she slid out of it and rushed through the door.

"Fuck!" the man cried still on the ground.

Diane raced out of the door and briefly paused to watch her attacker as he crawled toward her. But she didn't waste any more time. She ran to her car and drove off immediately.

When Diane parked in front of her house she still hadn't managed to calm down. Shooting out of the car, she raced into her house.

Thirsty and tired, she rushed over to the refrigerator and grabbed a bottle of beer, popping it open and taking a rather long swig.

"What the hell is going on?" she mumbled.

Her heart wouldn't stop pounding and the thought of the man she had just assaulted continued to toil in her mind. He had shown her a badge, but she didn't get to see if it was genuine. Torn between what to believe and what not, she pulled her curtains closed, walked tiredly to the living room, and fell onto the couch with the bottle still in her hand.

"Catherine," she whispered, trying hard to remember the beautiful vibrant girl she was and not what the killer had made her.

Images of her defiled body stuck in her mind, and the horrid sight of her missing eyes lingered in Diane's mind. She sat back up and picked up the notepad she had used that morning to make a shopping list before heading out.

"What are the things I know for certain?" she asked herself, pressing the pen against the page without writing anything. She was feeling overwhelmed and afraid to write down anything.

Taking in some calm and relaxing breaths, Diane finally found the strength to write, as she listed the three odd facts about the murder that needed answers before anything else would go on. There was the door, the smell of bleach, and the question of where the assault had begun. One more thing lingered in her mind while she wrote, prompting her to let down her pen and paper and reach for the cell phone.

Dialing the numbers she had stuck in her head since the day she fell ill and couldn't go out for coffee, she held the phone to her ear and waited for the familiar voice from Alan's shop to answer, but she got the voicemail again.

"Where are you, Alan?"

She assumed that someone so involved in Catherine's life would already know about her death or at least would have tried to reach out to her for more information. It wasn't like Alan to go AWOL. Even when he got sick and couldn't go to work, his shop was still open. He had plenty of employees to keep the shop running when he was out.

Diane dialed Vivian's number, needing the support of her best friend but halted from calling as a roar from a car engine suddenly burst to life right before her house. Its lights dimmed, and the engine slowly died before the sound of the car door being slammed shut reached her ears.

Gently putting her cellphone down, she closed the last blind in the living room before racing to her bedroom to retrieve her gun. Diane yanked off the safety, pointed it at the front door, and waited patiently as someone marched up to her front porch.

"Easy now," she whispered. "Take it easy."

She tightened her grip around the gun she hadn't held in about two years since she stopped being a forensic criminologist. Life had gotten far safer for her for some time now and she had not found the need to arm up again.

The visitor softly knocked on the door. "Hello? Hello?"

Diane held her breath and steadied her aim with the magnum in her hands. Taking in all the training she had gathered from her father and through the shooting classes, she aimed for the head, knowing that only a clean shot would keep him from chasing her.

"Miss Diane Gates?" a familiar male voice called out from the other side of the door. The same voice from the bookstore that belonged to the intruder she barely escaped minutes ago. "I know you're in there and all I want to do is talk! Doctor Gates?"

She moved toward the door and stopped about eight feet from it. "I must warn you about how good a shot I am, and I'm well-armed too!"

She waited for a response, but the sound of safety being taken off from a gun from the other side of the door indicated her visitor meant business as well.

"Like I said! I just want to talk about something important. I believe we might have started on the wrong foot. My name is Detective Eric Barnes. I'm the lead detective in the murder investigation of your employee, Ms. Catherine Williams."

She was sure she had heard the name of the detective before possibly on a case file she'd worked on. Regardless, it still wasn't enough of a reason for her to open the door, so she held her ground and hoped he was telling the truth. For both their sakes.

"Can you please open the door? I found your ID in your purse at the bookstore and I know who you are now. We worked together on the Manhattan arson case a few years back."

"If you promise to put your gun away, then I'll do the same."

"Okay," he agreed, putting down his gun and placing it on the window frame.

Diane unlocked the door and threw it open, pointing her gun to his face. She looked unperturbed but somewhat surprised to see the Detective pointing another gun into her abdomen as they finally could see each other perfectly.

"Hello Diane," Detective Barnes winked.

She stared down at his gun momentarily before looking back into his deep piercing blue eyes and noticed the smirk on his parted lips.

"You lied," she stated in a displeased tone, forgetting just how she had done the same thing.

He smiled back at her, his hand steady and his eyes briefly glancing around, no doubt assessing her next move. "You cannot be in my line of business and not be the smartest one in the room."

Diane was barely able to stifle her laughter. He was right about one thing, though and that was the fact he was an officer of the law. She wished she could tell him just how wrong he was about being the smartest person in the room.

"So, are we to continue this standoff, or will you grant me entrance into your home as penance for almost ripping my nuts off earlier?"

With great reluctance, Diane stepped to the side, her gun still pointing at him point-blank.

"What a woman," he whistled for his ears alone.

But she heard him and that brought a smile to her lips.

Diane watched the detective place the fifth sugar cube into his coffee. Everything about him bore a sense of distress. He resembled a homeless person with his unkempt hair and wrinkled –albeit expensive –clothes He barely made eye contact until he took the first sip from his sugar-infested drink.

Eric sighed in satisfaction. "Why didn't you just step out and state who you were and that you owned the bookstore?"

Diane took her seat with her gun by her side but with the safety on. "Why didn't I think of that? Simply warming up to a stranger on an unsolved murder scene who'd snuck in after all the authorities were long gone."

He frowned at her snarky comment and his chiseled jaw tightened. He took another sip from his mug before gently setting it down.

"Where's my I.D.?' she asked.

He reached into his pocket and took out her I.D. "Your purse, by the way, is in my car."

She held out her hand and he gave her the I.D. For a moment no one spoke. Eric cleared his throat and sat up.

"Can you tell me anything you know which might be helpful with this investigation?" he asked. "I have a hunch that you might have picked up something while you were in there, but I need to know before I begin crossing my T's and dotting my I's."

She just shrugged, making herself comfortable on her couch. "Even if I did, what makes you think I'd want one scruffy-looking detective who doesn't seem to be stable to mess with my investigation?" she asked cockily.

His eyes widened. In the next instant, he broke through the silence letting out a ringing of rather odd and annoying laughter. "You… you." He couldn't stop laughing. "Your investigation?" He finally asked and Diane felt the urge to ram her gun into his head. It took Eric a while, but he finally managed to compose himself. "You aren't the detective on this investigation and you definitely shouldn't be having anything to do with it either. You're too close to the deceased not to mention the fact that you're retired."

"Yes, and I am also a person of interest," she stated, showing him that she was fully aware of the facts.

He might be right, but she still knew nothing and telling him that would mean the man could walk out of the door without giving her any information.

"I was getting some information when you came in," she replied. "Also—" she paused while he played with his finger.

"In other words, you don't have anything for me," he rubbed his temple.

Diane could tell she was dealing with a man unlike anyone she'd ever met. He might look scruffy, unkempt, and unstable but he seemed to be thinking fast and that alone helped a lot of detectives. Yet, she didn't know much about him. Not yet anyway. Her interaction with him on the one case they worked on together was brief, limited to just a simple exchange of files and data. She remembered a less scruffy and rather handsome detective, not that his current disheveled state wasn't sexy…

Diane shook her head, forcing her mind out of her dangerous thoughts.

"See… I need all the help I can get," he cleared his throat. "I need all the information you have about Ms. Williams and any you might not remember right now, but when you eventually do."

Diane wished she could remember a whole lot or even knew anything helpful. Aside from the fact the killer had entered the bookstore unnoticed and without triggering the alarm, there was nothing else to say.

"For what it's worth, I can help you if I get proper information on the autopsy performed on the deceased body and any other forensic discoveries," she informed him. "I want to catch the bastard that did this and make sure he pays for his crime."

He frowned at her and slowly got to his feet. "You sound so convinced about the killer being a man."

She wondered if he was trying to test her.

"I saw the body, Detective. I told that to the police officers on the scene, but I don't mind repeating myself. I recognize that sort of a kill. It's personal. The killer took his time to torture and sexually assault her, none of the visible wounds were a result of a rage attack, they were too…precise. And there was a robbery at the store not long ago and all that was taken were Catherine's belongings. It makes sense to believe these two crimes are connected. The killer knew her and took his time learning her routines, making sure he wouldn't be interrupted."

Eric reached into the breast pocket of his jacket and took out his notebook. "I'll get the report on the robbery. Is there anything else you might know which could be helpful?"

Diane shook her head. "That's all I know without having access. Now, will you be kind enough to share anything you get with me?"

Eric stood and walked to the door. Her question made him chuckle. "*I* will catch this killer and you don't need to worry about that. Meanwhile, stay safe in your home and give the police as much information as you can."

His smile never wavered as he exited her house, bearing the same egotistical persona she had come across in many investigators since her time in the force. He grabbed her purse out his car and placed it on her door handle.

"They will never change," she murmured somewhat impressed with the detective's quick wit while his smile lingered in her mind.

He was no different than the rest, wanting nothing but an arrest, a victory, refusing to share the spotlight with anyone when the case was finally solved. Captain Larry had been that way and she wasn't sure that the man that had just left her house was any different. When she returned to the living room, she grabbed the gun to return it to the safety box, but the blinking light from her answering machine caught her attention.

Diane approached the machine and pressed play, waiting to listen to the message.

Alan's voice came through the machine. He seemed out of breath. His panting could be heard above a car horn in the background.

"Diane. I need to speak with you… It's urgent. Please, come to my house. You alone."

The recording came to a stop, and she played it over and over and again until the words registered in her mind. She was now genuinely concerned about the local coffee shop owner.

"Shit!" she huffed out staring at her gun. Diane ran to her bedroom to change before grabbing a jacket and heading out. At the last minute, she remembered her purse and yanked it off the knob before rushing to her car.

Chapter Eight

Diane's head was swimming with questions as she drove to meet Alan, the greatest being whether she should call the police or not. She could be very well asking for trouble but there was no turning back now. Diane drove down to Creek lane, to Alan's address. At least that's where he'd told her he lived from some conversations they had over the years. His family had lived there a while and he had taken over the property after his folks passed away, making him the sole owner.

"I'm doing this for Catherine," she told herself with a frown, tightening her grip on the steering as she pulled into a dirt road. "He might know something. It can't be a coincidence he went missing the day of Catherine's murder." Diane shook her head to clear her mind. "Stay with the facts, don't make any accusations or assumptions, yet. Perhaps… he might… need help."

She couldn't hide her trepidation, and her perspiration didn't help any. But a great part of her wanted justice for her friend above all. Leaving her fears aside, she used her training to calm herself down.

Glancing through the rearview mirror she thought she saw a car tailing her earlier, but she quickly dismissed the thought. Diane found herself a less-conspicuous spot to park along Creek lane where the houses looked relatively new compared to the street sign. She stepped out of her car and a waft of cool air greeted her, making her feel as if she'd entered a ghost town.

Crows lined the telephone poles, and nothing moved aside from an old swing jostling away in the distance. She felt her heart beating loudly in her chest and she nearly yelped when a storm door suddenly opened a few houses away. A young man stepped out and looked in her direction.

"Excuse me," Diane went after the young man who seemed bewildered by her presence in the neighborhood.

He moved closer, weary in his steps but with a smile on his young face.

"My name is Samantha Brown and I'm looking for Mr. Alan's residence if you could be so kind to point it out to me," she spoke politely with a self-assured smile without giving him the chance to doubt her words.

The boy turned and pointed to a blue house with a green door just opposite the dangling swing she could still hear making its bizarre noise. The swing set must be old and rusty.

"Thank you," she smiled and headed for the house the boy had pointed out.

Diane's knock on the door went unanswered and she wondered what to do next. Choosing to be cautious, she circled the property in the hopes of finding him or anyone else around back, before returning to the front door and crouching so she could be at eye level with the rusty-old lock.

It took her seconds to open the door. Drawing out her gun, she slowly walked into the home.

She closed the door behind her gently, mindful of any noise, not wanting to make her presence known. The living room looked spotless, with a nice sofa and a modern fireplace which she could guess was recently installed. On the center table was a large weekender bag with items strewn around it. Diane went closer and saw two pairs of shoes sitting by the side of the bag.

"Where are you headed?" she whispered, looking around the room to see if there was something else that seemed out of place.

When she was finished with the living room, she headed for the bedroom. The door was open, and the bed looked neatly made like it had not been slept in. Only his wardrobe seemed ransacked. Quite perplexed she put her hands on her hips and looked around the room for clues.

Judging by his house, Alan was neat and particular with his things, and the one thing that seemed out of place was the wardrobe. Everything else in the house was tidy neat except for the closet.

"What got you in such a hurry?" she asked, hoping for an answer. "What is chasing you, Alan?"

Turning around she found herself at the other end of a barrel of a gun. Her heart raced and sweat formed on her brow as the man in front of her smiled and shook his head. She thought of making a run after dodging the nozzle, but that could be suicidal, and she wasn't trained for taking silly risks.

Raising her hands and with a look of dismay on her face, she cursed herself for not spotting him tailing her. She scoffed. "Detective Barnes."

He smiled at her. "Nice night for a break-in."

Diane frowned. She was getting sloppy. If she'd paid better attention to her surroundings, she'd seen him following her. In a flash, Detective Eric grabbed her gun and motioned her to the living room with his gun still pointing at her. "Do you enjoy stalking me?

"I know your kind," he said. "I could tell you were lying from the first word that slipped out of your mouth."

His tenacity was somewhat interesting. What was even more intriguing was that she could make out some aspects of his personality without knowing much about the man.

"I'm guessing you don't have much of a life outside of being a detective," she concluded but didn't expect him to comment.

He motioned to her to have a seat and he did the same, sitting opposite her with his legs spread. He might have his gun out, but his relaxed posture told her that he didn't view her as a threat.

"What aren't you telling me?" he asked. "You can make this investigation easy because I am good at what I do, or you can make it hard and I will see to it that…"

She burst into laughter but quickly checked herself when he stopped speaking. Someone so disheveled would either be lazy with the case or trigger-happy, a man seeking a high end to his life too cowardly to pull the trigger himself, which would ruin the case as well. Diane could easily assume that detective Barnes –like Catherine— had demons to battle with.

"If I am to share anything with you, then you must agree to help me in return," she demanded.

He took a few seconds, but he eventually shook his head. "I could just arrest you for trespassing."

"Come on," Diane yelled in frustration. "Your ego cannot be the size of your manhood!"

He adjusted in his seat, drew closer, and finally put her gun down on the coffee table closer to him, before putting his away. "I guess that's a compliment, but I cannot include a civilian in this case. Even more so, you cannot keep running around like a vigilante. Why are you even here?"

Diane was barely able to stifle her laughter. "You believe I'm a civilian? To think after all my awards and the cases I've helped solve that I would be insulted in such a manner. If I'm just a civilian, why was I called to consult on the copycat case a few months ago? Not to mention the continuous calls I get to help. I guess in your case I *can* judge a book by its cover, and I conclude that you're just as disordered and confused like your appearance. You don't work well with others."

Detective Barnes leaned back to think. Diane wasn't going to tell him anything and it was obvious her trust issues might be more than his.

"How about a trade?" he proposed.

Diane sat up, but her face gave away nothing. "You tell me why you came here and why you broke into this house and I'll let you see the autopsy report once it's out."

She shook her head. "I want this case solved as soon as possible, but *you* people have an annoying habit of wasting time. I want in all the way." Diane already had an inside man who would give her the information she needed, but if she could go through the detective, she'd have first-row tickets to the day-to-day operations.

He looked at her as if he was pondering what kind of stubborn woman he was dealing with.

His shrilling phone brought him out of his thoughts. "Just a second," he nodded at her before taking out his phone. "Detective Eric Barnes."

Diane stared at him the whole time, studying his body language. She could imagine his agility being off the charts and she got somewhat distracted by his biceps until she noted the worried look on his face.

"Thank you," he responded. "I will be there shortly." He got to his feet. "I pulled up this address before I came in and I know this house belongs to one Alan King."

"So?" Diane asked dismissively wondering why he didn't say that earlier.

"It is a rather disturbing coincidence that the same Alan King was found a few minutes ago, drowned in a river, just up north, a few hours' drive from here."

Diane's heart sank immediately. "No!"

Glancing at the weekender bag on the table, she wondered what happened to Alan.

"I don't know what it is about you, but dead bodies seem to be dropping and—in some way— they are related to you," Detective Eric spoke in a louder voice. "If you didn't have such a good reputation and only just retired, I would drag you down to the station. But my gut tells me you're one of the good guys."

Standing up he motioned for them to leave and his forbidding glare told her he didn't want any fuss.

They hurried down the porch and Diane stopped and looked around perplexed. "Where is your car?"

"We'll take yours," he announced and stretched out his hand.

Huffing, Diane folded her arms across her chest.

"*I* know the location. So, hand me the keys," he demanded.

Reluctantly, she tossed him the keys and grumbled her way into the car as the detective impatiently started the engine without putting on his seat belt. He pulled the car into gear and sped off immediately.

The car's groan made Diane want to curse, and she turned to him, unable to hide her discontent. "I am okay with you driving my car, but not flying it."

He ignored her and after he'd reached the highway he headed south toward the outskirts of town.

"Where on heaven are you headed?" Diane asked impatiently.

The Detective remained silent once more, and she fumed at his stubbornness. That man would be a difficult nut to crack and Diane tried to remain unperturbed. Admittedly, she had handled far worse and, in the end, she knew how to make them dance to her tune.

The blue and white police cars parked just some feet away from the river were an ominous sight. As Eric parked the car, he motioned for Diane to step out before tossing the keys back to her. Diane mumbled something she was sure he didn't catch, while remaining rooted to her spot, taking her time to appreciate her surroundings.

Thick with shrubs and trees, the path leading to that section of the river was barely noticeable unless someone used the road with logs and potholes dented into the offbeat road frequently.

This has to be familiar terrain to our killer, she thought then saw Detective Barnes waving at her.

She stepped closer, clearing through the mass of police officers swarming the body, before coming to a halt at the sight before her.

"Alan," she whispered.

"He seems to have committed suicide. There are no visible signs of foul play," she overheard an officer say.

That didn't sound like the man she knew, but she wasn't sure about anything anymore. Diane crouched closer to the body, looking for scratches or any signs of foul play, but came up with nothing. Judging by the color of his skin, she could deduce that he had recently died. A few hours at most.

"What do you think?" Eric asked her.

Ignoring his question, she looked around her, and after a brief walk to her car, she returned with a pair of gloves slapped on both hands. She knelt closer, examining both hands and every visible part of his body without much luck.

"There are no physical signs of him being forced into the lake in any way or injuries." Diane checked his mouth and noted that his tongue was swollen. "Without an autopsy, it's hard to tell. There could be internal injuries. Did he walk out here? I can't see his car and I highly doubt Alan had the stamina to walk all this way. You need to find his wife and learn when was the last time anyone saw him and see if there's anything that explains how he got here. There are no close bus routes and I doubt a cab drove him here. Also, his tongue is dark, which can be a sign of poison. The medical examiner needs to check for toxins and see how much water is in his lungs. Anyone who drowns has a moment where they struggle and end up swallowing a certain amount of water. He might have been killed then thrown in to make it look like a drowning."

"Detective," a police officer called out holding a bagged note. "Our men found a suicide note a few feet down the ravine not far from here. The wind must have blown it away from the body."

Detective Eric handled the bagged note in his hand and mumbled the words out without much effort.

"I am sorry."

He handed it over to Diane who read it perplexed and then stared at the dead body.

"It doesn't feel right," she muttered. "Why would he kill her? They had a great relationship; you have to trust me on that. Catherine sometimes would chat for too long with customers, myself included. Another employer would fire her. She spoke highly of him and he did the same. It doesn't make sense. The reason I was at his house is because he left me a voicemail, frantically asking for my help. That doesn't sound like a killer. He sounded afraid for his life."

Eric opened his mouth to speak but stopped when his phone rang. Excusing himself, he walked away to answer the call, and Diane looked at the note again. Nothing seems to be out of place and with a resigned sigh she handed it back to the police officer who took it away as evidence.

Alan liked Catherine. He would never do this to her, she tried to reassure herself.

The possibility that the man could act out on violent impulse was a human possibility, but even at that, Diane trusted in her ability to read people and she was certain Alan wasn't the type. What would get him so mad? Catherine's death wasn't one of rage, it was a passion kill. What motive was there for Alan to kill her? The entire plot felt twisted and even more disturbing, but not as disturbing as things were about to get as Detective Barnes approached.

"Diane," he called out to her and nudged his head to the side, indicating that she should come over.

Unsure of what to expect from the man who now had a look of fury and disgust on his face, she inched closer.

"I just got a call from the Coroner, concerning Catherine's autopsy," he whispered. "She was raped."

The possibility of rape was already in the back of her mind. The way Diane had found the body stark naked when she arrived along with the blood and bruises on her thighs, indicated as much. Diane could not believe Alan King had done it. He was a family man and a perfect gentleman. She looked to the dead body being carted away and then back to Detective Barnes.

"So, what now?" she asked.

He tucked his hands into his pockets. "Now, you go home, try and find peace with everything that has happened, while I get busy with a stack of paperwork that's bound to keep me awake for a few nights. You can send me a copy of the voicemail, but it might have been a diversion, or he just wanted a friend to confess to."

Diane tried to protest, but he raised his hand promptly silencing her.

"Just go home."

Diane marched back to the car and zoomed off immediately. As she drove off, she could see him from the rearview mirror still staring at her car, but she didn't have any kind words for him. His readiness to agree in such a solution to the case without taking into consideration other evidence or parameters enraged her.

More so, the most disturbing and damning aspect of those discoveries was the belief that Alan was capable of such madness. Diane needed to think. She needed a copy of the autopsy.

Chapter Nine

Two days passed, and the world didn't feel like it was ending, even though there was an air of uncertainty that Diane Gates just could not shake off. She tried to sleep at night, only to end up staring at the ceiling until the small hours of the morning. It wasn't just Catherine's murder that ate at her anymore. It was the way her friend's case had been closed.

Diane realized how very little she knew about Catherine. Why had it taken so long for her to open up to Catherine? Over a year of wasted time holding the girl at a distance. Only a few months ago had their friendship begun to deepen. The police hadn't been thorough because of Captain Larry's insistence for the case to be closed.

She turned in her bed for the umpteenth time before getting up and heading for the kitchen for a cup of tea to help calm her nerves.

Diane was feeling trapped like a mouse in a cheese box with nowhere to go. The bookstore would remain closed until the funeral. Her options were limited, and she opted for another day in her house, ordering pizza and drinking her heart out. Diane grabbed her phone to call Vivian, knowing her best friend would keep her company.

"Good morning, sweetie," Vivian greeted her with an overly sweet tone. "How are you feeling?"

"I feel as if I don't need my best friend coddling me. I called my annoyingly energized friend not an imposter," Diane grumbled and grabbed her tea, taking it over to the sofa.

"Well, we all know you woke up alone this morning. I told you, you need to let someone find those happy endorphins hidden deep, deep within your dark cavern." Vivian laughed and against her will Diane did too, feeling some of the tension leaving her body.

"I have no idea why we're friends," Diane teased, taking a sip of her tea before placing the steamy mug on the coffee table.

The table was cluttered with the case files Ian had copied for her on Catherine's murder. A few seconds went by and Diane realized she was still on the phone with Vivian yelling her name.

"Sorry, I got distracted. What were you saying?"

Vivian sighed. "Looking at the case files again? Sometimes you can't have a satisfying ending, babe. Are you going to the funeral?"

"Her family, what's remaining of it wants to have her buried in her hometown. I covered the cost of flying her body there. I don't think I'm going, it's just too hard. I talked to Alan's wife yesterday and she's distraught. She got a weird call from him as well and has to plan a funeral for a man people believe is a murderer." Diane ran her fingers through her hair, willing herself not to cry as a tear rolled down her cheek.

"You'll get through this. If you need me to come with you, you know I will. We'll go to both funerals and I'll kick anyone's ass who tries to give you shit about it."

At that moment, a male voice in the background spoke letting Vivian know that the judge would see her now.

Diane's smile turned into a frown. "Vivian, are you in court? I've told you before that you don't have to answer my calls when you're working. Go save the day and put the assholes away."

"The judge can wait. Family always comes first," Vivian stated strongly.

"Right, like the time we were in Venice and you ditched me for two days for some fake Casanova." They both chuckled at that one, but the shrilling sound of Diane's doorbell broke the spell. "Someone's at my door anyway. I'll talk to you later."

Diane hung up but chose to ignore the doorbell as it continued to ring, assuming it was yet another journalist looking to pick her brain about the murder. After all, Catherine's murder and Alan's alleged suicide was the biggest thing that happened to the area in a while.

Looking over the files and the notes she made to some random thoughts or questions that needed answers, she tried to concentrate, but she couldn't block out the annoying and endless ringing in her ears.

"Whatever it is you're selling, I'm not buying," she grumbled, before cleaning up the table and putting the contents away in a drawer. Picking up a baseball bat she had handy, she marched to the door.

Yanking the door open she came face-to-face with the last person she expected to see. Trapped in what felt like a standoff, she stood with the bat still raised until she noticed his eyes scanning her body. Diane gasped in outrage and promptly shut the door in his face, putting her back against it.

"Oh my God," she mumbled, taking in her semi-nude state.

Bringing her ear to the door, she hoped to hear him laugh, but a rather disturbing silence came through.

"I'm sure I didn't see anything," Detective Barnes assured her from the other side of the door.

Somewhat embarrassed, she rushed to get her robe on.

"He saw nothing! He saw nothing," she chimed over and over again before placing the bat to the side and opening the door once again.

The blank look on the man's face was what she noticed first.

"Good morning," Diane ran her fingers through her hair and waited for him to get on with whatever he'd come there to do. "Aren't you going to invite me in?"

She briefly glanced at her living room before turning back to him. "That depends on several factors."

Surely, he didn't expect a warm welcome from her, did he? Without speaking he held out a brown file to her.

"Whatever that is, I don't think I want it."

With a smirk, he pushed the file closer to her. Reluctantly Diane took it but didn't open it. Being handed a thin envelope brought back memories. That brought a smile to her face even though she suspected that this envelope might not have the information she wanted.

"I had the coroner do another thorough examination on both bodies to see if there was anything we missed and the results just came in this morning," he explained. "I figured since you seemed connected to this case, you could use some closure."

She looked from the man to the file in her hand whose seal had not been broken yet and sighed.

"I guess you could come in," she muttered, holding the door open for him.

Eric eyed Diane before stepping in and taking a good look around. On the walls and mantle were a few paintings, but what seemed to draw him in were the plaques and awards congratulating her Forensic Criminologist work first as a forensic science technician specializing in crime scene investigation, then as a forensic medical examiner before she retired early at the height of her career.

"Let's sit by the fireplace," she suggested.

He obliged and sat in the armchair opposite hers. The air between them suddenly felt thin. They were both clueless as to how they should break the conversational ice.

"Err…," the detective started but stopped.

He finally motioned for her to take a look at the file, choosing to see it after her. Touched by his consideration, Diane tore off the flap and unveiled the contents of the envelope, gently placing them on the center of the coffee table in front of them. The envelope contained some pictures of the dead bodies of Alan and Catherine.

Staring at the pictures from the crime scene on Catherine's violated body, still made her eyes water, and feel a sharp pain to her heart. It helped some that Alan's body remained clothed in the crime scene photos, but Diane frowned at Alan's photos. She had gotten a copy of Catherine's case files but not Alan's, so she never had a close look at his crime scene or the Coroner's report.

"What?" Eric asked anxiously as he drew closer.

Diane wasn't sure if she was onto something but, without a doubt, there was something about Alan's picture that stuck out in her mind. She got up to fetch a magnifying glass. Diane examined the images spread across the table while Eric watched a different side of her he hadn't noticed before.

"Do you have a copy of the handwritten note?" she asked him.

Eric appeared unsure of what to make of the woman's actions, but he rifled through the contents of the envelope until he came across the photo of the note.

"What exactly are you getting at?" he asked, sounding impatient that she wasn't including him in her thinking process.

Taking the photo from him, Diane took a good look at images of Alan taken after his death, before picking up one photo in particular.

"He was right-handed," she whispered excitedly. "Alan was right-handed… do you have any idea what this means?"

Eric shrugged. "No."

She held the photo of the suicide letter to his face and the photo in her other hand by its side so the man could look at it himself.

"If you're skilled in the art of penmanship, as I have grown to be, then you can tell the difference between letters written with either the left or right hand," she explained. "This has to be a forgery and I bet if we get an expert on handwriting to test this out, it will prove that Alan never wrote this letter! I cannot believe I didn't notice this sooner! Look at his belt, how it's put on. A right-handed person did that. You get dressed with your dominant hand." She grabbed another picture. "Look at this wound and this one on Catherine. Those marks were caused by a left-handed person.

"So, you're saying there's someone else out there who is the killer?"

She nodded excitedly. "I remember seeing Alan's right-hand trembling when he served coffee at times when the shop was swamped with customers," she relayed. "I asked him once about it and he said he has bad arthritis and the nerves in his hands were damaged from an old burn from hot coffee."

Eric pressed his hand against his temple. "What if he was ambidextrous?" he asked. "He could have learned to use his left to write."

She paused and shot him a look of indignation.

"I would think he'd have preferred serving with his good hand and not the bad one. If his dominant right hand was so messed up and he could use his left hand why not use it and keep from hurting himself? That means he was most likely only right-handed and whoever *did* the killing and forgery of this suicide note is left-handed."

Detective Barnes gave Diane a look she'd encountered before. Her reasoning and keen observations didn't seem plausible against the obvious facts, and he wasn't ready to believe her. On the other hand, he did order another autopsy to be done and is in her living room so he might have had his doubts as well.

Diane made the decision for him. "I'll get you some coffee while you maul everything over," she suggested and got to her feet, disappearing from sight.

The detective picked up the photos and looked at them once again.

"What if she is right?" she heard him muttered as she went out of sight.

Diane knew if she was right it would mean some serious trouble, as well as panic for the community as a whole. Captain Larry specifically would have some serious answers to give, considering he took the plaudits for the investigation's success. No doubt he'd be enraged when he saw the new findings.

Diane hurried with the coffee.

"Diane," the detective called out.

Diane came running over, holding a mug of coffee in her hand.

"Your girl fought back," he informed her before holding a photograph up for Diane to have a look at it.

She could not tell him she already knew that from her copy of the files she got illegally. "I assumed so by the way the scene looked."

"True, but nothing in the medical examiner's reports or Coroner's reports say she managed to get any DNA. The Coroner didn't make note of what the substance was under her fingernails during the autopsy." He took the mug, passing Diane a photo. "Look, one of her nails is chipped off and there appears to be blood which can be from the chipped nail but the other fingers have something as well under them but for some reason, there's nothing in the report that states what the substance is, even if it's her own blood. We need to know. It isn't enough to re-open the case, but it gives us something to hold unto," he chuckled.

Diane hadn't smiled so broadly in a while and without realizing it, they shared a tight hug before pulling apart when they settled down.

"So, what next?" he asked.

They returned to their respective chairs. Diane closed her eyes, trying to collate every data before her. Blocking out everything else she focused primarily on the photos.

"We need to see the bodies ourselves and ask the coroner to run some tests on the DNA underneath Catherine's fingernail," she stated once she opened her eyes. "It's a rookie mistake not to run tests on everything. The DNA can break this case wide open."

Standing up, Diane rushed away while Eric sipped his coffee.

"Nice shave by the way," Diane smirked while the feeling of her body within his embrace lingered.

That brought a smile to his face and a blush gathering on his cheeks by her compliment. She had noticed the difference from the moment she opened the door. It was impossible not to since he was a far cry from the unkempt figure she'd come across before.

Diane soon returned, wearing a rather form-fitting dress and a wide smile on her face. Without preamble, she headed for the door

"Does this mean we're working together?" he asked her.

She paused and shrugged her shoulders. "My services don't come cheap, but in this case, I could work pro bono. Even though, I am yet to get an official request to work with you."

She held the door open for him.

"Okay, Doctor Gates the smartest woman alive, who earned a bachelor's degree in Criminal Justice and English Literature at the age of eighteen, then went on to get a Ph.D. in Psychology and Forensic Criminology. Will you please, work with me on this case, which is supposed to be closed and will have me riding a desk for years if we're wrong?" he asked dramatically.

Diane was a little impressed by his words as she locked the door behind them. "Someone has done his homework," she observed with a chuckle. "I will give your offer some consideration."

The air was tense within the room as the coroner slowly unveiled the dead bodies previously stored in the coolers. Diane went to Alan's body first, examining his entire frame for any other clues that might point to what exactly had caused his death if there were any aside from drowning.

"If we are dealing with a serial killer, why would he kill Catherine in such a violent manner, but simply drown this man?" Detective Barnes asked.

"When my store was broken into, only Catherine's personal belongings were taken. I believe this killer took those items as trophies, but he waited a while before coming back to kill her. Why would a killer take items so far in advance? Seems he already has a history with her. He's awkward, not confident enough to be a psychopath. And the report, her vagina walls do not appear to have any tearing as if he was rough in that department. The injuries are horrific, but they are not ones you find from someone in a blind rage or emotionally cut off. This killer took his time, even after she fought him to the very end, he didn't break any bones, her face is barely marked except for her eyes. In my opinion, this guy is a sociopath." she explained. "Alan's death is truly a mystery though. If we didn't have the note their deaths could be unrelated but we know they aren't. Maybe Alan saw what happened? Or could point out a connection to the killer and Catherine and the killer was just eliminating anything to connect him to Catherine."

The detective nodded just as the coroner left them alone.

"We should check Catherine's history and anything from her past life that might have come to haunt her. Also, can you get me copies of receipts from the day of the break-in and the day of the murder? Eric asked as he jotted down on his notepad.

She agreed and slowly began to turn Alan's body over examining it for any injuries when she felt what appeared to be a dent on the back of his head. "Hmm… this feels new."

She shone some light on the spot and tried to guide the detective's fingers to the dent in the basal part of his skull to the detective.

"Something knocked him out, possibly before the killer drowned him," she conjured. "Something else that was not in the report. I want to shave this area and see if there's any indication of what type of injury this is for sure, but my best bet is a Basilar skull fracture. It would cause bruising though around the eyes."

"All this is still speculation until we can actually get a weapon, a motive, and—most importantly—a suspect. He could have gotten that head injury in the water." Eric pointed at the desecrated body of the young girl. "Why did the killer scoop her eyes out?"

It was a question which Diane had wondered about too. It seemed more than the usual trophy grab.

"The eyes are often said to be the window to the soul," she explained. "Maybe by taking her eyes the killer attains some powerful feel that makes him believe he is superior to her or that he owns her soul."

She slowly began circling the body, before taking Catherine's hand to examine her fingernails. They were cleaned like the rest of the body, prepared for the family, and trip back home for the funeral.

Diane huffed. "I still want to beat that coroner for not running a test on what was under her nails before cleaning the body. He needs to lose his job."

"Nails!?" the detective sounded shocked.

They briefly shared a look, almost as if their minds were in sync, before racing off to Alan's body to examine every inch of it.

Diane called it with a definite tone as they found no scratches whatsoever on the man. "Alan didn't kill Catherine! We have a serial killer on the prowl. We're so stupid to have missed this!"

"This person might have done this lot of times," she muttered to herself. "I don't know what links Alan's death with Catherine, but it is safe to say Catherine was the major interest of our killer."

Eric looked perplexed as he asked. "Why?"

She paused and looked in his direction, wiping any calm smile off her face, before pointing at the dead girl.

"Firstly, he took her eyes, then her clothes. To me, it seems as those are *his* trophies for this kill. He took nothing from Alan, which tells us the man wasn't of any worth to him."

Eric huffed. "Maybe Alan was at the wrong place at the wrong time? He visited your bookstore before or during the murder."

Diane clamped her hands together, contemplating his words and fell silent once again as her mind waddled on the packed bag in Alan's house, the spot his body had been found and how everything related to Catherine's death. A whole lot still made no sense to her. If Alan was at the wrong place at the wrong time why did he pack his bags? Why did he want to talk to her? Had he witnessed Catherine's murder or there was something else that troubled him? It would explain things more clearly but that would mean the killer was someone in the area. Someone both victims knew and definitely not an outsider.

"We know our killer is a man and that he had a personal motive against Catherine," she mumbled softly. "How good are your informants in the red district uptown?"

Eric folded his arms and looked at Diane sternly.

"I confiscated a stash of weed from Catherine with this odd insignia almost like a gang-related kind etched on the back," she replied. "What do you say we make some inquiries about the dealer and see if it is somehow relevant to the case?"

Eric smiled. "You're the complete package, I must say… brains and beauty."

Turning around, he yanked off the disposable gloves, tossing them into the bin on his way out. Diane did the same, hiding a smile and blush on her face as she walked behind him. She had heard the same type of compliment before from others but from his lips, the compliment sent an involuntary spark through her.

"Are you hungry?" he asked.

"I could eat."

Chapter Ten

The world felt still and peaceful and despite the evil lurking around, Diane smiled to herself for the umpteenth time since she had woken and rolled to her side. The other side of the bed felt warm. Laying her head to that side, she heard the thudding heartbeat and soft snore from the man next to her.

They had both slept late, and it was worth it in every regard. She ran her finger along his side and noted the softness of his skin. He seemed at peace.

His lips had felt perfect when they first met hers, and his firm grip on her waist had sent shivers down her spine even before he even lifted her up, allowing her to wrap her legs around his waist.

"You're awake," he spoke in a soft voice, before bringing his hand up to caress her hair.

He bent closer and planted his lips on her forehead, as he slowly sat up, mindful of her head on his chest.

"I told you, putting away those glasses of Henny was a bad idea," she mumbled softly.

When he didn't comment on that, Diane looked up and found him observing her.

"You put away more glasses of it than *I* did," he reminded her with a smirk. "I was only following your lead, young lady!"

Diane giggled and lifted her head from his chest to sit up. The sheet slowly slid off her breasts. Eric smiled broadly and Diane yanked the sheet up to cover herself. She frowned at him, before cracking a smile. Eric, on the other hand, seemed unperturbed as he scooped her into his arms and brought her closer to him.

"What plans do you have for dinner tonight?" he whispered.

"Anything aside from last night's shenanigans," she bluntly replied. "It was a one-time thing I don't expect to happen again. We have to stay professional and get these cases solved."

Eric frowned as she slid out of his arms and got to her feet. Diane looked around for her top and located it in the corner but couldn't remember how it ended up there. She put on her top and began looking for her skirt.

Diane jumped when she felt a hand on her hip, but quickly recovered and sighed as the hand glided up finding her breasts.

"Why don't I believe any of the words you just said?" he asked.

Diane had hoped he would believe them, considering she remembered everything from the previous night's events. His charming nature had warmed her up during their dinner, and her walls had slowly lowered before he asked to come in for a cup of coffee after he dropped her at home.

What happened after that was quite out of character for Diane. She wasn't in the habit of sleeping with people she worked with, but Detective Barnes felt too perfect to ignore. Especially after almost finishing a whole bottle of Hennessey together.

"It's not as if you have somewhere you have to be this morning," he whispered into her ear, before planting a kiss onto her neck.

Waves of electricity raked Diane's body and her pulse picked up as if connected with every nerve ending in her body. Her knees suddenly felt weak. His touch had such an inexplicable effect on her, just as she had first noticed when their hands touched over dinner when she asked him to pass her the salad.

"I enjoyed last night," he admitted into her ear.

"It was a drunken one-night stand."

Diane enjoyed every bit of it too and most of all, his lips and rough hands that could use a mani-pedi. She turned around and wrapped her arms around his neck while their eyes locked. His beautiful blue-rimmed eyes shone, while his slightly crooked nose gave him a touch of imperfection in his otherwise perfection.

"So what? Imagine what my tongue can do without the numbness of brown liquor."

His smile took her breath away a moment before his lips crashed into hers, demanding entrance. He pulled her closer in a commanding manner, tightened his grip around her lower back, and swept her lips between his.

As Vivian kept telling her, she needed to stop being so uptight and let a man rip her sheets to shreds. There needn't be any strings attached. Diane pushed aside her logical thoughts and thought only of the lovely morning coming her way as they slowly returned to bed, panting heavily.

Two weeks after Catherine and Alan's murder Diane was no closer to solving the case than she was with figuring out why she was missing Eric whom she hadn't seen or heard from in three days. After spending everyday seeing each other under the ruse of the cases only to end up on lunch or dinner dates that, more often than not, ended with him in her bed until morning, the distance shouldn't matter, she should be grateful for the break.

Diane took another look at the pictures on her cellphone. She flicked through the screen and stopped on a picture of Catherine she had taken while the girl wasn't looking. She smiled and was a bit startled when her phone began to ring.

"Hi Eric," she greeted, answering the call.

"It's a dead-end," he replied without further explanation. "The insignia on the drug bag belongs to the South End boys who peddle drugs, but it's sold almost everywhere, and nobody has any ties with Catherine from what I gathered."

Diane had not entirely pinned her hopes on the weed bag, but it was a start and a good lead which had been successfully struck out.

"I'm sorry," Eric apologized. "I know you were hoping something positive would come from there."

Everything seemed to be moving at a snail's pace. Alan's coffee shop remained closed and the investigation on his death still seemed like a slam dunk case until they had new evidence to prove otherwise.

"What about the tests on the letter? Was it proven it's a forgery? It should have taken just a few days, but we're way past that mark."

"You know the politics linked with cases that have been labeled closed. They don't tend to them as fast as they should. With the evidence we have, there's room for reasonable doubt, but we have no leads, no suspect in custody, or a murder weapon. It'll be hard to reopen the cases, you know this. But I will get over there later tomorrow to speed things up. The cases will be reopened for sure."

His reassuring words somewhat calmed her heart, but the lack of progress angered her. It didn't feel like they were taking Catherine's case seriously, even when everything pointed that there was a sociopathic killer on the prowl.

"Are we still on for nine?"

"Yes, I believe we are. I'll pick you up," Eric replied. "I have to go… bye!"

As soon as the call ended, the bookshop's door opened and the bell on top dangled as a customer walked in. Diane got to her feet to welcome her customer, and she smiled broadly at the blind man who was making his way into the store.

"Steven," she greeted him warmly. "It's so nice to see you."

Steven stopped walking and folded his cane back into place while Diane approached him and helped him take a seat. He looked rather pale and his face was scratched but wore the usual smile that accompanied his charming persona.

"What happened to you?" Diane asked worriedly.

"It's nothing, some young guy robbed me on the way home a few nights ago. I wasn't sure you'd be open, considering the tragic thing that happened to your assistant. I'm sorry about her untimely death."

Diane smiled faintly. "Thanks, Steven. That's sweet of you."

He slipped his hands into his pockets and lowered his head toward the ground.

"So, what book are we getting this week?" Diane asked in a more vibrant tone to lighten the atmosphere. "Your daughter is picking fast on her reading list and I love that."

Steven smiled. "She is a sucker for books, that one… almost like Catherine and the way she put away all those novels."

Diane chuckled and folded her hands together.

"She was a lovely girl," he sighed, before getting to his feet and weaving his way toward the counter from the sitting area by the door. "I'd like to pick up the fifth and sixth volumes for now."

Diane hurried off to make the listings available. She soon returned with the books, but Steven was nowhere near the front desk and certainly not on his chair. She looked around her and spotted the blind man's cane on the front desk.

Tightening her hands around the books she raced toward the rows of bookshelves and began to look past each shelf in the hopes of finding him. When she finally spotted him, he found him with his back turned in the adult section, holding a book to his face and unaware of her being so close. Steven gently raised his glasses, placed it on his forehead, and cleaned his eyes.

Baffled by the sight before her, Diane subtly cleared her throat to alert him of her arrival. "Are you okay? Is there something I can help you with?"

Startled and completely caught off guard, he fumbled with his glasses, before knocking them to the ground. Diane stepped forward and picked them from the floor, handing them back to him. Being up so close, she caught a good look at his eyes and face without the glasses, which made her take a step back and frown.

"Sorry… I was trying to get a feel of the books and loved the texture of this cover," he stuttered, putting the book on the shelf incorrectly, and then hurried back to the main area with his hand trailing the shelves to his left.

Diane stepped out of the way and watched him continue his walk, before slowly tailing him. They both arrived at the reception area and Diane set about ringing the books before putting them into a bag. Her head swarmed with too many questions, while her eyes continued to dart from the books back to Steven.

"Your eyes bear a striking resemblance to someone I used to know," she stated in a quizzical expression.

Steven laughed off the claims as he handed her his credit card. "What are the odds of a blind man sharing the same eyes with someone you know?"

They both laughed on that one and soon enough, Diane handed him his books and walked him to the door.

They exited the store together before Steven raised his left hand and smiled. "Thanks for walking me this far, but I have things covered from here."

"Are you sure? I can call you a ride," she insisted.

Steven waved off her proposal and with his cane on his left hand, he tapped his way through the crowd around him. Diane watched him until he rounded the corner and left her line of sight.

Turning around, she walked back into her store as more customers followed her inside. The day was about to be a long one for Diane, and Catherine's absence only made it drearier.

Taking another glance at her watch for what felt like the umpteenth time, she took a sip from her white wine and waved at the man standing by the entrance. He hurried over, unbuttoning his suit jacket, and wearing the most apologetic and guilt-ridden face any man who had stood a lady up could have on him.

"I am extremely sorry," Eric leaned closer to Diane and planted a kiss on her forehead.

She smiled to herself, still wondering what exactly was going on between them. The lack of definition brought little to no threat to whatever they had, but she understood the unwritten or undefined terms of their relationship bordered around some really serious emotional responsibility to one another which had grown over the time they met.

"You were on a stakeout, weren't you?" she asked with a thin smile.

He looked down on his shirt and frowned. "Okay, tell me how you knew."

She shook her head, taking another sip of her wine.

"Don't make me beg," he implored.

The truth was that she loved it when he begged, and he wasn't above doing it to get what he wanted from her. He went to speak but stopped when he saw Diane adjusting in her seat and putting her elbows on the table.

"Firstly, your suit is mainly rumpled on the back, and it wasn't done in an office chair. If you had been in the office all day, you'd have hung your jacket. Secondly, you couldn't pick me up and when you were late getting here, I called your office."

Eric shook his head and smiled. Diane was right again. "Well, since the cases are officially reopened, I've been staking out your store to see if any familiar or recurrent figure visits the premises or lingers in wait around it at night."

The waiter brought over two plates of pasta Diane had ordered for them. Eric looked up confused manner while the waiter walked away.

"I ordered for you," she explained to him. "So, did you find anyone or see anything interesting? Many of my customers are regulars."

Eric shook his head in dismay while he placed his napkin on his lap. "The closest thing to anyone moving closer to your door was when a bunch of drunk elderly ladies mistook your store for the coffee shop and began knocking on your door, yelling for coffee."

Diane burst into laughter and barely kept her voice down before stopping suddenly. She looked right back at Eric with a soul-piercing gaze and gently laid her cutlery down by the side of her plate.

"We have been looking at this whole thing wrong," she whispered with her eyes widening. "Damn! We haven't considered other varying factors. We have only been focusing on the region of occurrence."

"The region of what?" Eric asked baffled.

"Region of occurrence refers to the murder scene… We have been concentrating on the murder scenes, the bookstore, the lake, and not extending it past the fact that whatever could have brought about the murder, might have occurred outside those scenes."

Eric nodded and took the first scoop of his pasta. "Is that it?" he asked.

Diane looked straight at him and shook her head. "Oh, no honey… We have a profile to build tonight."

It was her way of telling him he was spending the night with her.

Chapter Eleven

Diane hurried around her office putting a whiteboard on a stand she had filled with information and moved the copy of Catherine's case files onto a table closer to them. Then, she took out the files Eric shared with her from Alan's murder and her notes. She rarely used the office in her home unless she wanted to read old case files or assist in a case when she was pulled back into the job. Diane rolled a big blank board closer to their seats and grabbed a marker, while Eric sat with his legs crossed and his arms folded in the chair opposite Diane.

She looked at him and smiled. "So, so far, we have nothing but the crime scenes in my bookstore and the lake."

Eric nodded but remained silent, his attentive gaze solely focused on Diane.

"What you said at dinner about the women mistaking my bookstore for Alan's coffee shop had me thinking… Catherine had only been working at the bookstore for a short time before her murder but we already established that the killer somehow knew Catherine before she worked at my bookstore. That was a murder of passion and such passion doesn't happen in a short amount of time."

"Which means the killer might have been on her tail a long time, considering he did such a perfect job with his surroundings and knew Catherine and Alan were close," Eric continued for her.

Diane snapped her fingers excitedly and turned to the board, scribbling down 'Alan's coffee shop.'

"What if the killer not only has a connection with the bookstore, but with the other place Catherine had a strong affiliation before coming to work for me?" Diane asked and finally stepped aside, letting him what she'd written.

The detective looked like he had been smacked on the face.

"We were so focused on Catherine's murder we only did short interviews with Alan's close relatives and friends for a motive, we never looked at his store for evidence." He looked through the papers on the table in front of him.

Diane nodded. "Alan's coffee shop should have surveillance, too. In fact, I'd bet he has one of those cameras overlooking the street and almost adjacent to my bookstore. What if he *did* see something and felt threatened?"

The look on the detective's face grew and he sat up immediately. Diane smiled and took a step back to look at the information on the board.

"We need to check the coffee shop, make inquiries about any customers Catherine might have had an altercation with, and find out everyone who worked at the shop while she was there, and hopefully we will have a lead," Eric sounded excited.

Diane waved his words and insinuations away and he arched a brow at her.

"This is a crime of passion, Eric. The killer took a lot of time being patient and even took his time with her on the night of her murder so I doubt our killer would be one to challenge her or have a public altercation with. It's too rash and this guy seems too much like a pro. I'd bet quite a lot on her never even knowing he has been watching her from a close distance. Possibly a fellow worker, but that doesn't seem plausible as they'd have the opportunity to kill her when she worked late at Alan's shop."

"So, he is in disguise?"

Diane shrugged her shoulders and looked back at the board. The missing pieces remained unclear to her too. While her speculations and deductions were majorly based on human behavior and the working knowledge of the minds of psychopaths and sociopaths, there was always the possibility of being wrong when profiling killers.

There was a lot she might be missing or not even be able to bring into the mix yet.

"I'll check the coffee shop out tomorrow once the search warrant pulls through from the judge for the surveillance tapes at Alan's coffee shop," he explained. "I think we are building enough information to reopen this case and get back on track even with Captain Henwick trying to stop us. The case will be reopened but quietly. He's not going to want a panic in the streets."

Diane laughed before placing the marker in her hand on the table. She walked over to him and gently found her seat on his lap as he wrapped his arms around her.

"You're an amazing woman, you know that right?" he muttered with a twinkle in his eyes as their gazes locked.

Diane wore a disinterested smirk on her face.

"A little too arrogant, but brilliant nonetheless," he added.

She cupped his face in her hands and drowned her gaze in his. "You're a silly man," she whispered.

He smiled wildly and reached over to lock his lips with hers. Kissing him never felt stale and each time came with the alluring feeling that his lips were about to melt hers.

He pulled away gently and they both panted. "I never get tired of that."

His whispered words echoed through her ears and her heart raced in her chest.

Diane smiled and closed her eyes, bringing her mouth to his once again. "Neither do I."

She led him away from the office, hoping the night would trickle past slowly.

Laughing and smiling, Diane and Eric stepped out of the car. Still intoxicated by last night's high emotions, they rode together to prolong their closeness before work would separate them. Eric moved around the car and handed her a pair of gloves.

"Really?" she asked surprised.

He looked toward the coffee shop and shrugged. "Since you're here, you might as well cast an eye over to the scene."

Diane looked across the road and at her bookstore, before taking a glance at her wristwatch.

I still have an hour until I open, she thought, looking back at the detective. "Lead the way."

Eric approached the front door but stopped some few feet away to look up. "Lucky us."

Diane followed his lead and noticed the camera still blinking its indicative red light. She turned her gaze and approached the door with the detective but stopped when she noticed something strange. "We've been beaten to the race."

Eric approached the door and tugged at it as hard as he could. "This looks pretty solid to me."

He unlocked the door with the spare key Alan's wife had given him and held the door open for Diane. She took another look around the room, going back in her memories to the days she'd find shelter in the coffee shop and how Catherine would almost tear her ears off with stories and talks on books.

Maybe if I hadn't hired her, this might never have happened, she thought, as a pang of pain sliced through her heart.

Eric placed his hand firmly on Diane's shoulder and she turned to face him. "Don't."

"Don't what?" she asked perplexed.

"Please, don't beat yourself up on how things turned out," he pleaded. "We will catch this bastard and you can get justice for Catherine."

Diane nodded and continued walking about the room. "And Alan! We will get justice for Catherine and Alan!"

Eric patted her on the back, slipped past her and headed toward the back where the office was situated. Diane looked around the room, citing track marks on the floor but without much clue on whose it was. Several boot prints were along the floor and it was apparent that Alan had not cleaned his store as he normally would have before going home that night.

"None of these makes sense," she whispered.

The bold and commanding voice from the detective broke her focus as he returned. "You were right… the bastard beat us to this place and took the tape."

Diane tried not to smile, but she had seen faint scratch marks on the lock and could tell it had been tampered with.

"This leaves us with a big whoop of nothing," Eric raged, kicking into a stool, sending it across the room. "I hate playing second fiddle! Weeks of nothing!"

Diane remained standing unphased. "You still have something, possibly. The lock has been tampered with, so you should have a forensic team check for fingerprints and run them through the database for any hits. Then take some pictures of these footprints and see if they match any of the two crime scenes."

He shoved his hands in his pants' pockets and chuckled. "Yes, Ma'am. So, I guess I'll see you later then?"

Diane stepped out of the shop and shrugged. She wasn't sure if he had picked up on her mood, but not seeing or getting anything solid from the coffee shop, felt like an arrow had been lodged further into her heart. "You can see me once you have some results."

She hurried across the street with her thoughts buzzing in her mind. Her steps felt misdirected as she wished she could do more to help with the investigation. Her decision for early retirement never felt so wrong than it did now.

"Good morning Miss Gates," a familiar voice called from behind.

Diane almost dropped the front door keys as she struggled to catch her breath. The familiarity in the voice had done nothing to help her already unsettled nerves, but she managed to turn around with the widest grin even though it didn't matter much for the blind man. "Steven! Good morning. I must say it's quite a surprise seeing you around this early in the day or at all. Your daughter can't have read all those books so fast," she said as she helped him up the stairs.

Steven adjusted his glasses and smiled warmly. "I came to return one of the books I bought a while ago and pick something else, it was the wrong book."

Diane nodded and turned to open the door.

"Thank you," Steven said graciously while Diane helped him through the door.

She hurried to turn on the lights. "I don't usually do refunds but for you I can make an exception, considering you got the wrong book."

Steven held out his right hand and slowly tapped his way back to find his seat by the door. Someone hurried through the front door, looking somewhat sweaty and rather lost until he caught sight of Steven.

"You dropped your keys," the teenager said, before handing a key ring with a bunch of keys over to Steven.

Steven held out his hand and hurriedly slipped the keys into his pocket while he thanked the young man.

Diane spotted what appeared to be a car key. "Do you own a car?" Diane heard herself asking without really thinking.

She might have been rightly perplexed, but she sounded intrusive if not downright insulting.

Steven shrugged and bowed his head with a small smile. "It's the spare key to a Jaguar I inherited which is dust-laden at home in the garage."

Diane nodded and turned away.

"The irony in owning what you cannot use," he added as in afterthought.

Diane turned her attention to the man and successfully stacked the book he'd returned. "Which book are you swapping this for?"

Steven remained silent, with his head still lowered and his cane tapping nervously against the ground. She called out to him twice and still got no response, prompting her to circle her counter and approach the blind man.

"Steven," she called out louder before touching him on his shoulder.

Steven jumped and grabbed her wrist. After a while, his grip relaxed but he didn't let go of her.

"I need something with fewer pictures, maybe a good space opera," he said vaguely. "I heard the coffee shop across the street isn't going to reopen. The wife of that Alan guy Catherine used to work for is going to sell it."

Diane nodded. "So, I heard."

She wasn't about to get into details with what she thought to be a civilian, even if it was her favorite customer. She returned to the shelves and looked over her selection in the genre he'd requested before deciding on one. None would be within the reading level of his daughter, but she assumed he has someone else to read for him too, or maybe it was a gift.

Diane returned to the sitting area to meet with Steven, but, once again, he was nowhere to be found. She looked around the room, wondering where he had gone to. He visited the bookstore so frequently she wasn't too worried he had fallen somewhere but still, his actions worried her. Her insurance premium would spike if he got himself injured.

"Steven?" she called out before doing a quick search around the bookstore.

Her search for the blind man was to no avail, prompting her to wonder if he had stepped out in a hurry. It wasn't uncommon for customers to change their minds and leave.

"I guess I'll just leave this out for you," she mumbled before going to her front door looking across the street. Seeing Eric's car was still parked outside Alan's shop made her sigh, remembering the cold words she said to him earlier which might have prompted him to stay on the scene longer.

Diane took out her phone and sent him a quick text.

Diane: *Are you thinking of buying the place or just drinking all the coffee before it goes stale?*

Eric: *Just protecting the scene until the forensic team gets down here. But coffee does sound good. I'm sure I can pour some beans and handle the machines myself.*

Diane laughed at his silly words.

Diane: *Fire up the oven too and bring me some bagels with that coffee.*

The forensic team hadn't arrived yet, but Eric could have a police officer protecting the scene. She decided to make up to him for her coldness later.

Five people walked into her shop distracting her. She greeted them and busied herself with the day's tasks. She was hosting a book signing, children's reading hour, and had to do inventory she hadn't done since Catherine's murder.

The day was going to be a busy one for her to get sidetracked.

Chapter Twelve

Her mind fluttered with thoughts, but her blank expression hid her distraction from the man across from her. Quite frankly if Diane didn't feel guilty about being harsh with Eric earlier, she would be at home, studying the information she had on both murders. Even the fancy and intimate environment of one of her favorite restaurants did nothing to entice her.

A hand cupped hers, bringing her to the here and now. She looked at the man opposite her and smiled faintly at him. "I'm sorry," she muttered.

Glancing down at her watch she realized that it had almost been ten minutes until she had spoken with her dinner guest. Still, the time didn't feel enough to pull her out of her funk.

"It's about the case, isn't it?" he asked, doing just about enough to smile at her.

She shrugged and slowly withdrew her hand from his, bringing it to her lap. His touch lingered on her skin as their eyes locked for a moment.

"I don't know," she replied sincerely.

She swept her gaze around the room. Everything looked normal just sitting there, with a small quartet playing in the background. No one seemed concerned, knew, or thought about the real horrors of the world, the murders that were happening every day.

"It is one of the reasons I left, you know," she muttered without looking at him.

Eric reached his hand across the table again and Diane could see him from the corner of her eyes as he stopped.

"No matter what we do, and no matter how far we go, the extent to which the evil resides in the world is never truly understood or defeated," she continued with a tight expression.

A small commotion claimed her attention and she turned her head in the direction of a couple getting engaged as the man went on his knee and the woman screamed her heart out.

"If you think about it, the world is a game, but not everyone is dealt with a fair hand," she continued.

Diane looked back at Eric, somewhat angry with herself without really understanding why, and at the same time feeling sorry for the man before her.

She peered into her wineglass. "I must be a terrible company right now. A terrible date for sure."

Diane had ordered the second most expensive bottle of wine they had, noticing Eric shifting uncomfortably in his seat. She had become accustomed to eating out alone. She didn't always bother with a date when all she sought out was sexual relief. Diane considered proposing they leave and go somewhere else, but dismissed the idea, thinking that if her relationship with Eric was to last, he would have to accept her as she was. Thankfully, she still had enough money from her past career, the money her father left, some stocks and bonds she had invested in, and savings to maintain her lifestyle.

"Frankly, I understand you," he admitted.

His words brought a thin smile to her lips. "Catherine deserved something like that too," she pointed in the direction of the newly engaged couple. "She deserved a life with a happy ending or at least some measure of joy in it. She never seemed at peace."

Eric leaned closer, picked up his glass of untouched wine, and gulped down a good amount before letting out a sigh as well. "People like you and me do the dirty work so others can sleep easy at night. That's why we do what we do and why we are darn good at it."

They both leered some bit more in the direction of the couple before the waiter came back.

The well-spoken young man looked at Diane. "Will you like to order now?"

She looked at Eric who shook his head before doing the same. They had been too busy talking to decide on what to order. The waiter took his leave while they perused the menu's selection. Eric put down his menu on the table almost immediately, grinning while Diane took her time.

"You don't do this much, do you?" she asked without looking up at him.

He continued to grin as he leaned back into his seat. "Of course, I do."

She figured he didn't understand her question, or rather, didn't want to take his time to think about it. "You barely looked at the menu, which means you don't know half of the items in it. You only do that if you don't want to bother picking from a list of things you aren't familiar with."

The detective shifted in his seat, cleared his throat, and reached for the menu but didn't pick it up. "I don't need to see everything. I have already decided."

Diane chuckled softly, put her menu down, and snapped her fingers at the waiter.

"Have you decided?" He respectively looked at Eric and then Diane.

"We will both start with the Antipasti Misti, then move onto the spaghetti Bolognese with the special sauce," Diane replied.

She looked to her companion, whose jaw was dropped, and his eyes widened in what she could only assume was a shock. The waiter nodded and after thanking them he walked away as fast as he could.

"How did you know I like spaghetti?"

Diane tapped her fingers on the table smiling broadly at him. "That dish was the only recognizable one for somebody who doesn't fancy trying new things."

She was sure no less than eighty people out of a hundred would have picked the same dish because it sounded familiar and the chances of being served something they could eat were better.

"I cannot believe this," he mumbled in a mix of disbelief and shock. "You were psychoanalyzing me the entire time, weren't you?"

She shrugged, taking another sip of her wine.

"I try new things by the way," he said defensively. "Half the meals in that menu have nothing but weird names."

She chuckled, almost spitting out her drink as he took a sip from his as well.

"What were you expecting from a restaurant that serves international dishes?" she asked with an arched brow.

He shifted uncomfortably in his seat. "Well, when you decided we should go out to dinner, I wasn't expecting a place where I needed to speak foreign languages."

She chuckled some more and shook her head at him.

"I cannot begin to imagine how much toll this case is taking on you right now," he confessed. "You should know I never give up on a case. I will work it until we solve it. This isn't my first rodeo with cases that take a long time."

She knew that too well. She had read up on him after all, and his reputation as one who went above and beyond the call of duty preceded him. At times, he was so fixated that he didn't seem to have much of a life beyond the job.

"Is that why your wife left you?" Diane asked out of the blue, doing her best not to sound insensitive.

Diane saw that her question caught him off guard as he leaned back to his seat shocked.

"She left you, didn't she?" she added, sounding blunter by the second.

Those questions managed to distract her from her turmoil. Glancing down at his hands she saw the light impression on his ring finger, indicating that something had been removed from there recently. She had noticed it when they first met.

"I don't understand your question."

She scoffed and downed the last of her drink. "You've been hiding it from me, and I don't do well with secrets," she explained. "You can choose whether to answer or not, but don't lie to me."

Eric clamped his mouth shut and donned a stern expression on his face. The air between them had suddenly changed and it wasn't for the better. To make things worse, Diane had her 'game face' on and she wasn't ready to stop her questions until she got the answers she sought.

"Have you been spying on me? Have you been through my stuff?" He paused, tightening his fists and did his best not to look away from her.

Diane remained silent on purpose.

"I never lied to you, and you aren't one to talk about secrets either," he said angrily. "Whatever happens in my private life is *my* business and mine alone and you can stay the hell away from it!"

Standing up, he yanked his jacket off the back of the chair and walked away. Refilling her glass and taking another swig, she wondered if she had accomplished anything other than pissing off the one person who had as much interest in solving Catherine and Alan's cases as she did.

"Men," she grinned and looked to the couples still enjoying the euphoria of the moment. His abrupt departure drew some curious glances her way, but she was not bothered by them.

The waiter finally returned with their meals, looking perplexed at Eric's empty seat.

"You can go ahead and serve his meal," Diane informed the young man.

She gently laid her napkin on her lap and picked up her cutlery, ready to dig into her food. Looking up she saw a figure standing by the empty seat.

"Thank you for coming back," she muttered, knowing it wasn't an apology per se, but it showed she meant no harm.

Eric didn't respond, and quietly took his seat and began eating his meal.

He came back, was all that Diane could think about as she dug into her meal in silence.

The air around the table had dulled considerably, but even in that drab moment, she could still catch his eyes stealing subtle glances of her every chance he got.

"You won't get rid of me that easy," Eric stated without looking at her.

Diane realized he was right. She wasn't going to scare this one away that easily. Diane decided she shouldn't interrogate him but use a more delicate touch. She could try again later in private.

Still charged from the intense moment, Diane purred softly while she ran her fingers along Eric's damp chest. After the third round, their bodies felt like lead, a sweet heaviness that begged them to rest. Her lips were still parted with awe.

"You were right," he whispered, planting a kiss on the side of her head. "But I didn't lie to you."

He tightened his grip around her while Diane readied herself to hear about the man's relationship with his wife or ex-wife, and why he always took off his ring before having a meeting with her.

"I was young when I got drafted into this life," he explained. "I was young, married, and daft enough not to see how I chose one marriage and constantly neglected the other."

"She left you because you weren't at home often?" Diane inquired.

He nodded and slowly pulled away so they could both sit up.

"She left me because I was never at home, and the family time I had, I spent it with stacks of case files in burger joints and fast-food restaurants. I messed up that life and, I guess, she couldn't have any more of it. Even when I was home I went over case files, had a hard time letting go when things weren't solved, and got into trouble more times than I could count. I hate it when any of my cases end up in the 'cold case' section."

Diane had figured as much but it'd be better for him to tell her.

"The divorce papers are already signed, and things should be sorted within the coming week, but I…do, did have a problem with taking off the stupid ring for too long. I always put it back on. I feel like a failure. But since we've been together, every day is easier, every day I keep the ring off for longer periods of time."

Diane smiled and reached over to his ring finger, placing a kiss there. "We all have things we cannot let go of. I won't fault you for it."

"How about you?" he asked.

She looked at him with a frown and absolute loss on her face. "How about me, what?"

"Your father's murder case, have you let that go?" he asked.

Almost as though a can of old worms had been let loose within her, Diane slowly drew away from the detective, slipped on her robe, and walked out of the room.

She wanted him to leave sooner rather than later.

Chapter Thirteen

Glancing at her phone one more time, finding no new messages or missed calls, she slipped it back into her purse and stepped out of her car. Donning her shades, Diane walked across the street and stood behind the line with five people ahead of her.

It was one of the things she didn't fancy about the situation and she had to pay every month in person which meant dealing with the condescending jerk behind the counter. She glanced at her watch and figured she should be off for work within the next hour, provided she didn't get delayed again like the last time.

Do I really need to be here? she asked herself.

Paying monthly for something she wasn't ever going to open, or rather, a place she felt too scared to even get within four feet felt ridiculous, but her past wasn't like every other person's. She would rather keep a lid on it and allow the future to pan out as it wanted to. It was the reason she walked out on Eric the night before.

He was prying about her father and she wasn't willing to open up to him. It was still too early.

"Miss Gates," the chubby fellow with the large hands and dark brown hair called out to her, raising his right hand.

Diane rolled her eyes and stepped forward, placing her hands on the counter. She didn't bother with greetings. "Storage space 5C," she announced before taking out a bank envelope from her purse and slid it his way.

The man looked at her with a bizarre expression on his face. He had things to say, or at least, the man had his head filled with thoughts and she could just see it. He eyed her some more, before scribbling some nonsense into his record book and handing her a receipt.

"You have to pay for maintenance," he informed her.

Diane wondered what sort of maintenance they needed for a space she had never visited. More so, maintenance costs were billed every year and not halfway through it.

"I wasn't informed of any pending maintenance cost."

She watched him sniff, get up from his seat, and press his face closer to the glass separating them. "Whatever shit you got back there can rot under the rain for all I care, lady, but you gotta pay the cost or you don't get the space!"

She felt her fists clench and her anger bubbling up, but she had readied herself for whatever madness the man would dish her.

"Hundred bucks," he noted, reaching his hand out through the pay hole to receive the money.

The wild smirk on his face was enough to tell her there was no maintenance being done. He was simply extorting her, and he knew darn too well she would never know.

"Can I see it?" she asked.

Hearing herself say those words sounded both strange and alien.

The look on his face grew sullen and he immediately froze, tightening his grip around the cash in his hand. Diane cocked her head to the side, motioning for him to step out and lead the way since she had never been to the storage room before and had no idea where to go.

"Show me," she spoke boldly and stepped back.

Since she was the last one in line, there was no excuse for the man not to leave his post.

"Err, you don't... we still have guys working in there," he stuttered without giving her a clear response.

She ignored his words and marched along as the man dallied in his steps and seemed reluctant to show her the unit. With each step taken toward the unit, Diane felt her heartbeat slowing down and her desire to see the space wavering by the minute.

"It was his," she mumbled.

Yes, it was *His* and that was one of the many things about *Him* she wasn't about to let go. Like a box of tricks, bound to leave whoever opened it, unsure of what they were about to face, the storage space felt familiar and the walls of her heart clamped at the thought of being anywhere near it.

The greasy, plump man trotted in front of her. "Diane, I must insist that you don't go in there right now."

Before she could tell him off, her phone rang interrupting her.

"Jesus Christ," she mumbled before yanking out the cellphone. Looking at the caller ID brought a frown on her face.

Considering they had sex no more than twenty-four hours ago, she felt little to no excitement seeing his name across her phone's screen as it continued to ring aloud.

"What?" she asked, sounding as hostile as she could be as she answered.

A loud sigh greeted her in response. "Drop whatever you're doing and meet me at Alan's shop right away!"

Diane slowly removed the cellphone from her ear to look at it, before putting it to her ear again.

"What?" she asked befuddled.

"Stop being so goddamn stubborn and hurry over here," Eric yelled.

She watched the man ahead of her stopping in front of a red door, leading to the storage spaces. He seemed nervous, judging by the amount of sweat on his face, the redness of his chest and cheeks, and the fumbling of the keys. Everything screamed that something wasn't right.

"Are you checking it out or what?"

Diane turned around, slid her phone back into her bag. "You owe me a hundred bucks, you swindling crook!" Diane grabbed a hundred-dollar bill and tossed it over her shoulder.

His response never came though as she exited the building and headed for her car. A part of her was thankful for the detective's call. She wasn't sure if she was brave enough to see what was in that storage unit.

Diane sped off into the distance, wondering what the workaholic she was falling for had discovered.

Eric was still wearing the same clothes as the day before and paced beside his car, halting almost every five seconds to glance at his watch. He must not have gone home after he showered and had breakfast with her. Why didn't he change, considering he needed to go into work today? Was he looking for an invitation to leave some clothes at her house so soon? Diane took her time observing him while parked just around the corner and in a blind spot from the man's view.

When she had seen enough of his agitation, she stepped out of the car and waved her hand at him until he noticed her. He caught sight of her and hurried over, holding a brown file in his right hand.

"Hey," he greeted casually.

"What did you find?' she asked, sounding less cordial.

He shot her a disapproving look and scanned their surroundings in case they were being watched.

"We should do this somewhere safe and without prying eyes," he whispered while holding a file in his hand.

Diane nodded and pointed to her car. Eric hesitated for a moment before agreeing and as he rounded the car, he waited for her to unlock the passenger's door before hopping in. Diane took her time to look around as well, ensuring nobody was watching them.

"Drive," he commanded.

Diane turned on the ignition and rounded the corner going past her bookstore veering toward the Manhattan bridge until she was certain they weren't being followed.

Eric flipped open the file and laid bare some gruesome pictures for her to see. Diane felt her stomach grow sick almost immediately as she struggled to keep her eyes on the road. She veered right, barely missing a side railing, before flashing her blinkers toward a safe patch on the road and slowly bringing the car to a halt.

"Who is this?" she asked, taking the file from the detective's hands.

Eric remained silent, while she tried hard to comprehend that the images were of the same person, she was thinking it was. Gruesome seemed to be inappropriate to quantify the monstrous dealings the victim's attacker had done to her.

"When did this happen?" Diane asked without looking away from them.

Eric moved closer and replied. "Her attacker did this to her while she was a freshman in college. Right on campus grounds at night and she left school some months after recuperating. We closed the case so fast we didn't interview Catherine's family and friends about previous incidents. But there were things in her home that led me to reach out to them to learn more about her."

Diane closed her eyes and tried to remember Catherine for the sweet, gorgeous girl she was before the incident that took her life, and before she came across the gruesome images in her hands.

"Any leads on who did this to her?" she finally looked at the detective.

He shook his head. "I cannot really say."

He cleared his throat and reached for the file in her hand before flipping over some more pages of paperwork he had printed out to show her another photo on the back page. Diane seemed confused while she glared at an image of what appeared to be an eye.

"I don't understand."

"They found that at the crime scene, somewhat damaged because something had been stuck into it, but intact enough to be recognized to be someone's eye. Someone like her attacker but there was no one in the system matching the DNA back then."

The explanation and findings finally garnered enough interest from her, prompting her to reach for the file once again and stare at the partly damaged organ.

"Catherine stabbed the entire thing out with a stick," Eric noted, while he pointed at the image.

"Whoever lost an eye on that day is our killer. She fought back then, too. I always wondered where her scars came from. Was the person caught? Maybe it's the same person."

There was no doubt they had just found a potential motive for the murder against Catherine. Yet, there were still many unanswered questions.

"Unfortunately, there were too many suspects. There was a party that night and she was seen with many people. A rape kit was done, and the blood samples taken from the scene of the crime confirmed two different people were there on that night. Catherine was blind-sided, she couldn't make out who was her attacker since it was too dark. Another problem is that the scene was contaminated by the school's security. They messed with the scene walking in it and they moved Catherine inside to their offices to wait for the police, so the crime scene was left unattended for a while."

Diane closed the file and rested her head into her seat.

"He raped her, she fought back, and made him lose an eye," she mumbled. "He finds her years after, finishes the job, and took her eyes as her punishment for defacing him."

She was thinking out loud, but the pieces were finally falling into place like a jigsaw puzzle.

"She never forgot about him," Diane suddenly sat up and turned to look at Eric. "She never forgot about him and the years after that assault, she still remembered that night."

Like a lunatic speaking utter nonsense, Eric stared at Diane and wouldn't look away. She could see the expression and understood what it meant, but it didn't bother her and started the car.

"Where are we going?" Eric inquired.

Diane pulled the car back on the road. "Her poems. She always mentioned this incident in her poems."

She scoffed and wondered how she could have missed the correlation between the words scribbled from a broken heart and the damaged soul writing them. Often her poems were unusually dark, and Diane had pointed this out once or twice to the young lady.

"We need to get back to my store," Diane said, finally answering the detective's question.

He fumbled with his seatbelt as Diane drove off like a crazed person. "Don't get us pulled over."

As though the skies went blind,

as though they just didn't mind,

in the darkness, he continued to loom,

just before pouncing on the helpless stag

Diane stopped reading the fifth stanza of what she could tell was turning out to be a disturbing poem for the detective.

"He was watching her, and she knew it," she explained to him. "Catherine knew her attacker was stalking her and if she knew he was stalking her, then she might also know his face or maybe have even seen him again."

The detective finally understood her. "Which means she might have documented her findings or fears down somewhere."

Diane snapped her fingers. Eric was right.

"Unfortunately, I have read and gone through all her stuff here and nothing points out to a name or what her stalker's face might look like."

"How about the things she might have stashed away in her house?" he asked, grinning.

"I wonder what we will find in there," she mused as she walked past the man.

She could hear him grumbling in displeasure as he trailed after her, and it brought a rather mischievous smile to her lips.

Chapter Fourteen

They drove in silence. Diane knew Eric had many questions for her and her behavior was colder than usual, but she didn't want to get into their problems. She wanted to solve Catherine and Alan's murders.

One thing that kept bothering her as she drove was how the detective got all this new information. The district attorney had told Eric they were not going to help anymore until there was hard evidence Alan didn't murder Catherine, so how did Eric get his search warrants or convince the college to hand over details on the assault? How did he get the police in that county to share their files?

"How did you come about these findings?" she finally asked.

He tightened his grip around the file and seemed rather unwilling to speak. After some seconds of silence, he diverted his gaze out of the window and began to hum to himself in what Diane could tell to be an evasive technique meant to dispel her interest in the answers she sought.

"If you don't want to tell me, that's fine," she snorted, before ramming her foot into the gas and zooming off.

"I got the files from her school and not entirely in a legal way," he admitted.

Diane decided to ask no further question not wanting to be an accessory to a crime. Diane could only guess the detective might have hacked into their systems, possibly even threaten someone. Any of her guesses could get him fired.

"Did I do something wrong last night?" he finally breached the question she could guess had been dancing on his lips for quite some time.

Diane pulled the car into a side road and made another turn arriving at their destination. There was nothing but old buildings scattered all around. The area seemed busy, easy to blend in, and not to be noticed. Diane smiled, feeling Catherine's personality in the buildings. She loved literature and old historical things. With her salary increase working at the bookstore she would have been able to afford one of the renovated apartments.

"Seems just like yesterday we were having a sleepover and partying in her apartment." Diane mused as she stared at Catherine's old building.

"Crowded, just the way she must have liked it. Easy to be just another number, another face," she said to Eric as she got out of the car.

He got out but marched around the car, blocking her path. "What on earth is going on with you?" he demanded, confusion and irritation clear in his tone.

She shrugged and smiled at him. "We should keep our business professional as best as possible from now on."

The words didn't resonate well with the man whose face flushed red and his nostrils flared.

"We should ask around for anyone who might have known her or seen her come and go from her apartment," Diane suggested as she marched on. "I assume that while you were breaking in for evidence you didn't do that."

She could hear his footsteps slowly begin to head in the opposite direction as she approached a couple getting groceries out of their car. Clearing her throat and doing her best not to startle them or seem like a creep, she snuck her hand into her jacket and held out a photo of Catherine the detective had printed.

"I don't mean to bother you, but do you happen to know this girl?" she asked, looking from the woman to the man and then back again.

The man stepped forward, took a look at the picture, and nodded. "Yeah, I know Katie. We had her over for dinner one night as a welcome to the building sort of thing. She lived up on the third floor, right by the elevator. First door on the left after you get off."

Taken aback by their willingness to answer her questions, Diane nodded in appreciation, but couldn't find anything else to ask. She turned around to leave but thought better of it and turned back to the couple again. "I just have one more question and I will be out of your hair."

The couple exchanged a quick. "Shoot," the lady spoke.

Diane cleared her throat and laced her fingers together. "Did any visitors come around or anybody, in particular, you might have seen regularly with her?"

They both shook their heads before the woman spoke. "She was pretty quiet and half of the time she was never around. Most of us even assumed she had some boyfriend she lived with, with her gone so much. We were all shocked about what happened to her."

Diane thanked them for their time and turned away. She would take their word about Catherine never having any visitors. Glancing around her, she tried to find Eric.

"Diane," he called out, a little further of where she stood, panting as he raced toward her. "Not many know who she is, just her face in passing or from the news."

It wasn't anything she had not found out already.

"Her room is by the—"

"Elevator," Diane completed his sentence. "Like I said, I've been over here before."

They tried to enter the building but found the doors locked. Eric knocked on the door, getting the security guard's attention, flashing his badge on the glass. That worked like magic and the security guard came over to let them in.

He was a man in his late fifties and looked at them perplexed. "What can I do for you?"

Eric read the guard's name tag and smiled. "Mr. Thomas, I'm here to escort Mrs. Hall to her daughter's apartment to get some things. Her daughter was involved in an accident and wants a few things at the hospital. I hope that's ok."

Mr. Thomas face quickly turned solemn as if his daughter had been injured. "Of course, it's ok, Ma'am, I hope your daughter recovers quickly."

Diane smiled and thanked the man before walking off to the elevators. Once they were inside the elevator, she smacked Eric's arm. "You could have said she was my sister. I'm not old enough to have a daughter living on her own let alone able to afford a place like this."

She huffed before a smile found its way to her lips. Eric chuckled and held his hands up in surrender. Diane pushed the number three button and turned to face the closing doors.

"You don't do well with sharing, do you?" he asked, glancing the back of her head.

Diane could feel his staunch gaze locked into her skull as she offered him no answers. He sighed, somewhat restless as the air between them began to grow thinner.

"If I did something, I am truly sorry, but you're not the easiest to understand. I thought we were at a point of being able to share important things in our lives, like my divorce. You pressured me to talk about that."

"I wasn't comfortable with your question about my father's murder. But you're right. I *did* open that door I just didn't expect you to ask about him. Listen, we are fine. Ok? I was just having a hard time and… I'm just not ready to talk about it. But I'll try. I don't want to mess up finding this murderer because my head is in the clouds."

The doors finally chimed open, indicating they had reached their destination. Diane stepped out and walked down the hall to the left.

Eric hurried after her. "So, we are good?"

Diane nodded. "I was nervous. I haven't allowed any man into my home and my bed in a while and the entire thing felt fast, and then you went and popped the question about my father and I just wasn't ready." She turned to face him. "I'm sorry about my reaction."

Eric only smiled at her and took her face into his hands, bringing his mouth down for a kiss.

"Diane Gates there's nothing you can do to make me stop falling for you." Eric placed a light kiss on her lips before taking her hand to walk to Catherine's door.

Eric glanced around to make sure they weren't watched and tested the door handle before lifting it and slamming his shoulder into the door. It gave way immediately and he smirked triumphantly at Diane. "Before I left, I tampered with the locks to make sure I could get back in."

He proceeded into the apartment then took out his tactical flashlight and clicked it on, while Diane closed the door behind them and turned on the flashlight on her phone. The blinds blocked out enough of the natural light in the room, so she used her phone to get to a light switch and discovered the electricity was turned off.

"Should we risk opening up the blinds? I'm sure no one will see our faces." Diane suggested as Eric handed her a pair of gloves.

He shook his head as he put on his gloves. "No, we don't want anyone to know someone's in here at all. Hopefully, the security guard won't mention our presence to anyone."

The stench of cannabis greeted her nostrils. She saw the center table in the room had a good amount of weed on it. She knew Catherine liked to smoke weed so the sight wasn't shocking. Diane walked over, wondering if her assistant smoked anything else, but she couldn't find evidence of something like that. Nothing about the place other than the weed screamed Catherine.

"She had nightmares too," Eric explained. "She couldn't sleep without having nightmares."

He held up what seemed to be a diary with a rather gloom expression on his face. Diane could tell the man had struck something important and she found her interest peaked. She leaped toward him and slowly retrieved the book from his hand to skimp through the first few pages.

"This is far worse than I first perceived." Diane slowly found a place she could lean on while checking out the content of the book.

Catherine's journal had been meticulous in every word, from her meeting with people over the past year, to even what she ate and drank and above all, every single haunting thought that coursed through her mind.

"She wrote everything about her life from the day she began working at Alan's but nothing about college," Diane slapped the book shut and looked at the detective. "The most worrisome entries are dated after she left the coffee shop. Before she came to work for me, she always talked about parties and her friends. I knew something haunted her, but it never seemed to change her life other than sleep and not wanting to be alone too long, which her diary backs up."

Diane tossed the diary onto the shelf behind her and rubbed her face. "The date of the entry when her poems get dark again don't ring a bell to me. I don't recall anything while she was working for me that hinted at a customer bothering her around that date."

"When I was here before, I saw a laptop on her bed. I couldn't get in and I can't get help with it or I'll be in deep shit. Catherine's lease isn't over until the end of the year. Her parents want the money for the rest of the lease, but the landlord won't give them the money and insists on selling this place. Catherine's parents got a judge to halt the landlord from touching this place, so we must be really careful not to get caught. The parents or the landlord can sue us."

Wordlessly, Diane headed for the bedroom to look around. The laptop was exactly where the detective said it was. She opened it right as he entered the room. Diane tried her luck with the password and with the fourth try she got in.

"Her favorite book title and the last name of her favorite author." They looked through her files and nothing was of much interest. She had pictures of family members and friends, but none showed anyone lurking in the background. There were more poems and stories too. Diane opened the most recent poem.

Eric stood from the bed and leaned against a dresser. "This stuff doesn't seem to help. We need something to point at her killer. We have a great lead so why can't we find a name for him? I think we need to find and interview the security guards and those who were at the party the night of her rape."

Diane moved closer to comfort him when she noticed a small blackboard with cursive on it and she moved closer to get a better look at it.

A part of me wonders if the night owl still exists…

if it still lurks in the dark,

waiting to pounce on unseeing mice for dinner.

How well can a night owl function when it's ocular?

Diane looked at the words carefully.

"She wasn't sure he was still following her," Diane explained. "The owl is her attacker and the ocular vision being mentioned relates with the culprit having just one eye now."

"Then we need to find something that remotely tells us about who he is or what he might look like," the detective stated.

Diane liked the fact he was now thinking along with her and she nodded in agreement. It would mean a trip to the college where Catherine was first attacked.

"I feel sorry for the girl," Detective Eric mumbled just before dragging her dresser away from the wall. "She managed to get over with what happened to her the first time and worked so hard for nothing."

Diane folded her arms frustrated and determined to find the killer. "She worked her ass off to never come home because of terrifying nightmares. I should have pushed her harder, realized that someone was stalking her. I'm going to make him pay."

Chapter Fifteen

The bookstore had been running slow for the past few days and the new influx of books Diane had yet to finish putting away was meant to bring more people into the shop. While business couldn't be booming every day, Diane could tell Catherine's murder deterred many from coming into her store. She had to figure out how to get people back in. A big event perhaps. She knew some reporters, maybe she could get them to write an article about her bookstore.

Casting her gaze across the street to what used to be Alan's coffeeshop, her heart felt weakened. The place had been bought was under construction. The bell above the door chimed as two young boys walked into the store. Diane straightened up and focused on the newcomers.

They glanced around for a while, not looking at any section in particular, or making a move toward the back and the young adult and teen sections. Diane stayed behind the counter checking her phone which buzzed with texts from Vivian. The boys approached the front desk just as Diane was about to text Vivian back.

"Good morning. How may I help you?" Diane inquired.

The boys looked at each other and chuckled looking at her. They remained silent for a moment before the taller one with dark brown hair stepped forward and parted his lips to speak. A loud honking noise from a truck pulling in front of her store alerted her of the arrival of the books she had ordered.

"Thank God! Finally," she gasped, hurrying past the boys. "I'll be right back! Won't be but a moment."

She raced out of the door and toward the men delivering the boxes with a scowl on her face.

"We had a minor accident on our way here, Ma'am," the driver apologized. "We are truly sorry for the delay."

Diane nodded and pushed her hair behind her shoulders as she heard loud arguing coming from inside her store. She turned around worried and saw the boys being held by the scruffs of their coats by none other than Steven.

She turned her attention back to the delivery men. "Bring the paper for me to sign inside. I trust you all won't have any more accidents and can find the door yourself."

Diane rushed back to the bookstore.

"Steven? What is going on?"

"These two were trying to steal from you!" He yelled while still holding them tightly.

The boys kicked and struggled as best as they could, but the blind man just wouldn't let go of them.

"We weren't stealing," one of them protested.

"We only wanted a souvenir from the store where the coffee lady was murdered," the second one added.

As much as she could not believe her ears, she could relate with their idiosyncrasy. "Please, let them go, Steven."

Steven obliged and the boys took off. Diane shook her head and moved closer to the stairs leading to the second level, while Steven continued to look at the direction the boys had run. The act made her pause a bit, wondering if he was looking to his right because the kids raced off in that direction, or it was simply a coincidence.

"I am quite surprised to see you, Steven," she confessed. "You left in a hurry the last time before I could give you a new book. Do you still wish to exchange the book?"

Steven chuckled. "I forgot I left the stove on at home and had to rush out. I haven't had the time to stop by and didn't want to call and bother you. Since I was in the neighborhood today, I decided to drop by."

Diane nodded and walked to the front doors to prop them open for the delivery men who had struggled to keep them open while rolling their dolly in. Diane went back to Steven who was sitting at the checkout counter. "I'm sorry for the wait. The books I ordered are finally being delivered so I just need a moment before I help you find a book."

She groaned as a box tumbled to the floor hitting the corner of a display, causing some of the items to fall out. "Hey! Watch what you're doing!"

In an attempt to stay calm, Diane ran her fingers through her hair and put it in a loose bun. "If I murder them, you won't tell, right?" She huffed as she glared at the men taking the boxes to the back room.

"A blind man is a terrible witness. So, do as you wish." Steven laughed making Diane follow suit. "Speaking about murder, I heard around that there was a CSI team at Alan's coffee shop a few days ago. Isn't that a closed case? According to the city police, that is."

"I don't think they got the right killer for him or Catherine," Diane replied. "I'm not satisfied with what they have and what they are feeding the public. I found some things that thankfully the lead detective listened to and went to have another look at Alan's shop."

Steven tapped his cane a few times seemingly lost in thought. "I didn't know you were helping with the investigation. But it figures with your brain. Smartest woman I know. Just be careful and let the police do their job."

"Thanks for apprehending those little rascals by the way," she thanked him while she scribbled down the number of delivered orders the truck had brought.

"I guess I'll have to come back to get a book when you're less busy," he said as he got back to his feet.

"I'm truly sorry. I might have to put emotions aside and finally hire another assistant. Next time you stop by, lunch on me." Diane smiled and hugged the man before jogging to the room at the back so she could make sure her order was all there before signing anything.

Diane barely made it there when her cellphone shrilled. Trapped between assisting the men and answering the call, she chose the former over the latter.

"I can always call them back," she reasoned.

She couldn't help but wonder if the caller was Eric though. They had not spoken or seen each other for the past few days, and she guessed it was his way of giving her some much-needed space. Yet, she had found herself aching for his presence in her home just the other night. The sweet scent of his cologne still lingered on her pillow from their last time together and as much as she ought to wash the sheets and change the pillowcases, she had found herself struggling to do so.

"Make up your mind," she whispered with a thin smile on her lips.

She wasn't naïve not to see that he liked her a lot but losing people after growing attached to them wasn't something she ever wanted to experience again. Past relationships aside, the one man she had truly loved, left her bare in heart and completely shattered when he died.

For some reason, she still had not found a way to move on after her father's death, and she wasn't about to let another man come into her life only to leave her again. She was a psychologist and knew her problems and how unhealthy it was to let them persevere, but helping others was easier than helping herself. She had the same friends for the longest time, never attempting after her father's death to make more. Not until Catherine and that turned out horribly.

"Ma'am," one of the delivery guys called out to Diane.

She looked up, glaring at the slender man and his lengthy tattoo running from his arm to his neck. "Your phone." He nodded toward her cellphone.

Apparently, it had been ringing for the last few minutes while she wallowed in her thoughts.

"It says Eric," the man said once again, prompting Diane to hurriedly straighten herself from where she was crouched opening the boxes.

Once she'd retrieved the phone from the computer desk, she clamped down hard against the "receive" button.

"Hey," she greeted casually, hearing the man on the other end of the line breathing somewhat heavily.

"I have some terrible news," Eric said immediately.

Diane looked around for the most comfortable place to sit, but the men in the room with her now had their eyes focused on her while she received her phone call. "I trust you all can find your way out." Diane quickly signed what she needed to, not bothering to check the rest of the boxes. Yearning for some amount of privacy, she excused herself, going into her office and slamming the door shut behind her before settling into her comfortable chair.

"What's going on?" she asked, her pulse racing with worry.

Eric wasn't helping matters either, as he panted and took his time to respond. "They are shutting the case on Catherine and Alan's murder again and I'm being assigned to something else. They didn't want to reopen it anyway but..."

The news was devastating. Diane thought what she and Eric found would be enough to keep the cases open.

"Did you get my assessments on the killer and his thought patterns? I faxed them to you this morning."

"Yes, I did. I looked through it and I believe you might be right. I've scheduled a meeting with some of the security officials working at the college at the time of Catherine's incident and I should have tracked them all down within the next few days."

Diane believed him. Observing him so closely the past few days, she saw how dedicated he was on his job. He rarely went to his house and he often slept in his car on stakeouts. Now she could understand why his ex-wife must have decided she had enough and couldn't go on any longer.

"But they close the case again and reassigned you. How are you going to meet with the security guards? Don't risk your job, Eric."

Diane wanted to keep on fighting, however, she was –or had been— a professional and had to accept things didn't always go the way they should. So many times, she would work on a case and not enough evidence was given. No matter how great of a job she did, a jury would let a murderer go.

"I'll keep you posted," Eric muttered before ending the call.

Almost immediately Diane felt a pang of guilt coursing through her veins. She wondered if she had lost touch with being a forensic criminologist. Her instincts used to be so sharp she would solve cases within weeks. Never as long as Catherine and Alan's case had lasted. Maybe she was too close to the case and didn't want to let go for all the wrong reasons.

Without a doubt, she was missing something. The picture remained blurry to her, the harder she tried to see. She let down her phone and took a glance around the room, remembering how Catherine would dance and sing as she unloaded orders and got them ready to display. She was so full of light and energy, and no matter how standoffish or scary Diane could be, she kept reaching out until she grabbed hold and yanked Diane out of her own darkness. Diane had started to heal. She had talked about everything with Catherine, even things that were a trigger for her.

"Whatever it takes," she told herself. "Whatever it takes."

Like a movie getting interesting by a dramatic turn of events, Diane entered the backseat of the police vehicle without a fuss. It wasn't her first rodeo with them, and she guessed it might not be her last for as long as this case remained unsolved. The day had drifted by fast and noon had rolled on her in the oddest manner with two police vehicles stopping in front of her bookstore.

"We were asked to bring you in," was the only information she got.

It was enough to tell her all she needed to know. Someone high-up wanted to meet with her, and it would most presumably be someone she had met before and not in a pleasant manner if they chose such an aggressive tactic.

They wished to unnerve her. They could have asked her to come in. So, maintaining her composure and with a smile on her face, she agreed to go with them, humming along the way as the car swerved through traffic and past stop signs as though someone of absolute importance was on board.

She leaned toward the driver, hoping to strike a conversation that would provide some information. "May I ask why I am being brought in?"

He shrugged, feigning ignorance as he spat out words of lies. "Nothing trivial Miss Gates."

Diane nodded and sat back. At least, she wasn't being cuffed this time around. She hated being driven in the back of a police car though. It had always been a position she didn't fancy. Thankfully though, they arrived at the precinct sooner than she had expected, with the car making a round turn and heading for the parking lot behind the building reserved for the staff.

She snickered "We aren't going through the front door, are we?"

The men ignored her as the car finally came to a halt behind a black SUV with an official plate number.

The officer occupying the passenger seat got out and open her door. "You can exit the car now Miss Gates."

"So formal." She shot a smile in the direction of the gentleman, deciding to play along.

Their calm demeanor and courteous actions could only mean they had been instructed to act appropriately. It meant she wasn't in trouble, and for whatever reasons she was brought to the private parking lot could only mean someone wanted to talk to her in private. Her amusement increased.

"Leave us," a familiar cocky voice commanded the officers as the door to the black SUV opened and a man stepped out.

Drenched in expensive perfume and with a smile, the police Captain approached her. Diane scoffed and met his hand halfway in a firm handshake.

"If it isn't Larry Henwick," she mused.

He gushed back at her smiling and held the SUV door open for her to step in. She obliged and he followed her as the driver stepped out and stood just outside the vehicle.

"If I didn't know you had a thing for theatrics, I'd say you're planning some form of espionage," she teased him.

Dealing with someone as cunning and manipulative as Larry Henwick came with its hassles and the need to remain atop of the situation at hand. Allowing him to trample all over her wouldn't be the wisest thing to do.

"You haven't lost any of your beauty since we first worked together," he complimented her.

"I know this rodeo too well to understand this isn't some form of a social visit, so what do you want?"

He cleared his throat and adjusted his blue tie. She waited without getting excited or antsy as she watched him reach into the back pocket attached to the driver's seat to take out a padded file with metal clips holding the edges together.

"I need you to have a look at this before we discuss anything," he demanded, handing her the file, and simply resting his back into his seat.

Puzzled, yet curious Diane took her time to open the file, feigning disinterest as she parted the pages open and glanced Eric's passport pinned to the top right corner of the first page. The passport held a younger image of the detective, but he was no doubt the man in the picture.

She read through the first page, taking in details about his growth amongst the ranks and how sporadically fast the man had risen to where he was. In fact, his record was impeccable and something any man in his position should boast of, aside from the glaring dark patches that plagued everything after that. Carefully, and making sure she took her time, she read them all, making sure to take into account these dark patches and paths the man had found himself wallowing throughout his career.

Surprised Captain Henwick was showing her such confidential information on a remarkable detective, she closed the file, deciding she had read enough.

"To what end?" she simply stated.

He coughed and adjusted his tie once again. "I have had my eye on you two since you got yourself arrested after your worker's death."

"You mean her murder, which by the way, you still haven't solved," Diane snapped.

He scoffed and seemed to wave away her words before closing his eyes resigned.

"You aren't helping him," he continued. "You aren't helping him by indulging his obsessive need to work and never tend to his personal life."

Diane cringed and felt her fingers tighten around the file.

"There is only so far a man in Detective Eric Barnes's position can go and quite frankly if he wasn't as good as he is at his job, he'd be on desk duty already," he added. "I have seen him unravel and I have seen a brilliant man taste the depth of despair all for his career. You might hate me, but I care about my officers. I have put him on another case and that's the last thing I can do. If he continues to go against my orders, he's not just on desk duty, he's off the force."

She knew where he was going too, but it had never crossed her mind that the man would drown himself in their current case enough to jeopardize his life or job.

"Detective Eric is fine, and he'd be a lot better if you stop hounding him and preventing him from carrying out this investigation," she shot back. "There's enough information to cause doubt which means it should at least be a cold case, not listed as solved."

His smiling face suddenly turned into one of displeasure. "What investigation? You two have been chasing flies atop a dead body, claiming there is far more to the presence of maggots in it." The captain massaged his temples. "We found the killer. This case is solved and you two should give it a rest. I will not have you meddling with my detective or drive him down that road of insanity once again!"

"Were you ever interested in this case? Did you assign it to Eric because he is competent or just to have him occupied?" Diane inquired. "This has everything to do with the upcoming elections, doesn't it? You don't want to have an unsolved serial killer case on your hands, so you quickly closed the case."

He gave no response, but his demeanor told her all she needed to know.

"I can make his life a living hell if he continues to pursue this case, you know?" he threatened. "You two aren't going to mess things up for me. I allowed you two to foolishly work the case, let him quietly use police resources, but what you've given me isn't enough. That's not my problem."

Diane finally heard the words she wanted to. A confirmation that his decision to put an end to their investigation had more to do with his personal gain than anything else. She laughed hard and noted that he shifted nervously on his seat.

"I don't give a rat's ass about your election and I don't care if you become Chief of Police, Mayor, President, the fucking king of the world. I *will* find Catherine and Alan's killer and do your job for you while you run around playing politics."

She shoved open the door to her right and stepped out without caring for anything more he had to say. The police officers waiting outside approached her and blocked her path just before their boss stepped out from the car and walked toward her.

Bearing the file in his hand, he stretched it to her and spoke calmly. "I don't care how far you've come, and I don't care what you find, but don't be too delusional into believing that you have everything under control. He will unravel in time and you'd be the sole reason for pushing him out of a career. He's unstable and will do more harm than good to your investigation."

She retrieved the file from him and marched off into the distance, cursing him out to herself while she couldn't help thinking about the Captain's words.

Am I leading him down a dangerous path?

She wanted justice and so far, the detective was the only one fighting the cause with her. She sucked in a deep breath upon exiting the parking lot, before flagging down a taxi and slipping into the back seat.

"Gates' Bookstore," she directed the driver who nodded and sped off.

Her bookstore was the biggest and most successful in the area, so she didn't bother with an address.

She was worried about Eric, and wondered if there was anything she could do to keep him from being the person she had just read about. A part of her wondered what had made him spiral out of control in the cases listed in the report she had in her hand. He always achieved stellar results, but there was the problem of tipping over the edge and losing himself.

"What do I do?" she asked herself out loud.

She needed him and she had to accept the obvious truth.

Chapter Sixteen

Diane sat in Eric's house, trying to relax on his sofa as she waited for him to join her. His home was nice and not what she had expected. This was the first time she visited him at home, always wishing to maintain control and confidence, she made sure they spent their time at her place.

Yet, Diane felt impatient no matter how nice the home was. He had called informing her he had found something, inviting her over so he can tell her. The call ended too quickly for her to change the location, but some part of her was glad. She wanted to make the relationship work.

"Give me a minute," he called out from the kitchen where he had spent the past few minutes since she arrived.

Diane felt no rush while she sipped her glass of water and watched some television. She would have rather he came out to provide her details about his findings, but she will be patient. Having sent the man notes upon notes with her thoughts scribbled into every single one of them over the past week, she wondered if they played any substantial role in finding the clues he had.

She glanced around the living room, taking in the brown leather chairs of exquisite taste, and the mild-colored walls which gave the entire room a masculine aura but also a comfortable warmth. Nothing about the house depicted the rough and unstable personality Larry Henwick had tried to give Eric.

But there remained genuine concerns for her about Eric and how he hacked things when the pressure on him grew too much. The file remained safely ensconced in her house, partly perused and with enough details to make her want to ease away from him, but in there were heroic details of jobs done and sacrifices made for the good of his work.

"Tends to ignore life as it happens around him to focus on work and drown himself until there is no more outside of it for him to live with," were the words of the psychologist with whom Eric had taken some sessions with, years ago.

Eric finally came back into the room carrying a plate of French toast and an apologetic face. "Sorry I kept you waiting."

Diane waved away, smiling as she helped herself to some toast.

"No worries, dear. I *did* rush over before eating. So, what did you find out?"

He dropped into the single chair by her side and crossed his legs. "I went back to the apartment last night."

Diane felt the hairs on the back of her neck stand, while she struggled to hide the sense of shock now rapidly growing.

"I bribed the security guard and decided to see the room again for myself, you know, get a second perspective to see what we might have missed," he explained.

Diane nodded, took another bite from her plate, and waited for more information. He surely wasn't taking things slow with the investigation and she wondered if the fact Larry was putting him on another case was the reason.

"I don't think we were the first to visit that room," he continued. "For starters, the hair we found there doesn't belong to a human being, it was cat hair. There was no evidence that Catherine owned a cat. Then the small amount of blood was that of a chicken."

Diane let down her food and concentrated on the disturbing news she had just heard.

"Could someone be working with our killer?" she asked.

He shrugged and shook his head. For a moment he paused, possibly expecting Diane to try and piece the end together.

"Our killer has been smart and meticulous. He wouldn't be so dumb to leave himself exposed, so what you found might have just been planted. How did he get into the building though?"

Eric raised his right brow, obviously trying to infer that she shouldn't be asking such a question.

"He probably bribed a guard too, but you used your badge before. They could know our killer and let him in or someone else could have had a badge too."

"What are you trying to say? Someone on the force is a killer or an accomplice?" The detective's tone was harsh and filled with shock. "No way."

Diane put her plate down, trying to choose her words carefully. "The Captain has been very eager to close the case, not giving you the opportunity to solve it. If that wasn't enough when we gathered new evidence, he didn't give us enough time to go through all of it before closing the case again and assigning you to a new one. It's just all so suspicious.

"No, I don't think he's capable of this. Maybe he gets his hands dirty for those who can help him in his political endeavors. If there's anything, then perhaps someone is encouraging him to keep the case closed. We'll never know." He shook his head and snuck his hand underneath the chair to bring out some notes.

"Anyway, I found the security guards from the college Catherine went to."

He handed her his notes and list of findings. Diane eagerly flipped through his notes that detailed how he had tracked down each guard who had worked as security in Catherine's college, during the time of her first assault.

"Get this," he drew closer and pointed to a list of names. "There were six guards stationed in that area on campus that night, but I have managed to cross four off my list of suspects."

"That leaves two," Diane whispered as she ran her fingers over the names. "S.A. Fisher and Simon Clark."

He nodded. "I have worked my ass off trying to track those two down, but it simply feels like they've disappeared from the face of the earth."

He urged her to go through the remaining pages though, prompting Diane to skim through until she found pictures of men, she couldn't say she recognized.

"Those were the guards from that night, or at least, five of them while the sixth one was said to never really take pictures and the one for his file went missing," he explained.

Diane wondered if the sixth fellow was their killer.

"How do we locate these guys?" she asked herself, staring at the images as though something might scream out loud at her.

Eric suddenly sprang from his seat and began to pace the room. She watched him grow erratic in manner, before turning to look at her as thin crease lines appeared on his forehead.

"I didn't tell you everything about my meeting with the captain when he kicked me off this case and put me on another," he said.

Diane wished she could tell the man that it made two of them. They were both hiding things and hers would probably feel more condemning than his. She held her breath and kept herself from telling him about her meeting with Larry Henwick.

"He told me to steer clear of this case and I'd get a promotion once he leaves for the Mayor's office," he explained.

She wouldn't have expected anything less from the cunning and conniving captain, but even the offer he made sounded too good to be true. His offer convinced her that he was somehow involved in their case.

"Why?"

Eric seemed unsure about how to respond to her question.

"Why is he hell-bent on stopping us from finding the right answer to this mess?" she elaborated.

"I think we both know the reason why and considering we haven't been able to bring tangible proof to them they don't want anything to mess with whatever political plans he has. Maybe those in power he's trying to kiss their asses know something."

She felt bitter and somewhat betrayed by the force that had been created to protect and serve its people.

"Our hopes on finding this elusive killer hangs on identifying two strangers."

Eric nodded and pointed at the picture. "I had a buddy of mine run facial recognition scans on them and that bizarre tattoo of a skull on one of the two missing persons."

Her ears seemed to pick on the words immediately as she looked up.

"Skull? What skull?"

He pointed at the right arm of the somewhat odd-looking fellow in nothing but a vest and shorts. His face was blurry. The old picture and the poor condition it had been kept didn't make identifying him easier, but there was no mistaking the tattoo on his arm because she found it disgusting right off the bat after seeing it.

"Holy cow!" She exclaimed, immediately getting up from her seat and pointing her finger at the picture. "I know that guy! I know that man in the picture!"

Eric raced closer, took the picture from her to have another look at the missing face, but without understanding what she was talking about.

"His face is blurry," he noted.

She agreed and pointed to the tattoo on his arm. "I have seen that tattoo and the little scribbles underneath which says Gorge."

She was convinced but tried to hold some reservations because the next question she was about to receive might not be one she wanted to answer.

"How do you know this guy and why are you so sure?" He finally popped the words without preamble.

It would mean taking him to one of the places in her life she didn't like going to.

"We need to go on a little road trip," she simply replied before getting up from her seat and picking up her purse.

Wordlessly, he picked up his jacket and exited the room with her.

"You might want to take your breakfast along," she warned him. "You're driving by the way."

He made no move to decline or reject her orders. She held something up her sleeve.

One hour was what it took behind the wheel to get to the outskirt of town where Diane finally asked Eric to pull the car into a parking space close by the front doors of a rental storage facility with peeled-off paint and an unkempt appearance. He bore the same perplexed look as she did on the first day she learned of the rental storage building.

"I know you asked me not to ask any questions about how you know this place, but I feel the need to," he relayed to her, adjusting in his seat as he stared at her.

She shrugged as she stepped out from her side of the car and cast her gaze toward the payment booth their suspect often occupied whenever he was on duty.

"Do you see him?" the detective asked, turning off the ignition and remaining in the car.

The plan was simple. All Diane needed to do was point him out and the detective would do the rest. She scanned the entire area for the man but found nothing resembling his annoying self around.

"We might need to go inside," she advised.

With a subtle nod, he unbuckled himself from his seat and stepped out of the car with nothing but his car key, while his gun and badge remained safely tucked away in the glove compartment.

"We go in as a couple, do our best not to spook this guy and maybe even see if we can get enough information from him just by observing him," he explained.

"A couple?" she asked in jest.

He shot her a blank stare and replied. "Do you have a problem with that?"

"Not really. I should think we are already one. This guy knows me though, so he might not be willing to give me any information." Diane grinned.

He wove his hand into hers and nudged his head toward the booth where a man in tardy clothes had just stepped into. He was oblivious to their presence, humming to himself while he had his earbuds on, and his eyes affixed on a magazine.

"Here is our chance," Eric whispered and cleared his throat, adjusting his shirt to look a bit more casual.

Diane stuck her fingers into his and locked them there as they approached side by side and with her head placed atop his shoulder. The moment seemed to take on a rather odd motion as she found herself enjoying it more than she'd expected. His shoulders felt perfectly hunched, and his soft hands threatened to slip out of her just by holding unto them.

"I'm scared," she whispered without giving anything away.

Eric chuckled softly. "We can take him. He is just a weird dude with nothing on us both."

She shook her head, knowing he was misappropriating the message she intended to pass along. She fell silent for the moment, allowing herself to sigh intermittently as they got within few feet of their intended target.

"I am scared things will get ruined between you and me once they start going well. Relationships haven't been my strong suit and I wasn't expecting you and me to—"

He tightened his grip around her and caused her to forget what she wanted to say next as she locked gaze with their target up ahead.

He seemed shocked, initially allowing his widened eyes to give him away before his jaw dropped. Diane watched him glancing around, presumably to see if they were the only two approaching, before adjusting in his seat and tucking his X-rated magazine away.

"Why are you back?" he asked nervously.

Eric shot Diane a quizzical look but said nothing, presumably not to blow their cover.

"I need your help buddy," she said in a calm and relaxing tone. "My boyfriend and I need some information about a friend of yours who used to attend a college where you previously worked."

He nodded, looked from Diane to the detective, folded his arms across his chest, and remained silent.

"I think you've got the wrong person," he said rather convincingly.

Diane snuck her hand into her pocket and took out a picture of Catherine she carried with her. She held it against the glass and watched the man barely taking a look at it before shaking his head fervently.

"I don't know who that is. You two are asking the wrong guy," he said, remaining as adamant as possible.

Eric shot him a fake smile. "Give me a moment to speak with my girlfriend, please."

Diane stepped back as the detective urged her away from the booth and to a safe speaking distance.

"He is our guy," she said in an assuring tone.

He agreed, slightly tilting his head to the side. "I know, but he isn't going to tell us anything. I thought we were going to go with a delicate approach not gung-ho. What exactly is this place to you?"

"It's a storage facility I checked out once or twice for personal business."

The answer wasn't going to put someone as smart as the detective off, but it should do enough to stop his questioning for the present.

"What do we do about our guy?" Eric nudged his head to the side, while he did his best not to look in the direction of their suspect.

Diane frowned and looked toward the booth. "Which guy?"

They looked around and fast to see their suspect running in the opposite direction as fast as his legs would carry him. He had granted himself some good distance from them as he ran fast as he could.

"Shit!" Diane muttered, taking to her heels, and feeling rather glad that she wasn't wearing heels.

The detective did the same, gaining pace on the man who didn't think his escape plan through enough, considering he had to outrun two fit people with nothing but intent to get something out from him.

"You aren't getting away that easy!" Eric seemed to be enjoying the chase as he raced down his target.

Diane wasn't far off when she watched the detective tackle their man to the ground in a manner any football player would be proud of.

"I didn't do anything! I haven't done anything!" He protested, kicking and screaming while Eric overpowered him and placed cuffs around his wrists.

"Then why were you running, buddy?" Eric chuckled before pulling the man to his feet and turning him around so he could have a better look at their suspect.

"You're a cop? You didn't show a badge that's why I ran, I thought you were here to beat me up for your girlfriend." The slimeball struggled onto his feet helped up by Eric.

Eric yanked up the man's sleeve, confirming that his distinct tattoo was a match to the person in the picture.

"You're going to tell us everything you know!" Diane stepped forward, wearing a scowl on her face while the detective reinforced the words with a similar expression.

Their suspect looked at them, presumably bemused as he chuckled and eventually burst out laughing. "I know my rights and you cannot do anything to me," he boasted. "I haven't done anything wrong!"

Eric snuck his hand into the man's pocket, retrieving a handful of weed stashed in between paper notes and some other illicit drugs he was sure weren't prescribed by a doctor of some sort.

"Yes, I can buddy," he replied. "You're coming with us unless you cooperate and tell us all you know about Catherine Williams."

He suddenly fell silent and donned a bland expression on his face as though a new person had possessed him. Diane stared briefly at him, drawing the conclusion in her head that he knew something or at least, that he knew the victim one way or another even if it didn't necessarily mean he had anything to do with her death.

"If you aren't going to speak with us, then I believe you have a long ride ahead of you," the detective mused, before shoving his suspect ahead and tailing him back to the car.

Diane couldn't help but feel hopeful. They had their first proper suspect connected to the case and someone who could blow the entire thing open if they could get him to talk. As they got to the car something told her trouble was on the way.

She couldn't put her finger on what exactly but knew enough to trust her instincts.

Chapter Seventeen

Diane welcomed the endless gazes as they marched their way into the police station with their suspect. It was the highlight of the afternoon for her. No one seemed to speak no doubt shocked about the fact that she and Eric still pursued the investigation on Catherine and Alan's murder when they had been warned against it.

Thirty minutes had passed, and Eric was becoming restless and unwilling to take on Diane's proposed method, allowing their suspect to simmer in his thoughts and take his time to think about the ramifications of his actions. It could break either way from what experience had taught her, but quite often, suspects ended up speaking when they had nothing to do with the case.

All they needed was time to think and see that they needed to do the right thing.

"You can go in now," she informed the restless and pacey detective, who barely heard the last word in her sentence before barging into the room.

He needed to interrogate their new suspect before the Captain came back to the office.

Diane decided to observe and pick up certain facial cues and tells of his body language which would inform her of her suspect's sincerity or if he was simply messing with them. Eric pulled the only free chair in the room toward the opposite side of the table from the man being interrogated.

"I have rights, you know?" the man in cuffs snarled, but did his best to keep his composure.

"You are Simon Clark, correct?" Eric finally began his interrogation.

The man nodded, toying with his cuffs as he did his best to avoid eye contact.

"Did you, at any point, work at Wesley College?"

Simon shook his head, sniffed again, and replied staunchly. "No!"

Eric pushed some paperwork he had managed to obtain from the college with Simon's name clearly stated on it, and with his passport photograph on what appeared to be his application years ago while he was being interviewed for the job.

Simon seemed to mellow as he rested into his seat, looking defeated. "Maybe I worked there, but I haven't done anything wrong, and I shouldn't be here!"

Diane bit her fingernails, feeling nervous about whether they'd get anything before the interrogation was over, or the detective would have his ass chewed. It had been a while since she had to observe a criminal or a suspect's interview.

"During your time there, it is believed you were amongst those on duty on the night a student by the name Catherine—" Detective Barnes had barely completed the name when Simon got to his feet.

He turned around with his hands still cuffed to the table and began to shake his head fervently.

"I had nothing to do with that. I don't even know her!"

His yelling intensified and he began to yank his arm aggressively, making the chain attached to his cuffs rattle, and creating a commotion.

"He knows something," Diane murmured.

Eric managed to get the man back into his seat before continuing his interrogation.

"You cannot pin that on me," Simon whispered. "I was out on rounds on that night, but I didn't do anything."

His voice continued to shake, and his entire body soon followed as he shuddered and cringed without looking at the picture of Catherine set on the table.

"I need your help in identifying one more person who was on watch with you on that night," the detective pleaded. "I understand you were only one of six, but the others don't seem to know the last guy and they claim he had been hired, using you as a recommendation."

Simon looked up slowly, but without hinting at having any desire to answering.

"If you know anything, you can tell me and I promise I won't have to crack down on you for whatever illegal drugs you might be peddling in that storage area you work in," Detective Barnes tried to lure more information out of Simon.

Simon finally took a good look at the picture on the table. Closing his eyes and biting his lower lip, he remained silent for the next few minutes, in a manner that confused Diane and the detective.

"What is he doing?" Diane asked herself with her fingers resting on her lower lip nervously.

She was sure Simon would crack. She had underestimated him right off the bat to be the kind who would spill his guts the moment he saw the inside of an interrogation room. Yet, that didn't seem to be the case and she began to entertain the likelihood that he might have been feigning every bit of emotion he displayed the entire time.

"He is regaining control of the situation," she observed, alarmed by her conclusions.

She pinned down the intercom button to her right and called out to the detective. As he stood, he watched Simon remain still and without opening his eyes, before exiting the room with a pretty tired expression across his face.

"We might have underestimated him," Diane informed the detective.

Standing akimbo and with a rather highly raised brow on the right side of his face, he replied in a sarcastic tone. "You think?"

The duo took some moment to observe their suspect, but he barely moved a muscle as he continued to stall in silence, almost as if he was waiting for something.

"He isn't going to talk, but I bet he knows something," Diane noted. "We need to find out what he knows, or we might miss our only chance so far."

Eric nodded and rubbed his temple. He shot Diane a smile and hurried back into the room in a manner that set off her alarm bells, wondering what exactly he was trying to accomplish.

"Simon, you know what?" Eric smiled as he handled the man's cuffs and chains. "You're free to go."

Simon finally opened his eyes and glared at the detective. "Why?"

Eric looked toward the viewing glass through which Diane was watching everything going on in the room and turned his gaze back at the man before him.

"As much as I want to bust your ass and throw you in prison, I don't have anything on you right now," he replied. "I'm keeping the drugs I found on you, though, and you will be seeing me some time again if I have more concrete questions and evidence."

Simon scoffed and shook his head. "I had nothing to do with that girl being assaulted and the school cleared me before I left."

He sounded sure of himself, but with a cocky tone attached to his every word. Diane wondered why the detective had not asked of the name S.A. Fisher which was the last person on the list they still had not found.

"One more thing, I never recommended anyone to the school to get hired," Simon added. "I only worked there part-time and when my time was done, I left."

Simon tapped his fingers on the table and motioned to walk away before spotting the blurry picture the detective had placed on the table directly beside Catherine's. He cast his gaze on that in which his tattoo was visible, and immediately looked away as his finger rested atop the photograph.

"I don't understand why you're looking for six dudes when it's evident there are five in this photograph."

Eric remained silent. As Simon exited the room, he spotted Diane watching from the other side and he shot her a dirty grin that enraged her.

"I will be seeing you around, Diane Gates," he chuckled and walked away, much to Diane's dismay, a free man.

She stormed her way into the interrogation room, fuming red all over and barely able to let out her words to show how angry she truly was.

"You are letting him go?" she yelled.

The detective brought his hands to his head and closed his eyes for a moment.

"What if he disappears? He clearly showed enough markers to indicate he knew something he wasn't telling you because you didn't press him hard enough."

He slowly turned around with a faint smile on his face. "I love it when you get all fiery and pumped up, but I have this under control."

Diane felt herself simmer immediately as she took her seat opposite the man and waited for a better explanation.

"He was never going to tell us anything," he explained. "If there is one thing I know, it is people like him who have been in an out of the interrogation room and they know how the system works."

Diane cocked her head and bit on her lips. "He played us."

They could both agree on those three words and it seemed to dent her ego and leave her with questions as to whether she was losing her touch as a good criminologist.

"What happens now?"

"I know what he looks like and I know where he works. The moment I let him go, I had a police buddy tail him," he explained with a faint smile.

Diane chuckled softly and admitted to herself about not seeing his actions coming.

"Can we get something to eat, I'm starving," Eric muttered just as he got to his feet and turned around.

The interrogation room door swung open and standing in the doorway was the man they both had been trying to avoid. The Captain's displeased demeanor was more than enough to inform them both that he was aware of the situation.

"What are you two doing?"

Diane had always heard the phrase 'tables turned' but never literally happened to her. Detective Barnes had his defiant face on, but she could tell the man was simply putting on a show so as not to look weak. They were both trapped, like a mouse in Larry Henwick's cage and he alone held the key. He wasn't about to let them go easily.

"I'd ask again but, quite frankly, I don't think you two have been listening to me from the moment we came across Alan's body and his confession note," Captain Henwick continued.

Diane exchanged a glance with her partner. It was obvious the man needed her to remain silent for as long as she could.

Captain Henwick sighed and pulled his seat closer to the table. "I know this means a lot to you, Miss Gates, considering your relationship with the victim. To my knowledge, your involvement with my detective is also considerable, but this cannot continue to happen on my watch."

She snorted derisively, intending to anger the man as the action duly worked.

"Did he tell you?" He asked, looking from Detective Barnes to Diane.

Diane was lost but still managed to maintain a rather perplexed expression on her face.

"Did he tell you how he got whatever information he fed you about Simon Clark?" he asked.

Diane wondered what sort of question the Captain was asking, but the expression on Detective Barnes's face seemed to simmer into one with less pride attached to it.

"If this goes on and you don't put an end to it as I asked you to, I'll have your badge!" the Captain roared.

He got up from his seat and shot Diane a look of disgust, before turning away and heading for the door. In the split moment, right between when she felt they had the upper hand by being silent and the detective suddenly looking guilty, Diane felt her walls of resolve toward the Captain crashing down hard and fast.

Captain Henwick stopped by the door with his hand on the doorknob. "You didn't talk to him either, did you?"

Eric looked up at Diane, wearing the same perplexed expression as she had some minutes before. She had hoped to reveal everything she found out about the man as soon as possible, but the opportunity never seemed to arise. Captain Henwick exited the room and left his overbearing presence behind.

Like a poked bear from its slumber, the duo left in the room had their questions coursing dangerously across the fields of their minds. For Diane, it had more to do with what the detective had done to obtain the information he provided her with, while she could guess he wanted answers as well about what the Captain had just mentioned.

Diane took two steps forward and started feeling a whole lot of pressure overwhelm her as she attempted to figure out the right way to break her thoughts to the man she was, without a doubt, in love with. Relationships had never been easy for her and as much as she did her best to navigate this one, there always seemed to be something right around the corner, attempting to derail her.

"Eric, I was—" she stopped, not because the words clinging dearly to her throat wouldn't get out, but because his cellphone rang, breaking the moment.

"Hey Duke," Eric said to his cellphone with a rather excited look on his face. "Okay, buddy, thanks," he muttered, before bringing the call to an end and looking at Diane.

She weighed her thoughts and tried to voice the words dangling in her throat, but his demeanor seemed somewhat forbidding.

"The captain just pulled the tail I had on Simon and we don't know where he is right now," he whispered in a strained voice.

Diane gasped, inwardly cursing their luck. She yanked at the chair before her and tossed it into the far corner to her right in rage.

"Every time! Every freaking time!" She yelled.

Eric got to his feet and knuckled his fists into the table with his gaze affixed on Diane. "Is there something you'd like to tell me?"

She shot him a rather mocking glare. "You'd have to appreciate the irony in your question," she replied with a sarcastic smile.

He looked toward the door and then back at her, almost as if he was drained of strength to speak or any measurable resolve to argue with her.

"We need to talk, but not in here."

Diane figured he was right. They needed to talk, and she knew just the place.

Chapter Eighteen

Diane paced the room, waiting for him to speak while he seemed to be taking his time to come up with something tangible. She could recognize a deflecting personality and that was precisely what the man was doing, and badly so too.

"I got our guy, didn't I?" he asked, almost as if he meant to ask her if the end didn't justify whatever means he had taken to get his information.

Diane shot him a stern look, shook her head in disbelief, and continued to wait impatiently for an answer to the one question she'd asked, the moment they'd walked through her front door together.

"How did you get the intel?"

He had stuttered almost for a minute, before residing to cool off by sitting in the chair.

"Everything you sent me, profiling the killer and how Catherine must have been scared of authorities or speaking to them about her problems because she might have had a bad experience with one… ," he began but suddenly cut short his sentence.

Diane wasn't buying the words. There was more to it than he was telling her, and she could feel it.

"Okay, I didn't get the pictures from the college, following protocol," he confessed.

She still felt rather lost, whilst also doing her best not to vent out her frustrations just yet.

"I stole it, okay? They gave me some nonsense about waiting possibly three months before information on the case could be handed over to us," he sounded exhausted.

"They were worried it would open a sour spot for their school and tarnish their image," Diane said to him. "It still didn't give you the right to steal their files and lie to me about getting it through some bullshit stellar police work!"

Her rage couldn't be contained anymore. She willed herself to let it out as best as possible without caring where it would lead.

He got to his feet. "The damn files were there in their office and they wouldn't give it to me."

Diane snickered and shook her head.

"I pleaded with them and even tried to bring them into the fact we have an open murder case, but like Larry, they claimed the case was closed and that it wasn't their business anymore!" He said with a raised voice.

"It still doesn't explain the need to steal the files," she countered. "I would have believed a seasoned detective as yourself would know better! Anything we found would not be admissible in a court of law. We would not have been able to use it as evidence if found out!"

She turned her back on him, held her face in her hands, and felt her head threaten to implode the longer she thought about the implications of his mess. The entire case could be referred to as a joke if news got out about how he got his evidence or information. The fact Larry now had that weapon against them only made things worse.

"Why didn't you tell me about your meeting with captain Larry?" he finally saw the opportunity to ask his own questions. "What was that about?"

Diane walked away and soon returned from her room with the same files she had received from the Captain. She put them before him and watched his eyes widen with shock and his lips part to swallow enough air in disbelief.

"How did you get these?" he asked, flipping through the pages.

Diane remained silent, hoping to make him see her disappointment and how much she knew.

"Is everything in there true?" she finally asked.

He pushed the notes away and looked at her. "I get my job done and put in everything I have, which isn't a bad thing. Loads of great detectives make such sacrifices to be who they are!"

The passionate tone from his voice showed her by how much the man was missing the point. He was willing to burn relationships and sacrifice having any personal life for his work, without caring how the other party involved with him felt. To make matters worse, he had his limits and, as clearly stated in the documents, he didn't handle stress too well.

"I need to know if I should worry once those familiar patterns emerge," she sought his assurance.

He tossed his arms in the air, turned around, and began to shake his head fervently.

"You think I'm going to go nuts because of this little case," he chuckled. "How easy it is for you to take the side of a freaking shrink after reading a few fucking files about an ordeal you know nothing about!"

"Those files show how erratic you got after losing your—" she stopped mid-sentence, noticing his blood-red eyes and clenched fists.

He fumed and turned to the wall before him, ramming his fist into it three times before leaning against it with his head as he tried to hold himself from imploding further.

"I made one mistake and with that, everything changed," he whispered.

The files had labeled the man as driven, obsessive, and sometimes compulsive when he had a target to pursue or a lead on a case he found an interest in.

"I was meant to be his cover on a routine check in that old abandoned building. We had gotten a tip that a suspect of an armed robbery, who had killed six people, was inside," he sniffed. "All I had to do was double-check the freaking store and…"

He lowered his head before bursting into tears. Diane approached but watched him lift his hand, preventing her from coming any closer.

"My methods always work, and I never leave any stones unturned! The longer we wait, the harder it becomes to catch this damn killer!" he yelled. "Captain Larry doesn't understand what we do out there and he never will. Not when all he cares about is sitting in his big fucking chair and play politics!"

Diane tended her hand to him, hoping to bring him closer, but he refused.

"I trust you, Eric," she whispered as she neared him. "I trust you."

She took him into her embrace, and he brought his head to rest on her shoulder as he wept some more.

"I have a plan, but I need you to trust me," he whispered.

Diane pulled away gently and held his face in her hands as they locked with each other. His beautiful eyes seemed calm, yet she could tell that a storm loomed behind them.

"I need you to speak with the Captain again," he smiled. "He must stop holding us from this investigation. I have to work on a new case, but that doesn't mean you can't investigate. He has to let me work on the side with this case."

She agreed immediately and smiled back at the man in response. Diane didn't want to but maybe she can find a way to motivate Larry to back off. Not exactly blackmail, but she knew a lot from her previous job.

"You have to meet with him tomorrow," he stated.

She nodded, while his hand traced up her waist and settled beneath her breasts.

"I am sorry I wasn't entirely honest with you about the files, I just wasn't…" He stopped mid-sentence as her finger came to rest on his lips.

She leaned closer to Eric, planting her lips on his. "I love you," she whispered, hearing her words echo around the room.

Spilling the words felt like it was worth it. She led him by his hand toward the bedroom where more details about his plan would be discussed at length. He was worth it. He obviously would do anything for her and that in itself was what mattered.

Whatever Eric was about to do, she trusted him, or at least, he needed her to do just that. It was why she was back in the one place she had not planned to return to. The police station.

Chills of discomfort momentarily raced down her spine and her eyes continued to sweep around the offices as she waltzed by. The unnerving moment only seemed to simmer when she realized that she was the object of blatant gawking from almost every person in the room. Diane shook her head, knowing that what she wore was a tad too much for the men to handle.

The choice of a red dress tightly fitted onto her gorgeous physique, paired with black heels was distracting, but it was exactly what she was hoping for. It was basic psychology, distracting the other party's mind off what the main topic of discussion ought to be.

"Miss Gates!" Captain Henwick called out, sounding rather pleased to see her.

Odd, albeit acceptable, was the phrase she would have used if she had not called him earlier to inform him of her coming. He had been receptive over the phone as well, and she knew it had to do with the words she'd spilled right off the bat.

"We are willing to cooperate with you," she had said right out and without dally.

His lengthy pause meant he tried to think it through, but the sudden outburst of laughter from his end within seconds quickly dispelled that notion of Diane's mind. After all, she might have been giving the man too much credit. He wasn't that smart or even foresighted. More so, when it came to power, he was an insatiable beast with no self-esteem whatsoever.

It was exactly as Eric had said it would be. Stalling him would be easy as pie.

"It is good to see you, Larry," she greeted back as he extended his hand, leading her into the office.

Diane stepped into the large office which had recently undergone an immense redecoration. It was glaringly obvious that he'd rather waste resources to further his cause than get serious police work done. Diane felt her insides cringe but managed to keep herself in check as she took her seat.

"I'm surprised you decided to work with me or even listen to reason about what I told you and Detective Barnes," he leaned against the wall to her left and smiled wildly.

Diane shrugged. "Well, this isn't exactly a peaceful resolution but more like me coming to strong-arm you into doing what I want."

His smile suddenly turned into a frown.

"Or rather, what it is you should be doing as the head of this department," she rephrased her words.

He scoffed, doing nothing to refute what she had just said to him. He rounded his desk and planted himself comfortably into his seat with the cocky smile still gracing his lips and his eyes shooting rather daring glares at Diane. She had discussed doing what she was about to with Eric at large and the argument about it had been extensive, but the man before her wasn't about to give her any other choice.

She cleared her throat and drew closer toward his ebony tiled desk. "Larry."

He grunted in response.

"I need to find this killer and whoever did this is out there, having a good life because they feel we aren't after them. Detective Barnes needs to work on this case freely and I cannot do it with you cutting his resources."

He remained silent, before bursting into laughter. The longer he laughed the more likely he was to let out things and Diane remained calm, leaning back into her seat with a wry smile gracing the corners of her mouth.

"I thought you two had come to your senses," he said, bringing his fake laughter to an end. "I put my resources in cases that need them, and not some wild goose chase where the pair of you is playing Batman and Robin."

He swung in his seat, turning his back on her while his gaze settled out of the window and toward the larger city building outside of it.

"I have a shot at achieving something others who sat in similar seats as mine couldn't, through their tenure," he spoke softly. "I have laid down the groundwork, had extensive support from those that matter because they recognize my work and me being a swift, precise, and hardworking man."

Diane felt the urge to burst out laughing, possibly as hard as he had laughed earlier, but she refrained.

"Do you have any idea what it makes me look like when I go back to the same press I told Catherine's murder had been solved to tell them otherwise?" He turned back around with his right brow arched.

"They will see you as human and one who is willing to go the extra mile to get the right answers and not settle for crap?" she replied sarcastically.

"I'll lose my credibility."

Diane found it impossible not to snort or laugh this time around. It came out loud and in a condescending tone, but she was past the point of caring.

"Come on, Larry. Police officers make these mistakes all the time," she reminded him. "I've seen cases reopen and the glory goes to whoever thought of it in the first place."

He remained silent and said nothing while he turned around in his chair.

"You can take all the credit once we catch this guy," she assured him.

He snorted. "You mean the fantasy killer you two have been chasing for how long now and with no considerable result?"

She felt the jab strike her heart immensely, but it was the truth and it was bound to hurt.

"Did you even know why I didn't want you two dealing with or get anywhere near Simon Clark?" he asked.

She shook her head.

"We believe he's storing and moving drugs from his storage facility, a case that's active and a combined effort with the FBI and you bringing him in here will only risk our ability to gather more intel," he explained.

He sounded as convincing as he wanted to be, but not enough to fool Diane. She knew better and she understood why the man was trying to cover his ass. Hearing him mention the name felt like the perfect opportunity she had been waiting for and with that, she slipped her hand into her handbag, while his eyes trailed her every move.

"I think it's time we both cut the bullshit," she said seriously, tossing an article from an old newspaper page on the table.

"What is this?"

"You screwed up," she bluntly replied. "I have always seen you as incompetent, greedy, useless on the field, and I have everything I need to make others see how far you've simply been skating through."

Larry Henwick picked up the paper and looked too frightened to read it with his brows falling and his face growing pale just after seeing the headline.

"You snort bag!" she spoke without holding back. "This was your mess and you recognized her the moment she was murdered, didn't you?"

He shrugged, doing his best to feign ignorance as he looked at his door. He hurried to his feet and slammed it shut, leaning his back into it, and sighing out loud, betraying the fact that he was being backed into a corner he might not have a way out from.

"You don't understand," he reasoned

Diane slumped her right shoulder and leaned back into the comfortable leather seat. "Enlighten me on how you blamed a rape case on an innocent man, now in prison, while the real perpetrator is still out there."

He shook his head and waved his hands frantically.

"I got the right guy. He had a record and I got him, that's why he is in jail."

She shook her head. "You got the guy you wanted and you put him in jail because you couldn't find the real rapist, who happens to be the same person who came back to murder Catherine years after you let him escape. You rushed that case then just as you are doing now."

He stared at the newspaper and began to pace around the room while Diane bid her time.

"It is your word against mine and from where I'm standing, with you sleeping with that work junkie of a detective, I will easily discredit you both!"

Diane snuck her right hand which had been partially hidden in her bag out and slammed something into the table. It was a photograph of Larry Henwick with Simon Clark years ago meeting in a secluded warehouse.

"He isn't your informant," she tore his words into shreds. "You colluded with that bastard to help you win your case because his testimony would have been far more credible in court as a guard who worked in the school. If I show this picture to a judge the old case at least will be reopened, and you'll have to explain yourself. Last time I checked, bribing someone to testify is against the law. Your chances at being Mayor will be over."

The Captain yanked off his tie and collapsed into his seat in a loud heap. He had been found out and there was no doubt about it. As much as Detective Eric had done his homework, she had pieced a whole lot of the other information together. All she needed to do was dig deeper into the rape case years ago and find out why the college refused to give out information.

"You told the school not to provide us with the things we need, which was why Detective Eric had to steal them," she confronted the man. "You're a shameful bastard and I have always known it and as much as it had never been my business, it is now."

She figured everything she had laid bare would let the wind out of his tires. He struggled for words and his demeanor continued to bear enough grief regardless of how hard he tried to hide it.

"I did what I could," he whispered.

"No, you messed up big time, and that mess from years ago has come back to bite us in ways we could have prevented if you had done your job right!" she snapped. "How the hell did you even pick a suspect and successfully put him in prison for something he didn't do?"

He rubbed his temple and began to hyperventilate. Reaching for his drawer, he yanked out a paper bag and plunged half his face into it as he struggled to maintain a steady breath. All the time, Diane sat with her legs crossed opposite him, making no move to help him.

He paused after a good number of pants. "There were no witnesses, no suspect and nobody could identify the freaking guy! Not even your dead girl could give me something useful about him!"

"So, you picked a previous offender working in the school premise and sent him to prison," she concluded. "Well, your mess and inability to do what was right has cost us and I'd be damned to let it continue to cost this investigation any more setbacks. How can you be so worried about your ass that you don't care about finding a killer? Catherine would be alive today if it weren't for you messing up back then."

"What do you want?" he asked in a contrite tone. "This will ruin me if it gets out… is that what you want? Is this what you and your boyfriend want?"

Diane laughed, seeing the paranoid look on Larry Henwick's face threaten to cause his blood vessels to implode.

"Back off Larry!" she yelled right back. "Back the hell off and let us do our job! That's what I want."

The Captain held up his hands, indicating his compliance as he took another look at the article staring right back at him.

"You can do whatever you want with the case. I will re-open it, but I want things done quietly for now. When you're ready with actual hard evidence against a potential suspect, I'll even speak to the press," he assured her.

Diane stood, donning the warmest smile on her face, and not indicating how much of a beast she had just been with the man. "I would appreciate that."

She turned her back on him but could still very well feel his gaze locked on the back of her head. He was drowning in anger and if he had his way, he would surely fight back, but she had taken everything away from him. He was in no position to fight back.

"By the way," he called out and she stopped halfway through the door. "You still aren't out of the woods with Detective Barnes."

Diane smiled. "I will learn to hunt my demons, Larry."

With the words said, and his assurance given, even if they didn't count for anything, she exited the police station feeling both relieved and tired. She took out her phone and called Eric immediately, before getting into her car.

"How did it go?" the man on the other end asked.

"It was perfect! He is reopening the case, but we have to move quietly until we get hard evidence. Once we do, he'll go to the press," she replied. "How are things with Simon?"

Eric fell silent for a while. "Same old, same old, but I'm not letting him out of my sight just yet"

She sighed in relief and started her car before pulling off. "Can you come over tonight? With Larry off your case, you can have someone else stake the place out for you."

"Make it nine," he replied.

Chapter Nineteen

For Diane, nothing beat the smell of books in the morning, but even while her heart yearned to carry on with business in the store, the one unsolved distraction she seemed unable to find a way past, continued to trouble her. While she flipped through Catherine's journal, it continued to become even more apparent how disturbed the girl was.

She cited her problems with drugs as a way to ease herself off of the mental sufferings she endured every night when she attempted to close her eyes and rest. Night after night, she remained awake, diving into her job hoping it would keep her awake as best as possible.

"She was alive but not necessarily living," Diane whispered just before looking out of her store at the light rain pouring down.

"Nobody fought enough for you," she muttered to herself. "Nobody."

She looked up to the front door opening again as the doorbell rang.

"James took over for me for a while," Eric approached then leaned toward Diane and planted a warm kiss on her lips.

She wrapped her arms around him and held him tightly for a while, before easing off as he took a spot on the seat not far from her.

"Slow day?" he asked, looking around.

She nodded. "I had some shipment sent to schools and some orders should be ready for pickup by noon. Then the usual. People coming in to browse or sit and read."

She studied the man, noting his nervous ticks. He adjusted in his seat every chance he got and stuck his hand into his jacket only to take it out again and again. She watched him perform the act for the fifth time before clearing her throat.

"What is going on with you?" she asked.

He did his best to hide the nervous streak on his forehead. "I don't understand your question."

"Is the stress getting to you?' she took his hand into hers and inquired. "Something is bound to break soon with Simon. I am pretty sure of it."

Eric tightened his grip around her hand and nudged his head without showing that he understood what she was talking about or that he agreed with her.

"Has Larry been behaving?" she inquired.

"Yes," he sounded glad. "I'm still skeptical about letting him in on everything I'm doing, but the guys he sent are my buddies and they wouldn't rat on me."

It sounded like progress and it was precisely what Diane wanted to hear about. She got to her feet and began to walk back to her spot behind the counter, but he yanked at her arm and stopped her in her tracks.

"I have something for you," he said on a chuckle. "I was thinking of keeping it until tonight at dinner, but what the hell?" He took out a thick file from underneath his jacket.

He put it on the counter and began emptying it. "Everything in here contains my surveillance for the past two weeks and as much as I didn't want to blow my whistle too soon, I figured you'd be interested in knowing how far I've come." He seemed pretty jived up.

He laid out a set of photographs and then personal notes he had made. He pinned down the pictures with his hand and motioned to Diane to look at him.

"I tailed Simon for a week and the guy does nothing but cheat people, steal from them, and deal drugs in that place," he explained. "I mean, the guy is a total mess and nothing in his life seems consistent aside from these three things."

Diane sensed there was an interjection coming or some kind of revelation and she opted against jinxing it by speaking too quickly. The man had his markers and one of them was stressing a sentence when he had follow-ups to give afterward.

"One thing stood out, or one person rather," he continued. "There is this dude I see with him regularly at wee hours, sneaking stuff into the facility and heading out as early as six in the following morning."

"That's quite common with these storage houses," Diane reminded him. "People hide lots of stuff in those spaces that you'd be surprised what exactly they have in there."

He suddenly mellowed and the look of excitement on his face seemed to die within seconds.

"I know but I feel there is something to this guy," he repeated. "I mean, you need to see how really careful they get when they are dealing, and they seem to go way back too."

He finally began splitting the photos out individually so she could see them herself. Loads of the surveillance photos contained images of Simon Clark and a hooded figure whose face couldn't be seen from the pictures he had taken at night.

"This guy has been super careful all through and I never at any point in time got a clean shot of his face," he sounded in distraught tone.

Diane picked the photographs from the counter and began studying them. Without a doubt, there was something shady going on with those two and she didn't need to look far to see it.

"If you cannot identify this guy, and Simon is freaking well protected because of his pact with Larry, then we have nothing. Larry claims he is working with the FBI on busting Simon on drug charges which your photos prove there is something there with the drug accusations." She sounded both displeased and exhausted.

He remained silent and showed no signs of frustration. Instead, he tucked his hands into his pocket and smiled, almost as if she was the only one worried about their current predicament.

"What?" she felt compelled to ask.

She leaned closer and he wrapped his arm around her shoulder. Diane could feel it in her bones that the detective was up to something. He was unusually happy and in a good mood, unlike some days back when all she got from him were grumpy responses via call when they spoke.

"Well, it didn't matter that he tried his best to hide his face and remain hidden, because I got him," he chuckled.

Diane held her breath and waited for the line indicating that he was trying to mess with her.

"For real, I got him," he repeated, sneaking his hand out of his pocket, handing some papers to her.

"This had better not be some kind of joke," she warned him, trying her best not to get herself over the moon when in fact, there might be nothing to feel happy about.

She unfolded the notes and found her breath hard to come by almost immediately. Her fingers tightened into the edge of the paper in her hand which contained Eric's handwriting, but her eyes were glued on the photograph he had taken and attached to the note up in the right-hand corner.

"Are you okay?" he asked worriedly.

Diane looked up at the detective, feeling all the blood draining from her face and with her lips trembling.

"What is it?" he asked again, looking and sounding scared as well.

"That's Steven," she mumbled, fearing her words might sound too loud.

The detective relieved her of the notes and pictures to have a good look at it again himself. Diane ran her fingers through her hair endlessly, seemingly battered with what could only be a shock.

"Steven who?"

She tried to push down the feeling of dread rushing up to her throat and replied. "He is one of my most frequent customers. A blind man. He comes here often to get books. Since I opened the store, he's been one of my most loyal customer. I've had meals with the man, some days talked to him for hours."

It still didn't seem to register with the detective as he shrugged and looked back at the picture. She could see he was a little bit skeptical about buying into her words because of one major detail. The man in his picture wasn't blind, but in fact, there were pictures of him driving a car.

A Jaguar.

"Blind men don't drive cars," he reminded cheekily.

She shook her head and got to her feet. "I felt something was odd with him the last two times he was here, and I swear that the man in that picture *is* Steven!"

The detective got to his feet as well, at that point, more inclined to believe her.

"Do you have anything to identify him to make sure that he is the one in the picture?"

Diane frowned at him in disbelief. She would expect him to believe her and not be so skeptical.

"If I'm going to approach the Captain for a search warrant, I need to have my facts straight."

She stepped back and wondered what exactly seemed to be getting the man into a twist all of a sudden.

"I'm sure he's the one. I even introduced him to Catherine when she started working with me." Her voice was full of regret as she turned to search through her record books. "Our customers are asked to provide some form of identification when they make large purchases with a credit card. I'm pretty sure I have him on my security camera footage since he comes here so much."

She searched the records vehemently but found nothing relating to Steven.

"He gave me a freaking photo ID on the first day," she shrieked, kicking against the stash of boxes in her path while she searched thoroughly. "I'll send you copies of my security cameras.

"If you're right about him, then I need to get to the station."

Eric raced out of the room immediately without saying goodbye.

Frustrated and feeling like she had been blindsided and played for a fool, Diane searched her computer for a copy of Steven's ID. She was certain Steven had given her his picture, even though it would be with his dark glasses as a blind man.

"Did he take it?" she wondered.

The possibility of him being the killer seemed pretty high, considering everything they knew so far. Catherine had hurt her attacker by damaging his eye, and that justified the suspicions Diane had about Steven from the moment she saw his eyes after Catherine's murder. She still remembered how that made her feel as if she was looking at someone she knew. But he played blind even before Catherine's murder.

"He must have taken it," she heard herself conceding painfully. "The sly bastard must have cleaned up just as he did with the security cameras on the night of the murder."

Her heart sank into her chest and her breaths became heavy.

"It cannot be," she tried to tell herself in a defiant tone. "Steven cannot be Catherine's killer. He's so kind."

The pill would be hard to swallow if the detective's findings came out as true. It would only mean the man had played her and made an idiot out of her keen sense of judgment and instincts. He had always come off as sweet and a darling and that was what she saw him as, not someone with the potential to do something as diabolical as they had witnessed.

Why at her bookstore? So many questions ran through her mind. Steven was a customer before Catherine began working for her. He went with her a few times to get coffee at Alan's Coffee Shop and Catherine served them. Why didn't he kill her a long time ago?

There was a huge chance everything was nothing but circumstantial. Maybe he was just a drug criminal, but the other coincidences were somewhat baffling. She did her best to pull herself together and get through the workday.

Three hellish days passed, and her cellphone continued to chime with messages and phone calls, but not from whom she wanted to hear from. In fact, the days had trickled by slowly and with nothing but absolute torture every time she looked at her phone ring but nothing from Detective Barnes.

"What is going on with you, Eric?" she asked herself before placing the phone to her ear waiting for him to pick up.

The call remained unanswered until she got directed to his voice mail. Opting against sending the umpteenth voice message, she marched out of her living room and headed for the kitchen counter to pick up her car key. She knew where he would be or was most likely to be.

Diane rushed directly to the police station ready to give him hell for ignoring her. She thought they were officially a couple and a team on Catherine's case, but his distance proved differently. When Captain called her to let her know that Eric was at the storage facility, she made an illegal U-turn and sped there, hoping they'd finally found what they needed.

Slowing down as she approached the endless police cars parked outside the storage facility, Diane made out Eric's car in the distance, not far off from her preferred parking spot. She hurried out of the car to police sirens blaring aloud.

"I'm sorry, Ma'am, but you cannot be here," an officer stopped Diane in her tracks, while they cordoned off the area.

"My name is Dr. Diane Gates, and I'm with Detective Eric Barnes," she stated clearly.

She looked around, hoping to find the man but he remained out of sight.

"I am a consultant with..." She stopped as she spotted him ahead with a group of officers behind him. "Eric! Eric!"

Her voice felt strained while she continued to scream to get his attention. Eric looked in her direction and waved her through.

"Eric!" she called out while they got within touching distance of each other. "I've been trying to reach you for days!"

He looked pretty worn out, to say the least, and his clothes didn't appear to have been changed for a while. They were too wrinkled and dirty.

"I haven't been with my phone, sorry," he apologized. "Must have dropped the thing at home, and I've been too busy to go back for it."

She couldn't care less about his phone; she was relieved that he was alright after all and he was not intentionally ignoring her. Later, he'd still get an earful about not being home for so many days.

"Did you guys find anything?" she asked frantically.

He looked back at the site as more police officers carried out an extensive search of the entire property.

"We've been at it for a day now and nothing so far. Each space would need a warrant, so we've been tracking down owners of the spaces and asking them for permission to search their storages. But we just learned your customer, Steven has a rental space in here as well which he has been hiding out in," he explained. "We haven't located it yet because Simon refuses to cooperate, but once I find something, I'll let you know. We couldn't get a warrant with evidence on Simon as the judge wants him on the drug case, but we found another judge who signed a warrant to search Steven's storage space"

She cocked her head and leaned toward him to plant a kiss to his lips. There was no telling how much she missed him and she had almost committed herself into having a nervous meltdown just thinking about the worst possible things that could happen to Eric if Steven was truly the killer, especially if he perceived Eric as an enemy, trying to nail him.

"What about Steven? Do you know where he is?" she asked.

"Detective Barnes!" An officer yelled, waving him over. "You need to come and see this!"

Eric turned to Diane and motioned that he had to leave. Immediately, he hurried to the officer and Diane wondered if she should tell him that she had a storage unit in the same place they were investigating. It was her secret after all, even while she still had not summoned up the courage to go through it or whatever it contained. She still felt like holding onto the place.

"Shut it, creep!" Diane heard someone yell, prompting her to turn back around.

Simon grinned at her while they marched him off and placed him into one of the police cars. For a man being dragged in handcuffs, he seemed relaxed and she knew why. Thanks to the Captain being his friend, he was going to be out soon. She only hoped that the evidence was enough for both the FBI and the police to keep Simon off the streets.

"Get in the fucking car!" The officer restraining Simon yelled, shoving him into the back seat and slamming the door shut behind him.

The officer stepped away, allowing Diane to sneak into the front seat of the police vehicle.

"Hello Simon," she greeted calmly.

He looked up at her with the same nauseating and cocky grin on his face.

"Where is Steven?" she asked and pinned her focus on him without wavering.

His eyes widened and the corners of his lips seemed to twitch upon hearing the name, but he hurriedly masked his features with an expression of ignorance. "I don't know who that Steven is."

He was lying and that was a fact. She could read the deceit written all over his face and it made her want to reach over and yank at his throat.

"You worked with him at the college didn't you?" she asked again.

He simply chuckled, held up his cuffed wrists, and smiled at her. "I have nothing to say to you, darling, but rest assured that I'll be leaving here really soon because you got nothing on me. You all don't have a warrant to search the place and even if you did you think I would have left evidence around after the first time you and your boy toy brought me in?"

She was wasting her time. He wasn't going to tell her anything. She exited the vehicle, having established one fact. Simon Clark knew who Steven was and he was most likely covering for the guy. That was enough for her. Why a drug criminal would cover for Steven? It only provided enough speculation that there had been another killer out there as she had initially thought. Simon Clark was closely observed by the FBI so he couldn't be one of the killers. Steven was the perfect person for Catherine's murder, but he couldn't have acted alone.

"What sort of game are you playing?" she asked, trying to place herself into the criminal's mindset.

The killer wasn't an amateur and whatever experience he had with killing people had worked well for him when he dispatched off Alan with ease. She returned to her car and decided she still had an awful lot to try and decipher about the killers. Her one hope as she drove away was for Eric to find something useful, so they could finally have a face to match their second killer. She had to find proof there was someone else out there too.

"There has to be something here," she resided into telling herself again as she stared at the mural she made from pictures of dead bodies and ideas scribbled on notes pinned into the wall. The oven timer went off, forcing her to check on the roast she was cooking.

The cold floor stung her feet as she got up and hurried toward the kitchen to check the food and put it into dishes before placing them back in the warmer.

She returned to her position on her office floor, legs tucked in and her eyes glued to the wall all over again. Nothing could distract her at that moment, not even an apocalypse.

"Shit," she cursed, feeling her phone vibrate by her side.

Torn between keeping her focus on the wall and finding out who was calling, she picked the latter and saw the caller ID sprawled across her screen. Her heart leaped, and her hand moved faster than her brain could acknowledge.

"Eric."

"Hey! Steven gave us the slip, but we found some things in his storage room that you wouldn't believe."

She pumped her fist into the air in excitement then ran her hand through her hair and smiled. Things were coming together.

"I want to see them," she finally stated.

"Of course, I'm on my way and I was hoping we could celebrate," he replied, before ending the call.

As much as a celebration did not seem appropriate, considering their main suspect evaded them, Diane concluded that Eric needed tonight's victory. He had worked too hard not to deserve a night of celebration. She got up and decided to have a shower before he arrived. Dinner was ready for him and she had picked up an expensive bottle of champagne before she got home, hopeful of the search results.

When Diane walked back into her office, she found an unmoving Eric staring at the mural of information she had made on the wall. She had not heard him come in and he seemed oblivious to her presence. Sneaking up on him like a feline, she slipped her hands around his waist and held onto him tightly.

He turned around looking drained, and yet a thin smile was still on his face. "I thought you had gone to bed when you didn't answer the door."

He held up his spare key and smiled.

"I was in the shower. It's too early for tonight to end so fast after the breakthrough you had today." Smiling, she wrapped her arms around his neck. "You deserve to celebrate. I'll pour us some champagne."

He chuckled softly and lowered his head to meet her lips.

"I made dinner," she noted, leading him out of her office, and pointing at the table the man must have missed when he came in.

Set and ready to enjoy a nice meal before she would ask him to regale her all his findings, Diane had slipped on a sexy black gown with no underwear.

"I don't know which I want to have first, you or the delicious food I smell," he whispered warmly into her ear before planting another kiss on her cheek. "I'm surprised you aren't more eager to find out what I brought back with me from Steven's storage unit."

She shrugged her shoulders as though she wasn't excited to ask and led him to the dining room table. "We can do that over dinner. I'll go get the food."

He agreed and sat down as she went to the kitchen and grabbed the dishes already made and brought them back to the table.

"You know I ache to see what you've found right?" she asked, trying her best not to look at his jacket where they were bound to be.

He chuckled, nodding his head as he took out the notes and pictures taken from the site.

"Steven might be our guy after all."

"Might?"

"We're still running tests and fingerprints from all we took from his rented storage space, but so far, everything points in his direction. We found some articles on Catherine's rape in college in that room and some things that may have belonged to her. We just have to wait for the forensic results. The media has Steven's photo so hopefully, the public will help us find him."

Diane wasn't sure how to respond to him. She was under the impression that there were loads of condemning evidence, pointing him as the killer, but hearing Eric speaking in hypothetical terms set her alarm bells off.

"Did you find anything in there at all? Did you recover murder weapons, diaries, or personal belongings which can be traced back to Catherine or to him being the one who raped and murdered her?"

He seemed somewhat reluctant to respond and busied himself with his meal.

"We took all we got in for tests and we should know more soon," he simply stated. "The only leads we have are those items and the fact he happens to be a regular at your store and was also in contact with Catherine before she died. We have female items from the unit and

I'm sure the test will confirm they're Catherine's. There might be traces of blood, but we have to be meticulous and test everything."

Nothing made sense to her and Eric wasn't open with her. He continued with his meal and seemed disinterested in actually speaking about the case, while she looked through the list of hypothetical thoughts and the idea he had scribbled down. He should be more sure of himself. His behavior was unusual.

"You don't have him nailed as your suspect, do you?" she asked frustrated.

He looked at her and shook his head gently. "We got nothing on him for now, but things can change once the test results from the forensic team come from the lab."

Diane yanked her hand away from his as he reached out to hold hers. She perused all he had given her again and couldn't quite make sense of any of them. They had overwhelming evidence but waited for a test to bring Steven, and that baffled her. They should have enough to bring him in and keep him.

"The storage space," he looked at her. "How did you know Simon Clark worked there?"

She placed down the photos and notes. "I think the most important question is why Steven pretends to be blind when he visits my store, while in reality, he isn't," she turned the subject person and matter around immediately.

"He might be having difficulties with his eyesight at times, maybe he is partially blind. If he raped Catherine back in college then he does have one eye missing." Eric answered before wiping his mouth clean and getting up. "I need to shower and go to bed early."

She made no move to stop him. Their mood was soured, and sex was out without question. She continued to eat her food not bothering to get up with him, while Eric walked over to the living room entry wall. She thought he was going to head to the bedroom.

"Do you mind if I come back in the morning?" he asked.

Surprised but not willing to show it, she shook her head. "Tomorrow's Sunday and I'll be in all day."

Chapter Twenty

"You might want to wake up now, Diane," the calm, yet troubling voice caused her to roll out of bed and toward the other side.

Landing on the floor, Diane snuck her hand underneath her bed and yanked out her revolver, pointing it in the direction of the male voice she had heard in her sleepy state.

"Whoa! Whoa!" She heard Eric cry just before her vision cleared and his previously fuzzy frame came into focus. "Put the gun down!"

Diane exhaled relieved and flicked back the safety before dumping the gun on her bed.

"You seriously need to stop sneaking into my house," she warned him. "You were a few seconds away from having a fucking hole in your chest!"

He remained silent and looked at her with what she could read to be a displeasing and disturbing look. "It can't hurt to have one more hole into your chest by someone you love."

He turned around and exited the room. Still pretty drowsy and lost about what was happening around her, she brushed her eyes clean of sleep with both hands and dragged her feet along the same trail he had taken. Diane entered the living room to the sight of her profiling board torn to the ground and littered all around.

"What in the heavens happened in here?" she asked, without looking at the only other person in the room.

"Why?" Eric asked.

She turned around to see him with his hands folded across his chest and his eyes bearing enough rage to look demonic.

"Why did you decide to make an idiot of me?" he asked.

Diane was confused as she wondered what he was talking about. More so, she needed to figure out if she had been robbed or had a break-in through the night.

"Does he work for you?" he asked in the same ambiguous tone as earlier.

She motioned toward him but watched him stretch his hand out to stop her. "What are you going on about?"

He snickered with a hint of sarcasm in his voice, before shaking his head and placing both hands over his face.

"Did you think I wasn't going to find out? Did you think I wouldn't be able to pull the records of that place and find out your dirty secrets?"

She finally connected the dots and understood what he was talking about.

"I w… wasn't hiding it from you…" she stuttered, unable to finish her sentence.

"You killed her, didn't you? Or did you have him do it for you? It isn't uncommon for those who know the law to commit what they believe to be *the perfect crime*."

Feeling insulted and enraged, she yelled right back. "Don't you dare insult me!"

He held up images he took with his cellphone for her to see, scrolling through each one to reveal his findings.

"I had to go back and see for myself," he explained. "I just couldn't sit with the fact those two guys were so protective about keeping that place from being found out and for what, just some newspaper articles and a few female items that might just prove he robbed your place that night we met. There was nothing to put Steven away for life, so why did they protect it so much."

"Where did you take these?" she asked, staring at the pictures displayed on his cellphone.

He tossed his cellphone at her and tossed his arms in the air in frustration. "Don't play the fool with me damn it! That is your freaking storage space with you in surveillance I pulled up, paying for the bloody space with cash!"

Diane's knees gave way and she found herself falling back into the seat behind her. She gawked at the picture of two storage spaces linked by what appeared to be a false wall, with a video recording showing Eric making his way through Steven's and into another, apparently hers.

"I have never seen this place before in my life, and I don't know what you're talking about," she tried to make him believe her. "I've never been inside."

He only seemed to get angrier as he flipped the couch upside down and kicked the table lamp.

"You liar! You fucking liar!" He yelled. "You played me! You fucking played me and acted as if you loved me all along!"

Diane shot up from her seat and shot back at him. "Eric, I don't know what you're going on about and I swear that I have never seen this place before! I have never even been into that room! Surely the surveillance you claimed to have watched would prove I've never gone past the front desk!"

Aside from the clothing which was well recorded to be Catherine's as well as various disturbing items preserved in jars, the most glaring were the eyes presumably taken from Catherine and the nail to the coffin that the killer had something to do with the storage unit. All the damning evidence was in the unit she paid for. She was so confused.

"Do you deny owning that storage room? Do you deny paying monthly rent for that same room!?"

Diane felt trapped and the scenario wasn't one she had ever found herself in. Instead, she had been the one dealing people with such revealing information of how they had been made and how their dirty deeds were about to be thrown into the light.

"We found everything in there," he informed her. "You've been doing this for quite some time, and I promise you there will be no hiding place for you this time around!"

She had been blindsided yet again and there seemed to be no light at the end of the tunnel for her.

"You even pay in cash to avoid being linked to the damn place, then there is Steven, who I suspect works for you because why else would he frequent your store so much? Did you even love me?"

Eric had drawn his conclusions and Diane was certain that the man before her wasn't the same one she had fallen in love with. In fact, he saw her as nothing but a liar and a deceitful being.

"I want my lawyer," she simply said and planted herself back into her seat.

Eric fell to his knees, looking dejected and broken as he looked into her eyes. "If you truly loved me or if what we had meant anything to you, I want you to talk to me. Please, talk to me. I've asked you about the storage facility and you kept skirting around the truth. All the evidence is pointing to you. My heart says you're innocent. Tell me I'm right, please. Just tell me everything you know." He took her hands into his.

Diane freed her hands, looked away from him and back at the phone containing the video recordings and photos of everything he had seen in the storage rooms. She could finally understand what Larry Henwick had meant when he labeled the detective as one who would chase a balloon to the end of the earth once he got a sniff of it.

He had gone back to investigate and had he not done that he might never have found the false wall leading into her storage space. Yet, trying to convince him of her innocence would be futile. She had no evidence to prove her innocence.

"I need my lawyer," she insisted.

He agreed, retrieving his cellphone and walking to the door. He held it open for two heavily armed officers to come rushing into the room in a manner that sunk her heart and left her stomach sinking with despair.

"Miss Diane Gates, you're under arrest for the murder of Catherine..." the officer read out her rights but she blacked out almost immediately.

She watched the heavens threaten to fall as she made her exit from her home to the sight of her neighbors opposite the street shooting castigating and hypocritical stares at her. She wondered if telling them she didn't do it would ease their obvious opinion of her.

"It won't be of any use," she said to herself, just before disappearing into the backseat of the police vehicle.

It had begun to feel like a norm for her now, being escorted into a police car. She felt little to no worry the moment the driver sped off with a fleet of police cars blaring their sirens behind her.

Tables turned as they said, and the current situation Diane had herself in was the perfect example. Having a good view of the cocky-faced Captain smiling with Detective Barnes while they chatted like they were great buddies made her stomach churn with displeasure. His mood had been nothing short of happy from the moment she stepped out of the police car.

He had ushered her into the police station and ordered her immediate processing without listening to anything from her. To make matters worse, he was now approaching, with his belly swinging from side to side and the grin on his face threatening to blind her as well.

"It is funny how tides change, isn't it?" he asked cockily. "What is it you were saying to me the other day when you walked in here all so holy and self-righteous to blackmail me?"

She looked away, feeling too pained and distressed to listen to his voice.

"The icing on the cake is seeing your lover-boy drag you in here himself," he chuckled.

The words stung her and effected a response. "He was only doing his job, something you wouldn't know anything about, would you?" she concluded with a smirk to annoy him.

"You insolent thing. I will personally see to the end of whatever legacy you have managed to build so far. I will bring you to your bony knees!"

She continued to smile at him, knowing she had struck a nerve. "I still need my phone call," she demanded.

He shot her a furious look and turned around without acknowledging her words.

"Go talk some sense into your girlfriend," he said to Detective Barnes as he walked past him.

Diane turned her back on the man as he approached, hoping he would leave her be.

"Diane," Eric called out to her.

She closed her eyes and willed her thoughts to move elsewhere.

"If you don't talk to me, then I cannot help you," he pleaded.

She snorted. "Help me? You can only do that if you believed in me. How can you say you love me one moment then another believe me to be some monster?"

She turned around and locked gaze with the man without saying any more.

"You've seen the evidence we have against you. Even you know how this plays out. What would you have me do, falsify or hide everything I found out?"

He still sounded angry and betrayed and she could understand because that was exactly how she felt.

A little part of her questioned if he might just be capable of hiding evidence for her. The thought scared her. If he *did* love her, she didn't want him to go down with her. She had to keep him away from her. "I want my phone call and I have nothing to say to you or any of the rats in this freaking place. You can rot in hell for all I care!"

He stepped forward and tightened his hand around the bars of her jail cell. "I will destroy you if you don't cooperate with me, so this entire mess can be brought to an end."

Instead of indulging him, she dared him. He turned and walked away, ignoring her demands for a phone call.

"Take a few hours to think whether you are ready to speak or not," he threw over his shoulder.

Chapter Twenty-One

Maybe it was her life or maybe there was some other kind of force trying to teach her something, but Diane was not seeing it. What she understood was that life was screwing her over. She hated the way it seemed like she had found something in Detective Barnes she could hold onto and then it slipped away, leaving her with nothing but a hollow feeling.

Despite her better judgment, Diane had fallen in love, and life decided to take him away from her. Take away everyone she cared deeply for. First, it was her father, then Catherine, and now Eric. She wondered if there was something she did. If there was something she could have done, or maybe this was her bad luck for sticking her nose in Captain Larry's business. Maybe he was involved more than she thought and he's the one setting her up.

She could hear the officers talk from where they had put her. Eric hadn't come to her with another one of those half-baked and insincere lifelines. She didn't know why this was happening, but she knew they had to let her call her lawyer.

She turned against the cell wall and slid down. She had put people in there so many times. She didn't think she would be on this side of the barricade. It was funny and weird she could not help but smile.

The case was swirling in her head and she worked up a certain kind of crazed anger. She stomped her foot on the ground like that would do any harm and then closed her eyes. She tried to calm herself. Being angry would not help.

Diane could not have known this was going to happen, but she could have known earlier that it was Steven. He had started to show signs and if she was paying attention, she would have caught those signs. He kept asking about Catherine's case, the police, and seemed to have his theory. There was so much she should have done that would have kept her away from this situation.

Diane chuckled at the irony. The one person who had been somewhat a distraction to her had been the one to put her in there. She wondered if he knew how much that hurt. Then she concluded that he *did* know, she had seen the pain in the way he shouted before dragging her to the cell. Betrayal was something she was new to even though she understood that he was just doing his job.

Diane shook her head and wondered how long she had been there. They had not allowed her to make her call yet and that was a violation. They could not charge her with anything, they didn't have any real evidence that those things in the storage room were put there by her. Things were circumstantial at best. Diane knew they wouldn't find any forensic evidence with her DNA or fingerprints on it.

The case was one intricate web of dead-ends and baits. If the murder had not occurred in her bookstore and it had not been Catherine, Diane wondered if she would have given up already. Hell, she would never have gotten involved. There was a probability that she would have. She hated the truth in that voice. She was passionate about justice, but this was the life she had tried to run from before. She had slowly walked back into it like she had not tried to run from it before.

She ran her hands over her face. She was tired and she felt like her stomach had nothing in it but air.

Fuck food, I need to get out of here. She stood up again and held the bars. She had hated people who did what she was about to do but, she hated police officers who did what they were doing to her more. It was a kind of laziness.

"I want my phone call!" Her scream bounced off the walls.

She was about to scream some more when Eric walked to her. His eyes were red. She wondered if he had been crying or if he was just exhausted. She wanted to act like she didn't care but she did. If it was not because of her insistence, he would be on another case and this would have been closed. She hated that she felt bad for him since he was not the one on the other side of the iron bars.

He looked at her like she was something dragged from the gutter. No, it wasn't disgust, it was pity. Was he sorry that he was doing this to her? She shook her head and turned away from him. It was just his acting. People who cared about other people wouldn't throw them into a prison cell. She was not going to let the man in front of her get to her.

"You ready to talk?"

Eric's face was flushed, and his voice was hollow, none of the usual bounce it had when he said something sweet to her in her living room or when they kissed, and he mumbled something romantic. The man in front of her was not her Eric. This was Eric, the detective, the angry man who felt like his heart had been toyed with. There was no hope in it. She realized how fast she needed to make the call, how badly she had to leave there before things got worse. What if they booked her and moved her without her phone call? It would take longer for her to get help.

"I have a right to a phone call, Eric"

"Yeah? Who are you going to call? Someone to clean up any other evidence we might get on you?" he asked.

His voice was laced with every shard of anger available and his eyes held all the rage she could imagine. He was not just passionate about this job. It was not just something he drowned himself in. It was his oxygen, it flowed in him. Some people were considered workaholic, but Eric was something else. He had completely become the thing that every detective was warned off. He had completely become his job. She could not believe what she just heard and tried to say something, but nothing came out.

"What?"

"I can't believe what you just said. Have you forgotten how much I wanted to solve this case with you? All the help I gave you examining evidence and that I helped get Larry to reopen the case?"

She was angry and was beginning to see that there was no use trying to get through to him. There was no hope in that. She would have to get out of here and then try to clear her name from the puddle of mud that she had found herself. She hated this but then she could not do anything about it from a jail cell.

Diane had enjoyed working together with him, and she should have kept it at that. It would have been easier if they had not gotten involved. What he had said would have stung less. She would have felt he was just another one of the brain-dead detectives the country churned out mostly. But she had kissed that same mouth and held those hands. That had to count for something.

"Eric, I need to call my lawyer."

There was no need to talk to him further. There was nothing left to say. No more of the familiarity that seemed to be burning him up. She knew she would probably feel the same way though. She would be hurt that someone she had trusted with so much had been the one killing.

"Why would you kill her, Diane? You said she was good to you. She was sweet and kind. Why?"

She didn't reply. She just looked at him with pity in her eyes.

"If you won't give me my phone call, Eric, I have nothing to say to you. I hope you know that this is wrong and remember the consequences of not allowing a suspect to call their attorney."

"If what I do now is wrong, how would you call what *you* did to that girl?"

"Seriously?"

He reduced his voice to a whisper. "You think this is wrong?" he asked once again.

She shook her head at him, she could not believe what he was saying. That she had anything to do with Catherine's murder. She wanted to get her hands-on Steven. She wanted to strangle him so bad that the feeling made her shake. She was not just angry; she was furious at what was going on.

Diane could picture him hitting Catherine, raping her and the girl being helpless on the floor while Steven smiled at her when he was done. Then he would have fished out a knife or something, killing her and digging out her eyes. The agony Catherine must have gone through, the stress of wanting to die quicker because she could not take the pain anymore.

It felt like someone had decided to play golf with Diane's stomach and the strike sent sharp pains to her brain. She doubled over and started to sob. Eric watched her for a while and then he walked away. She stayed there crying for what must have been about twenty minutes. There had been some nights where she had wanted to dodge Catherine and her questions. Some nights she didn't like talking about books or characters or the flow of sentences. She just wanted her cup of coffee and maybe a bite to eat and the girl would still bring her questions. Diane's shoulders shook with guilt. For all those times and more. For not knowing that she had trouble. Her friend didn't seem to have much happiness before her cruel death. She lived her life scared, worrying that a piece of her past had not floated in her present, and yet, it still succeeded to get to her. It was a cruel way to live.

Diane could not imagine how that had been. How Catherine was able to always smile and be the uplifting light of a room. Diane had gotten so much out of being friends with Catherine, she hoped to give her some happiness too.

"One call, Miss Gates," a voice instructed.

It was another officer. Diane closed her eyes and slowly stood. Suddenly, she was too tired to walk. It seemed like she had been in the place for days instead of just hours. She wanted to go home and have a warm bath. Being in that place made her feel tainted. She needed to sleep and then she was going to make sure she proved that she was not their suspect

Keys clanged against the iron bar as the police officer tried to unlock it for her to come out. He was not smiling or trying to taunt her.

He was not even looking at her. He was not someone Diane had seen there before. He was probably new or maybe he was not, and she had been too engrossed in her own business to notice him when she came by on her own free will.

Diane could not tell if he was not looking at her because he couldn't bear the sight of her or maybe it was nothing, just awkwardness. She wanted to say she didn't care but she did. It hurt to be accused of doing something as sick as the death of Catherine. She had loved the girl like a dear friend maybe even a little sister. She was surely going to make someone pay for what had happened to her and that was a personal promise to herself.

The officer finally opened the door and let her out before locking it again. "Over there," the officer pointed, and she nodded.

The phone was old and dirty from passing through so many hands without being cleaned. She turned and the officer was watching her. Trying to catch what she was saying, she guessed. She dialed the numbers and then waited. She had never felt so impatient for someone to take a call as she was that few seconds before she heard the voice.

"Hello?" the voice demanded.

"Vivian, I need your help. I've been arrested."

"Diane? What? why?"

Diane told her everything that happened since that morning and then dropped the phone. For once ever since she got into the station, she was able to breathe properly.

Chapter Twenty-Two

Diane had her eyes closed when she heard footsteps approaching her. It had to be early in the evening. She had heard the change of shift from where she was made to sit. She didn't open her eyes, there was too much in her mind and she didn't want her eyes to wander to where Eric was sitting. She didn't know why but he didn't go home. He had been looking at her before she closed her eyes and she felt he was still looking at her as the steps approached.

"Diane?" someone called out from afar and then started to run to her.

She could recognize the voice in a sea of other voices and that brought a wash of relief to her. She let out a breath that she didn't know she had been holding. It was so good to hear Vivian's voice and somehow, she felt bad for that too. Vivian was her best friend, yet Diane was always too busy. Aside from quick phone calls, they had not seen each other for a long time.

She was walk-sprinting and then she was holding Diane in a warm hug. It was the best thing Diane had felt in a long time. Closing her eyes, she soaked in Vivian's smell. Her hair had the mixture of autumn and a sweet fruit she could not remember its name but could taste it on her tongue. She wanted to cry but she could not. It was neither the right place nor the right time. She would have plenty of time to cry later but now she had to put on a brave face.

But for who?

"Are you alright?" Vivian asked. Her voice was strong and warm. "Are you alright?" she asked again.

"Not really." Diane shook her head.

She had been there way too long to be alright. She wanted to go home and fall on her bed for a while and then, she was going to get the son of a bitch that was trying to frame her. She would need to purge herself off everything she was feeling at the moment and that was what was more important. A clear head would help fix what has been done to her.

With a nod, Vivian turned to the police officers. "I want to see the captain now, please."

She sounded different. There was none of the emotion her voice had before. It was clear, cut, and direct. She was not playing, and she was not going to beat around the bush on that. It made Diane smile. They all turned to her.

"My name is Vivian Ginsberg of Ginsberg and Carols and I would like to see the captain," she said again.

Diane could see Eric standing up and walking toward them and she looked at him.

"He's not in now, Miss. Ginsberg." Eric said as he got closer. "I'm detective Eric Barnes, can I help you?"

"I know who you are. I would like to take my client home now." Vivian stared Eric down

Eric's jaw dropped before he frowned. "She's the main suspect in a murder case, I can't let you do that."

"Right, I'm sure you have something on her, right? What do you have? A storage unit leased by my client, but no DNA or fingerprints placing her in that room. And you know the unit is hers from surveillance cameras but none of the footage shows my client ever going into that unit. From what I was told it only shows my client in the lobby then right back out." Vivian confidently laid out all she knew. "The only actual forensic evidence you have belongs to Steven Anderson, not my client. The same Steven Anderson that has a unit right next to my client's and could have easily along with Simon Clarke made the false wall and put that stuff in there. Again, not my client."

At first, Diane was somewhat annoyed it had taken Vivian so long to get down to the station, but now she understood why. She had gathered ammo before coming down. She looked at Eric with a smile that showed she knew they didn't. Eric looked deflated. He turned from Diane to Vivian and then back to Diane. He could not say anything. He turned to the others that were looking and listening to the exchange. Vivian shook her head. Her face had disgust written over it and Diane could not blame her.

She had felt the same thing when the case started. They were all a bunch of incompetent people who would take the easy way to close a case. It was sad that Eric was, after all, like the other lot behind him.

"We are waiting for forensics. We can hold her some more hours," Eric said and at once closed his eyes like he regretted saying it, but he could not take it back.

Vivian scoffed. "I would like to think you guys are humans, but I might be wrong. On my way here, I spoke with the District Attorney.

I suggest you call him before I do. He agrees with me that you cannot hold my client. And doesn't recall you having a warrant to enter my client's home and take her. She is a respected person of the law, has an award-breaking career, and deserves to be treated with respect until all facts are found. A career that includes recent assistance to the police to put away that serial killer copycat. Such accomplishments could be reexamined and overturned if you all are not careful. The District Attorney would hate for criminals to be back on the street because of false accusations of my client. My client will hand over her passport and any firearms to show her compliance."

Diane wanted to tell Eric again that it was not her stuff that he'd unearthed. It was not her prints they would find when the forensic report was out. It would be someone else's and that whoever had put those things in there must have thought they were going to get her to go down for something she had no idea about.

She wanted to tell him that he was running frustrated because he was not letting himself think and she wanted to kiss him and tell him that she forgave him, but she didn't. She wanted to believe that if he loved her, he would see through the haze of the set-up.

All of her wants were weaknesses that couldn't protect her. She had to stop wishing he would see the hard truth. She made a mistake opening up her heart to the detective.

"Since you have nothing on her, she is leaving. If something comes up, you know where to find her since you already barged into her place. And expect to hear from me real soon if you and your incompetent team also searched my client's home illegally without a proper warrant signed by a judge. Anything found will be inadmissible and I will be filing a complaint as soon as I get back to my office."

Eric couldn't take his eyes away from Diane. She could not decipher the look in his eyes. Was it anger? Hate? Fear? Remorse? It was cold and she tried to avoid him.

"Did they take anything from you?" Vivian asked and Diane shook her head.

"Diane… Miss Gates, you're free to go, for now." Eric said and walked back to his office.

She could tell he wanted to say more. But she didn't care for his words anymore. Knowing what she felt for the man didn't change the fact that she was angry. She walked out and behind her, Vivian told him not to worry. Diane wondered if Vivian had caught the tension between them. Vivian knew everything about her relationship with Eric, and Diane was planning a date for them both to finally meet.

The sun was barely out but it was bright enough. She didn't know she could miss seeing outside so much even if she had been there for only half a day. She wondered how those who spent weeks, months or years behind more serious prisons felt. No wonder they sometimes came out looking like they had just survived near death. She sighed and stretched. She was suddenly boiling with anger. Whatever tiredness she had carried in there seemed to have simmered and what was left was an agitation to solve the case.

"You want to tell me what happened?" she heard Vivian say behind her.

Diane smiled and turned to see Vivian was smiling too. They hugged and this time it was softer and warmer. Diane allowed herself to drown in the warmth of the other woman. She had never been so grateful to anyone as she was to Vivian at that moment. She would have held her there for longer if she could, but Vivian pulled away and looked at her face.

"Would you like something to drink?" Vivian asked. "Coffee? Something stronger?" She smiled and Diane shook her head. She would not be shocked if Vivian pulled out a bottle of wine from her bag.

Vivian wrapped an arm around Diane and led her to her car. "Come, let me take you home since you don't want anything."

"How are you?" Vivian asked, but Diane didn't respond right away.

There was a lot she wanted to say but that would only keep Vivian, and Diane didn't want that. She had done more than a lot already and it was not like there was anything more she could do for her. There was no need to burden her further.

Diane stared out of the window.

Everything now seemed to have happened so fast. The night before last, the morning and now. It was like she was looking through photo cards of herself. She had slept knowing she loved a man and that they were making headway in a case and now here she was, not yet out of a trap that she didn't know when she had fallen into it.

"What happened, Diane"

"I got framed"

"No shit, I want to know more"

So, Diane told her. She owed her that much and there was no way to shrug off the request anyway. When she was done, Vivian had her mouth open in a near-scream.

"That is a lot, hon," Vivian said, and Diane nodded.

She was thinking of the first day she met Eric back when her bookstore was still a crime scene. The thought made her chuckle. She was here now though, in a mess that she could not understand.

"What are you going to do?"

"I don't know yet, but I have to solve this case. That would be the only way they would believe I am not the one killing people like some psychopath."

"Yeah, but how?"

The question annoyed Diane but she saw it was coming from a good place. She shook her head since she didn't have the strength to think about it now. There were so many things she wanted to do and one of them was to take a bath. She needed to stop feeling dirty. It was not just being in there that made her feel sick, it was the fact that they had believed she could do something like that. It made her sick. She tried to imagine herself doing it and every time she did, it felt wrong.

"Will you be alright?"

"Yeah, I will. I just need to sleep a bit. I don't want your reputation tarnished by helping me. You've done enough."

"I win all my cases hon; you won't tarnish anything. I'm going to destroy that department. They won't come after you again so quickly, I'll make sure of it. Not having an arrest warrant is enough for me to hold them back for a while." Vivian reached out and squeezed Diane's shoulder.

They were getting close to Diane's place and fell into a familiar silence. They didn't talk much when they met. Diane thought that was why they didn't meet so much. They could go weeks without seeing each other and still, they would have each other's backs.

Vivian parked her car in front of Diane's house and Diane wondered if she wanted to come in. She got out of the car and when she looked on the other side, Vivian was getting out as well, yawning.

"I better go inside and check for any other violations the police made. And I haven't been in so long I'm sure you owe me a few drinks," Vivian reasoned, and Diane chuckled.

They walked to the front and Diane unlocked the door for them. The first thing Vivian saw was the torn down mural and looked at Diane who shrugged. She went straight to the kitchen and set up the coffee machine. She needed it. It would clear her mind. The smell of the coffee wafted to her and her mind went back to the station and the sweat and mesh of body odor and cologne. It was as if she was still there and it made her feel weak.

Slamming her hands down on the counter, she sobbed quietly.

"You alright, Diane?" Vivian's voice stopped Diane's crying.

Her friend was standing there, watching her bent over the kitchen counter, her shoulders shaking.

Diane sniffed. "Just shaken a bit."

"I understand. What you need is something stronger." Vivian opened Diane's refrigerator and grabbed a bottle of wine. Then she picked up a bottle of scotch on top of the far-right counter and hopped on the kitchen island with mischief in her eyes.

Vivian poured two cups of wine for Diane and poured herself some coffee before adding some scotch to it. They sat there and drank quietly. They were silent for a while and then Vivian told her about her latest court winning and the progress of her divorce.

They talked a bit more and they cleaned her house where the police had made a mess and then Vivian left with a promise to visit in a few days. Diane had a bath and then she walked to her bed and collapsed in it and in no time, she was swimming in a pool of nightmares.

Chapter Twenty-Three

Diane was sitting outside when dawn came. Sleeping was difficult. She could not stop thinking about being investigated, treated as a criminal, and when she caught small snatches of sleep, she was pulled out of it by nightmares. She saw herself carving Catherine's eyes out and with every scream, Diane would jump out of her bed like it was molten lava or like she was stung by a gang of bugs.

It was nearly dawn when she finally gave up and decided to sit outside and watch the stars. She felt as if someone was orchestrating her life and she was a marionette moving at his whim. The neighborhood was quiet in that hour. She imagined her neighbors were dead asleep. The isolation felt like a luxury at the moment. She was suddenly too poor to afford sleep.

"This sucks," she whispered.

The wind swept gently over the houses and the grass on the tarred street. She could feel it on her skin as it flushed her on the posh steps. Dawn was slow to come, or that was what she thought. When she realized its presence, it was a welcomed sight, a new beginning. She stretched feeling a bit hungry, but what she wanted more than anything was to get her hands-on whatever evidence the police claimed to have found in her storage. Diane knew if she had full access to a lab, she could do much more.

She needed help, but Eric was out of the picture. The thought of him made her ache in some places that she wished would not. Could she risk asking Vivian to include her in everything? This was a time she needed a clear head. She got up and walked back inside as the sun rose further and further. She went straight to her office to stare at the bare walls and decided then to stop being weak.

The police had taken everything she had on the murders of Catherine and Alan. There was no way she could continue without her notes. She needed Vivian to get her belongings back. The city officials and law enforcement had forgotten who she was, but she was going to remind them. Diane knew that if she refused to stay away from the case and stay minimally protected while investigating, she'd have to use old contacts and get back into her old life. Making promises and deals would cost her the quiet life she had sought.

"I guess there is no harm," she reasoned, but she knew it was a lie as she picked up her cellphone.

She was going back to a life that she had promised herself never to return to. Diane moved out of the room feeling frustrated and went to her living room. She was still hesitant to deal with her feelings. She couldn't even sleep without nightmares, couldn't deal with her father's death, how could she go back to work?

She could stay put and things could turn around. She shook her head. That was not how she was built. She was the best in her field.

"There is no other way," she said to the empty house, picking up her phone.

It only rang twice. "Yeah?"

"I need your help, Vivian."

Diane knew that her friend had told her to rest, but she couldn't just sit idle. Vivian chuckled but Diane sighed. She had expected this too. That was what Vivian did best. She was one of her best friends and knew her well enough to realize that she wouldn't just sit still. Sometimes Diane felt she was the biggest bitch in the world for not spending more time with her friend after she left her career. Before she did, they saw each other a lot more, frequenting the same places for quick lunches and the same courtrooms for work. Diane had worked hard to distance herself after leaving her old career.

"I thought you were done," Vivian spoke with a hint of humor. She was going to gloat. "You know I can handle things alone as always."

Not gloating as Diane thought, she was going to make her beg. Diane held back her sass with difficulty. "Yeah, well, that was before I had all my evidence and notes taken from my home."

"And before you got arrested as a suspect, right? I worked all day yesterday putting together a motion to suppress evidence found and to compel the return of your property obtained by the illegal search and seizure. I'm going to court in an hour to go before the judge and I'm sure it'll be a win for us. I'm trying to find some evidence of this happening before so there's no room for chances."

Diane knew Eric had stolen evidence before and cut corners. She didn't know if she should tell Vivian. A part of Diane still loved the man and didn't want to see him ripped off his badge.

"There is something you should know," Diane admitted and told her friend everything about how Eric got his information on the six security guards from Wesley college and that captain Larry knew.

"Girl, I'm so going to nail them. I'll have your stuff back to you within the day," Vivian adopted her lawyer's voice. "Anything else you're holding out on me about your boyfriend? We need to use everything we can to keep your ass out of prison. We must hold no punches back. If Steven visited your bookstore often as you say and had access to your storage unit, he could have gotten your fingerprints from anything in the bookstore. Could have gotten a strand of hair off your shoulder, we need to build a strong case against the department just in case things start to go their way."

"Don't talk to me as if I'm some civilian. I'm not, and I'm not some lovesick woman who is going to stand in the line of fire for a man who just runs away. Will you help me or is our partnership long gone? I need to finish this case for Catherine and Alan, not just myself." Diane bit out. She was working up a temper. Vivian chuckled again. Diane thought about dropping the call. If it was anyone but Vivian she would have.

"Of course, Diane but from now on, let's only discuss matters in person." Vivian sounded hurt and surprised.

Diane smiled. She knew how to play the woman too. Vivian had a fierce loyalty and when questioned, she felt pushed to a corner and eager to prove it. She didn't want to do it, but Diane was losing patience and it would not be a good idea to get into an argument with her new, but, in essence, old partner.

"You have a plan?" Vivian asked.

Diane made a sound and walked to the window, focusing on a squirrel running around a tree. The sun outside was already way up above a house on the other side of the street.

"Yeah, I think so, but first, I have to show them I had nothing to do with Catherine's death."

"And the others?"

"Others?" Diane asked.

"Yeah?"

"I don't understand. There are other victims?"

"Yeah. When I called to request that they send me copies of everything they have, I was told after a lot of bullshit that they found multiple body parts and pictures belonging to different people."

"What?" Diane was shocked.

Her guess was right, then. That was not the first murder. The killer or killers were pros.

"But they have Steven, right? And they still have Simon detained. Can't they get their DNA and try to match it to the crimes?"

Diane knew that was not enough. Catherine's rape kit showed that no DNA had been left behind. Steven must have used a condom. And the stupid coroner cleaned her nails of any DNA she got from scratching her attacker. Something must have happened that she didn't get. Did Steven deny it? Did he say he was not alone? What the hell was going on?

"You mean the one-eyed man, right?"

"Yeah, that's Steven."

Vivian was about to say something but stopped. "Hold on," and the silenced lasted for a while before she came back. "Look, we have to meet."

Diane nodded and then realizing Vivian couldn't see her, she said she understood and then they planned to meet that night.

When the call ended, Diane walked away from the window and fell on the couch. She wondered how much Eric had not told her. She had guessed this was the first killing, but why didn't they hear about the other killings that had happened? Or did those killings not happen close?

She could not think about other deaths like Catherine's. What was the world turning into? That was a stupid question, but she wondered every time she was assigned a gruesome case. Humans were the worst. Diane could do nothing but wait, so she got herself ready for work. She refused to be afraid or let her job suffer.

When she walked into the bookstore that day there were four customers and some children waiting for her.

Diane rushed past them to open her front doors. "I'm sorry for keep you waiting everyone."

"Is everything alright Diane?" Mrs. Baylor an elderly woman who enjoyed taking the children from her daycare to the bookstore twice a week for educational trips spoke out.

"Yes, everything is fine. Something came up. How about I order some pizzas for the children for lunch?"

The children cheered in excitement and hurried into the bookstore. It seemed as if the demons of the world washed away and she was left with the light of good people like Mrs. Baylor and the innocence of children.

Diane quickly got all the lights on and made sure the children were settled in the designated reading area before heading for the front desk to check her emails. She found herself stealing glances at the entrance of the bookstore wondering if the second killer would come in. Did she know him as she did Steven, or will the police show up to arrest her again?

She was angry and scared. She was a sitting duck, knew nothing about the case anymore. It seemed like she was spiraling out of control, alternating between anger and fear. The more time went by, the more desperate she became. It felt like she was going mad with idleness. Time moved slowly, and she could not wait to see Vivian.

Diane pulled herself from the front counter, deciding to spend time with customers and if they didn't want her help she would dust and reorganize the displays.

When evening came, Diane was still engrossed in changing two table displays. The only thing that took her out of her zone was the sound of a police siren in the distance. It startled her and she held her breath. The sound became distant, so she knew the car wasn't coming toward her. Glancing at her watch she saw that she had only a few minutes to meet Vivian.

They met in a diner called Sammie's Place. The label had red and blue cursives with neon lights. It was far from her bookstore, but she didn't mind. It was even far from Vivian's job. They didn't need to be overheard by anyone. Diane arrived about ten minutes late. It was relatively crowded and the smell of homecooked food swept over her. She didn't mind, she welcomed the new smell, a smell of comfort different from the expensive places she usually frequented.

She looked around, trying to pick a table when she caught sight of Vivian as she waved her over. Her friend had always been one to make her job look like it was one big, glamorous affair. She dressed as if she was a star but tonight, she dressed in a chiffon top with plain pants and remained stunning.

"You changed before coming?" Diane asked knowing the answer already.

"What do you think?" Vivian smiled and Diane rolled her eyes. "You hungry?"

"Starving," Diane moaned.

She had not eaten anything all day except coffee and breakfast. The children at her bookstore ate all the pizza before she even thought to grab a slice. Vivian looked at her and Diane could tell what she saw. She had looked in the mirror before she came, and she saw the exhaustion in her eyes too.

Vivian reached over and squeezed Diane's hand. "You'll be fine."

Diane didn't see how, but her friend meant well. She nodded and smiled. Vivian let go as a waiter walked to them to let them know the progress of their order. Vivian must have ordered for them both. The waiter took Diane's drink order and she requested a salad to be brought out before the meal.

"So?" Diane inquired when they were alone, decided not to waste more time without having answers.

"Five murders," Vivian whispered holding Diane's gaze.

"Jesus Christ!"

She had thought it was bad but not this bad. How far back has this been happening? Why didn't anybody say anything? How didn't they connect the other murders to Catherine's?

"Yeah" Vivian sipped her glass of water.

"When?"

"In the last two months."

Their orders arrived and Vivian took a big gulp of her sweet tea as soon as the waiter placed it down. Diane suddenly felt like her mouth was filled with ash. She looked at the burger in front of her like it was a lost part of a mutilated body.

"That's not the worse part, Diane. Eat," Vivian instructed her.

She picked the burger and took a bite and even though her mind was filled with anxiety the burger tasted good.

"What do you think?" Vivian asked.

Diane took another big bite and some fries. "Good, but I'll have to hit the gym after this."

They ate in silence for a while and when they were done Vivian looked at her. "You ready?"

"Yeah," Diane said as she ran her tongue over her teeth and took a last sip of water.

"They were cut open in one way or another and they were all females. Catherine's the youngest though."

"What do they have?"

"I don't know yet, but I'm guessing it's pretty good. We have to work fast, or you'll be in a cell again"

"Who are the others?"

"I'm expecting the names soon, but I don't think the forensics have anything conclusive yet."

Diane nodded. She had to think about what to do now.

"What about Steven and Simon?"

"The FBI concluded he had nothing to do with your storage or the deaths. He's just a sleaze who let criminals use his place. But the police figured out that Steven was not working alone. He hasn't said who the other person is, but with his limited eyesight, he's too blind to have done everything alone."

"Then who?"

Vivian shrugged, waving at the waiter to refill their glasses and ask for the dessert menu.

"We should check his place and then that storage," Vivian instructed, and Diane nodded.

I'll be going in there, after all. I'll be seeing his things again.

Chapter Twenty-Four

It was difficult to get Steven's address. Diane could tell from the way Vivian looked when they met. She had been going at it for two days. It seemed like Eric and whoever he was working the case with now kept the details on lockdown, but Vivian had her ways and she got some people who owed her some favors to stop the games. It was better to get the address from the case file than resorting to an illegal way. Especially since they were being watched.

They stopped in front of the house careful not to draw suspicion. The police had already gone through the house, but Diane needed to see things for herself. Steven lived in a neighborhood surrounded by houses with white picket fences. The lawn was well-manicured, and the porch was clean. The door was locked. Diane didn't know if the man truly had a daughter or if that was just another lie. She turned to Vivian who shrugged. Her hands were on the holster of her gun.

Diane nodded at her friend and knocked. "Hello, we are from the police department, and we'd like to speak to you."

They waited to hear for any signs of life, but there was nothing. It seemed like the house was empty, but Diane knocked again just to be on the safe side. When nothing happened, she took out her lock picks from her pocket.

Vivian kept scanning the area, making sure they weren't caught. The area was quiet and most driveways had no cars in them. "Hurry up."

Diane shifted and managed to work the bottom lock open. Then she tried the door and it finally gave way.

"I guess the police didn't bother to lock the top lock too," Diane murmured, stepping inside. They didn't turn on any lights and risk more exposure.

Inside the house smelt of cleanliness. It *was* clean except where the CSI team and officers had passed through. She could tell the obvious signs of where the CSI team searched and gathered their evidence. The cutting of a piece of rug, dust for fingerprints left on surfaces, and more. Diane played out the whole scene in her mind, visualizing everything from the time the officers would have arrived at the home to when they all left.

Vivian gave Diane gloves and they went digging. They had to search meticulously, but she didn't want Vivian to lose her job. The sitting room had two single-sitter couches and a TV. The black rug on the floor was soft to walk on, a detail that didn't hold Diane much as how spotless the black rug was. It took Diane a couple of seconds to notice but there was no dust anywhere on the rug which should be impossible after a whole investigational team had trekked through the house.

"Someone was here after the police," Diane said.

"What?"

"Someone cleaned up. But why bother after the police were already here?"

That bothered her. Diane looked for photos of Steven or anyone and could find none. They walked around some more. Then Diane walked to the kitchen and opened the fridge to find milk, juice, and beer arranged neatly. Whoever was here was super freaky about cleaning and arrangement. There were no dirty dishes in the sink. She was looking for real clues and this was what she was getting. She could not shake off the truth that someone had been there, though.

So, who?

She didn't want this to be a dead-end. That would mean they would have to start thinking about going to the storage facility and she didn't want to think about what would happen there.

She leaned over the sink and tried to think. Then she saw a juice mixer, but what caught her attention was that the device was not perfectly put together unlike everything else in the room. Diane went over and picked up the mixer, noticing how the bottom piece was not snuggly fitted so she twisted the top pieces to get to the base. What she found was a gold ring, possibly a wedding band. Hurrying out of the kitchen she walked to the sitting room where she found Vivian going through some books on a small stool.

"He got them from my bookstore," Diane smirked as Vivian jumped startled.

"What?"

"He was a regular at my bookstore. He was always coming to pick up books for his daughter. Sometimes even twice every week. That is where he met Catherine again, I guess"

"He started coming around the same time she came to work for you?"

"No, he had been coming before I employed her"

"That's weird"

"I agree. Another weird thing is this." Diane showed Vivian the ring she found in the kitchen before putting it in a plastic bag. "Maybe we can track down where it was bought or if there's any helpful forensics on it. I still have some people who are willing to do favors for me."

"I think it's best if you let me do that. We can't have anyone knowing you're involved in the case. We have some of the same contacts, I'll have the ring looked at. I can always say my private investigator found it and gave it to me." Vivian grabbed the bag from Diane and dropped the book in her hand.

Diane reluctantly nodded. They walked through the house and then got to the bedroom. The place was just as clean as the sitting room. Diane opened the drawers to find clothes. Another had knick-knacks. There was nothing important there.

"The clothes are not all the same." Vivian took out first a sweater and then a shirt and put them on top of the bed for Diane to examine.

"What are you talking about?"

"Look at the sweater, it's rugged and less expensive, and a different size and cut than the shirt. The shirt is sleek, expensive, and smaller than the sweater. The sweater looks more like a middle-aged man who loves to go fishing whereas the shirt would fit a young man who prefers only city living."

Vivian had a stronger taste for fashion than her, but Diane followed along what her friend was trying to say.

"You're right let's look at the other clothes. Maybe the second killer isn't an accomplice but the one pulling all the strings. An older male who took Steven under his sick wings."

They both put the clothes back and rummaged through the rest. After feeling the clothes proved their assumptions they went back through the rest of the house with new insight and noticed the place indeed had two different personalities.

"Let's go. We're not going to find anything else," Diane said now hopeful as her mind tried to calculate the possibilities.

"Yeah, let's go. I'll have the ring looked at and see if there's anything in Steven's life that might trace us to this mentor of his. Maybe their relationship goes deeper than that. They share the same bedroom, maybe they are lovers or this older male is a predator. I'll see if there are any reports of childhood abuse in Steven's records."

They rushed to Vivian's car and sped off. She turned on the radio and waited until they were a mile away before speaking again.

"Are we going there now?"

"We should," Diane breathed out and closed her eyes.

Vivian patted Diane's leg then continued to drive to the storage facility. Diane never thought she would have to go inside. It had been her decision not to and now it seemed like it was not anymore.

"You think we will be able t—" Vivian's phone cut her short.

It was a brief call. She looked at the road and then back at the phone and alternated until she could not carry on, so she parked beside the road and tossed the phone at Diane.

"The names and more of the other murdered women just came in."

Diane took the phone and when she turned it on, the first image was of a Nancy Gilbert. She turned the phone away because she could not look a second more. Learning the names and faces was too much.

"Christ!"

The storage facility was quiet. There were yellow police tapes, but they had not cared about that. They still had their gloves on so there would no prints left there when they leave. Diane was not worried about leaving shoe prints since the place had hundreds of visitors and it was filthy anyway. No one would be able to prove when she was there. They went through everything they could, using their phone flashlights as the place was rather dark.

"They cleaned out his whole office."

Diane kicked a chair and followed Vivian out to the storage units.

First, they went to the unit Steven had and found it empty. Then Diane led her friend to the other storage, only to find that room empty as well. There was nothing there, it had all been cleared by the police. Diane looked at Vivian who was scanning the walls. Diane never wanted to enter the unit, but now that she had and there was nothing there for her, she felt a great loss.

What had her father left for her in there? His personal things had been desecrated by body parts of dead women. Steven, a man she thought of as sweet and kind had violated her father's space. Anger and confusion bubbled within her. If her father was alive, he would know what to do. He always did. He was like a God, understanding when she was or wasn't happy and when she was hurt. She told him everything and then, one day, it just ended.

She was crying. She could not help it. It was like losing him all over again and it was not something she'd dealt with completely before. She felt her heart break. The loneliness returned and all she wanted to do was go back home and hold his shirt or his photo and weep. It was not going to help but it was what she wanted to do.

Vivian rushed over and pulled Diane into a hug. "You alright?"

"Yes"

"We have the names now. We can pinpoint when they went missing and were killed and match where you were during those times to give you a solid alibi. We can prove your innocence. We *will* prove your innocence," Vivian said. She looked at the time and gasped at how long they had been in the storage. "Come on let's get you home."

They got to the car and then drove out. She mustered up her courage and looked at all the victims' faces from Vivian's phone. Diane played the photos in her head. The different faces. Some were cut open and some slashed like someone clumsy was given a knife. Then thinking about it, that could be Steven's work.

"The cuts are clumsy, not professional as the ones on Catherine. He must have been practicing back then with those kills. But this one Heather Reed was killed by a different person, must have been the mentor." She stretched uncomfortably and yawned. She was tired and hungry.

"Want to grab a bite?" She asked Vivian who was lost in her own head.

"Who do you think would be doing this with him?"

"I don't know. There is not much to go on. I knew nothing about his life other than he talked about his daughter a lot."

Diane's phone rang and when she looked at the caller ID, her heart thudded hard as she showed Vivian the phone.

"What does he want?"

"I don't know," she said on a shrug, taking the call. "What do you want?" She tried to sound harsh, but her voice shook.

"No, thanks," she said. She listened for a bit and then sighed and looked at Vivian who shook her head at Diane.

"Look, I don't think that is a good idea," Diane spoke through the phone then began to listen again.

"Alright, the bookstore in ten minutes."

Vivian shook her head when Diane lowered her phone from her ear. She hissed and sighed and when she didn't know what sound to make anymore, she settled on just staying quiet.

"He said he wants to tell me something that can help me." Diane tried to choose her words carefully before her fiery friend cursed up a never-ending storm.

"You are so horny that you would believe that? He's been a pain in the ass with providing my office documents we asked for."

"No, Vivian I'm not, but we need all the help we can get. At least let's listen to what bull he's trying to push."

Vivian hissed again and just drove on. They were at the bookstore in twenty minutes. The area was relatively quiet with little bustle and hustle.

Eric was parked in front of her bookstore. He had his jacket in hand and was wearing a pale gray t-shirt. He still looked defeated as he leaned against his car. Diane didn't make a move to approach him. His wellbeing did not concern her anymore.

Vivian stepped in front of Diane and glared at Eric. "What did you need to discuss with my client?"

Eric glanced at Diane, ignoring Vivian completely. "I'm sorry, Diane."

"That's what you have for her, a pathetic apology? Some tactic of yours to get her to trust you and what, confess to something she didn't do?"

Vivian took a step closer to the detective, causing Diane to hastily grab her friend's arm so she wouldn't do anything to land herself in jail. Friendship and loyalty sometimes overruled the job, and she knew that if she didn't get control of Vivian, she would slap Eric and might not stop at just one.

Eric stepped back away from Vivian and looked pleadingly toward Diane. "No, I know you didn't do it and I may have a clue about who did… forensics came through…"

"What?"

"We better go inside."

Diane led them to her office in the back of the bookstore and flopped in her chair. "Speak." She waved at Eric who still seemed uncomfortable and hesitant to move toward a chair next to Vivian.

"None of the forensic evidence has your DNA on it so we can't charge you for the deaths of the other women. There was enough evidence linking Steven to one of the murders easily as well which takes you off the list." Eric finally sat down.

"Why don't you sound thrilled?" Vivian questioned him.

He rubbed his face leaning back in the chair. "Because she's not off the hook for Catherine's death. And since they think she did it she's also being blamed for Alan's death."

Diane remained silent.

"Diane, we also found your father's DNA which could have tampered with the evidence because a lot of his property was in there, but I wanted to let you know there's some tainted evidence on some of Catherine's belongings that Vivian can get thrown out. It buys you more time."

"Thank you for sharing this with me. I still don't understand why now you believe me when I'm still being investigated for two murders. And could still be pinned for the other women even if my DNA isn't there. My DNA wasn't on Catherine or Alan either." Diane tried to keep her voice bare of emotion.

Eric looked at her with sadness. "I'm sorry I accused you, the evidence was so overwhelming at the time. I…I believe you're innocent now because my gut tells me so. Since I came to your house to bring you in, I felt conflicted. I worked hard to be sure this whole time and at every turn, the results are proving to be in your favor. I should never have turned my back on you. I want to help."

Tears welled into Diane's eyes. She didn't want to trust him. The evidence was heavily against her.

"You didn't trust me. You didn't stand by me when I was at my lowest. I can't forgive that. But we could use your help. Professionally, and that's all."

Chapter Twenty-Five

She was back on her porch. She did it a lot these days. It was like a stage where she came to play all her thoughts, checking the ones she could trust and the ones she had to discard. The case was falling hard on her and she was not sure how she was going to pull it away from her shoulders. Vivian, Eric, and her had been going at it for about three days and they have had very little progress. The only big thing they got was that the ring Diane and Vivian had found in Steven's home was that it belonged to Alan. Now the police focused on Steven for Alan's murder and not her.

Diane hated the way it seemed like everything was against her. She appeared to be tangled in a web that was strong and stubborn and intent on dragging her down. When Eric said he had an idea of who did it, she had thought she was going to be getting out, but he didn't give her a name right away. Finally, after a few days, he spoke the name.

He had mentioned it like he expected her to be happy that he was suspecting someone else. She wanted to throw him out of her bookstore. It was not possible. Her father was dead and that was where it ended. It was funny that something as cruel as this would be why her father's name would be the conversation topic between her and the man she had cared so deeply for. A man she would have gladly introduced to her father. Her father who was nothing short of perfection. He was the kindest person when he was alive. She reminded Eric that her father was dead and hurried him out of her store.

The day was not far from coming but as she sat there, she enjoyed the coolness of pre-dawn. It felt like the day had its eyes half-open while she sat and watched like a dutiful guardian. She felt useful, appreciated. She shook her head because she felt like she was going mad. But then was that so wrong? She chuckled. She was going to see the others today. They had been trying to work on the case from their side as well.

She was the only one who was doing absolutely nothing. The others thought she had done enough. She wondered how Eric was feeling. Different news outlets were running stories on the deaths of the other women, it could not be avoided, there was a serial killer on the loose. Diane was happy that they had found a way to keep her name away from those news-hungry reporters. It would have been a disaster.

Every once in a while, a photographer would come to take photos of the bookstore. They were not doing any harm, but they were not doing any good either. One shutter sound was all it took to remind people that it was in the bookstore a girl was murdered brutally. And then with that one shutter click, people were feeling unsafe again. She had not been getting her usual flow of customers even. They were all worried about the increase in news reports. No one would want to be caught randomly and killed in a street that was already known as the killers stomping grounds and she didn't blame them.

She sat there until the sun showed up and then she stayed some more. Out there looking out to the street was the only way her troubled mind didn't suffer so much. She could smell the result of dew on the past day's dust on the roofs and ground and the grass and then she could feel the cool breeze on her skin and think of other things. But at the end of the day, with the sun up and the world removed from pause, she stretched and went back inside. The house was illuminated by sunlight and she glided to the kitchen. She was hungry, but she wanted a cup of coffee more.

As she took her first cup of coffee, she wondered what her father would say. He would give her the stern face for sure. She stretched and walked to the sitting room. She was not feeling like doing anything that would involve thinking, but it seemed to be her new reality. Thinking, solving, hypothesizing. Things had changed so fast and she wondered if they would ever go back to the way they used to be. She didn't even know what normal was anymore. She would always be the woman with the murdered assistant. The bookstore wouldn't be the same. It would be possibly featured in some writers' stories.

Her head was spinning. She had to get ready and leave for the bookstore. Eric said Steven had recoiled when he showed him her father's photo. He was going to question him further and then they would meet at the bookstore. Vivian was supposed to join them with whatever she had found out. They were fast becoming a solid team and Diane didn't know if she liked that. She was putting them in trouble, and they knew it. She was worried about Eric's health too. He didn't seem to be getting any rest.

They came in the evening. It made sense that they would come when they were through with work. Diane was feeling like she had waited all her life. When Vivian arrived, she sighed. The bookstore was beginning to feel cold.

"Took you long enough," Diane said with a smile.

She wondered if Vivian could tell that she meant it as a jest. It was getting difficult to stay as long as she used to and the books which were good company at a time were now witnesses looking at her for justice. She was falling, really hard, into despair.

Vivian shook her head and smiled. They were having small talk when Eric walked in. He looked tired. Diane looked away but Vivian didn't. Somehow Diane wished her friend would not say anything, but it seemed unlikely.

"What?" Eric asked when Vivian had looked at him for too long.

Diane never thought he was one to feel uncomfortable. He had always seemed like he could take everything but now it seemed as if he was fading.

"When was the last time you had a good sleep?" Vivian asked and somehow, the question stung Diane.

It was not fair, she realized. It was not as if she was sleeping well herself, but those demons were hers and it was only right that they would torment her. But it was like she was letting her suffering leak into those around her. There was no sign that Vivian was that stressed, but Diane knew she was taking on extra work and that was hectic too.

Eric shrugged.

"You should take care of yourself, pretty boy," Vivian said.

It was like she was burning Diane somehow, but she didn't think it was in her hands to stop the questioning. Eric could take care of himself.

"If you break down, it won't help the case. You know that."

Eric nodded.

"Let's get on with this," Vivian suggested.

Diane brought the pizza she had ordered and a bottle of wine. Eric brought out a file. It had Gracie Marquez written in bold on top of it. Diane had seen the name in the list of the dead victims that Vivian showed her.

"I'll have to take it back, but I thought this could help us take your hands off of Catherine's murder," Eric said, and Vivian whistled.

Diane understood why but nobody said it, so it was left there as it was. Vivian knew that this was not the first time Eric was getting things done outside the protocol. Diane could only sigh. Things were getting shitty and it was happening fast.

"She died not far from here. No one saw the killer. Her house is maybe a thirty-minute jog from here for someone like you. But she was killed with a fishing line. Unlike the others where the cutting was the cause of death, Gracie was strangled first before cut open."

The photo showed a line around her neck while another one showed the type of fishing line that it had been used. That type of line had been found in her father's storage unit. When Diane understood what Eric was showing her, she began to shake her head. It was not possible. Her father used that type of line for fishing, but it was a brand available to thousands of people. And there was also the fact that her father was dead. He could not have come back from the dead to kill this woman, could he?

"No"

"What?" Vivian asked looking at Eric and Diane.

"Why don't you think so?" Eric huffed

"Because it does not make sense," Diane said.

She was done thinking about it. Why was Eric not seeing that what he was saying made no sense at all? It would still make no sense if the man was alive even because he was nothing but sweet to everyone.

But he *was* dead.

"You think?" Eric asked.

His face was angry and frustrated. Diane had seen frustration before in the eyes of other men but somehow Eric's face shocked her when she looked at it.

"You think it does not make sense or you don't want to see the sense in it?"

"What are you guys talking about?" Vivian asked. She had a half-eaten slice of pizza in her right hand and the photo in another. She looked from one face to the other. "Are you guys going to tell me what is going on?"

"He is still harping on my father being the killer"

"What?" Vivian asked Eric. "You've slept with her and you still don't know her father is dead?" she asked. It was the second time she was asking Eric the question and this time she said it with throwing her head back. Eric felt like they were ganging up on him.

"The compass is pointing to him. From everything we've put together, the killers are Steven and some mystery man. An older man who is great at hiding himself, a dead man is the perfect ghost. They are trying to say you helped kill Catherine and Alan." Eric was beginning to convince Vivian.

"A body was ever found, Diane." Vivian carefully spoke. "There was only blood and a possible struggle

"What— There was too much blood, his blood, he could not have survived," Diane mumbled.

"Steven said they killed a woman and put her in your father's grave," Eric said as he took Diane's hands in his.

Vivian arched a brow at Eric. "How would you have found that out?"

"I know some guys in the prison Steven's at who could easily be bought. They softened him up when I went to meet him and be sure he's ok. He said that all I had to do was go and look."

"Then we go to the cemetery." Vivian shook her head as if she couldn't believe the words coming out of her mouth.

"What, with no warrant?" Eric grinned at Vivian who promptly shoved him.

The three of them knew they had nothing solid to get a judge to sign a warrant to exhume a body. If they wanted quick answers, they needed to get their hands dirty once again.

"Not tonight though, you both need to rest."

Diane saw the flicker of excitement drain from Eric's eyes, but she did not budge.

They all needed to rest.

Chapter Twenty-Six

In her heart, she wished that was not true. The next day came and went by fast with evening coming despite Diane's apprehension. Evening meant she was going to find out if her father *did* know Steven and if there was his body in that coffin. Eric was driving and Vivian was looking out of the window in the back of the car. She had been avoiding being close to Eric since they started working together again. Diane sat in the back with her. She could feel things stirring and she didn't want to. She was tired of feeling something as strong as what they had and then memories of him dragging her to jail causing her pain again.

She could sometimes imagine him looking at her at the station with those eyes that said she had betrayed him. She didn't want that to happen. She wanted to touch him sometimes. She wanted to stretch over and lay her head on him and hear him tell her that it was going to be alright and she didn't need to worry so much. But things were not going to be alright unless they caught whoever did the murders. She could not believe that they were going to be digging up her father's grave.

She barely heard Eric asking Vivian if she had anyone in the cemetery and Vivian nodding and then telling him about a grandma. She was locked in the thought of her father making breakfast and playing games with her when he was not working. She was convinced it could not be her father and she would love to see Eric's face when he realized they were wrong.

"...You guys moved here when you were little?" Eric asked Vivian.

"No, been here all my life"

"Wow," Eric exclaimed.

Eric still looked like he would keel over if someone punched him. He probably didn't sleep that much, even though Diane chased them home last night. Diane turned away from their conversation. She was removing herself totally and she didn't know why. She was trying to be careful. Seeing him hate her for that brief time had hurt her and yet here she was caring for him and she didn't want to drag herself into that again.

"Yeah. I didn't meet my grandpa, though. He died some time ago before I was born. I don't know much about him."

"How about your dad and mum, siblings?"

Diane's mind went to Vivian's brother, Stan. Hot-headed and wild, he was one of the people Diane didn't like when they were young and then he changed like a flick of a light switch when he became a banker and he was gone like that, off to own a bank. She smiled. They talked when they had the time. The internet was something else these days with its instant messaging and all that. She could hear Vivian telling Eric about her family, but she couldn't bring herself to participate in the conversation.

"You alright?" Eric asked as he parked the car under a tree closest to her father's empty grave.

Diane nodded, but she could not speak. There was something caught in her throat. Something that made it impossible for her to form words into sentences. She was scared, she realized. Terrified that it was going to be true. And she didn't know what she was going to do if they were right.

She was shaking and knew that they could see it. Raising her head, she looked at them. They were waiting for her to make up her mind. Absently, she wondered why they were even ready to go that far for her.

"You can stay in the car and let us go look," Eric said.

Diane shook her head. She was not going to chicken out of something like that. If there was a way to know for certain, then she wanted to be there when it happened. Besides, they needed all the hands they could get. She shook her head again and cleared her throat.

"I want to be there"

"You sure you ready for this?" Eric asked.

"Yes."

"Let's go then," Eric suggested, opening his side of the car as Vivian did the same. Diane closed her eyes and then opened them and followed suit. She refused to believe her dad was the monster they were talking about.

They went to the back of the car and when Eric opened the trunk, they all picked a shovel and a flashlight. She didn't know if it was the cemetery or just her, but it felt eerie. The shovel felt heavy in her hands as she walked in front of the other two. She could not remember when she came here last.

"Well?" Eric whispered. "No ghost so far"

Vivian chuckled but Diane kept walking in silence. She led them to her father's headstone and shone her light onto it. LAMONT GATES was boldly written on the headstone and below were smaller words Diane had asked to be inscribed still shone.

I'll watch out for you when stars touch the night sky.

She had heard it in a song when she was young. That was when they still battled over whose taste in art was better. Her mouth felt heavy again, she cleared her throat and broke the silence.

"Let's get to it. It is late already."

Eric nodded and they started digging. They dug for hours. They dug fast and silent. Finally, they reached the box and Vivian helped Eric pry the lid open causing Diane to gasp then clench her chest.

"Fuck!" Eric cursed.

"How? Why?" Diane said. Vivian just shook her head.

As Steven had informed them, the casket was not empty. The person in the coffin was a woman. She looked like she had been dead for a long time. Diane could not stop looking at the body in the casket. The woman's mouth, that was now devoid of tissues, had been open. She was probably screaming when she died. She could not control her mind creating the scene of her father and Steven killing this woman and putting her in there. She was lost in her head.

How it was that she had lived with someone who was this damaged and she didn't know it? Right until he died he had been the good father. How was it that she had missed everything? It was not easy to miss the signs. She had solved so many cases, saw through the mask many killers wore, and helped lawyers piece together the evidence. How did she not know her own father was a serial killer?

They covered the casket back. They couldn't go to the police with what they had found but the graveyard workers would have to report a dug-up grave. Then the police would have to investigate the woman in the grave. She didn't know if Captain Larry would believe Eric's claims that her father was the killer not her, but she knew what she was going to do. She was going to find her father and she was going to get him locked up if she didn't kill him herself. Her own father had implicated her in something so horrific.

"Hey, Diane, you alright?" Eric asked as they walked to the car. She nodded and kept walking fast.

She needed to get to her house and lock the world out. Her heart was beating so hard she thought she was going to have a panic attack soon.

"You're not ok," Vivian stated as they tried to catch up to her. She could hear them breathing hard. She felt Eric try to hold her, but she spun around, getting away from him. She was so fast that they knocked into each other.

"I am fine. What? You think I am trying to rationalize that in my head because he is my father? Or that I'm going to fall apart? I just want to go home." She didn't raise her voice. Eric took a step back and Vivian went to her to help her in the car.

That night she didn't sleep, she just cried, and Eric was there with her even though she told him to go home. She slept off as dawn came and he never left her side.

Chapter Twenty-Seven

"How do you find a dead man?" Eric asked as he moved around her kitchen.

He was still there, and she didn't complain when he knocked on her door after work. It was like before, he was not wearing a shirt, just the pants he had come in the night before. Eric being around was helpful. He had cared for her the night they dug up her father's grave then spent the rest of the day with her until he was called in about the report of the dug grave. He reluctantly left but within hours he was back at her place. Diane went through multiple emotions, mostly anger and sadness. She threw herself at him needing to feel something other than pain. She didn't want to admit it but sometimes sex was good to help take things out of her mind.

She felt like she was using him, but she could not stop, and it was not like he complained about being there with her. Even after she had broken a large bowl by throwing it at his face Eric stayed and let her lash out until she broke down in tears or clawed at his clothes.

It was the second day and Diane tried to control her emotions. She didn't answer his question. She stopped feeling anything for a while until Eric came around and carried her to the couch to just hold her. She was so still and pale he had panicked and called Vivian who didn't know what to do about her either. Vivian had spent the night with Diane like they were teenagers at a normal sleepover but had to leave for work before Diane woke up.

Vivian was going to show up soon and would have the same question. How would they find her father? There was no reason not to ask her. She had lived with the man most of her life. She had known the color his eyes took when he was sick, the movies and shows he could not do without. She knew that he had a sweet tooth and that he didn't like alcohol that much, so he drank light. He hated planes and loved to fish and go camping. But all these didn't tell her where to find him

She was blind.

"I don't know where to look for him," she finally admitted.

"It's fine, Diane," Eric assured her, running his hands over her thighs.

She loved him. She could not lie. She could tell that he loved her too. She didn't know if that was a good thing, but it was pointless denying how they both felt. It was so obvious when they looked at each other. She loved the way he smiled and how the smile stretched to his tired eyes. The sound of his voice had a quality that could be said to be cliché, but she loved it. It was manly and it was safe to wrap herself with. And yet she was finding it hard to verbally express that love to the man.

Diane could tell he was thinking. His face was still, and his eyes looked distant.

"What do we do?"

"We let the chief medical examiner do her job and wait. The captain has it out for you, but he can't ignore the evidence." Eric rubbed her shoulders.

Things were always like that for her. They got difficult whenever she thought she was getting to the end. She stretched and yawned, eyeing the empty coffee cup Eric had served her, and stood, heading for the kitchen.

"Let me—" Eric said, standing up

"Don't be silly!"

Diane walked to the coffee machine and refilled the cup. They had not done much since they woke up except eat, have sex, and talk about the case. She tried to imagine how her father had done his killings when she was little. Bile rose to her throat and she pushed it down with coffee. It was going to be difficult if she kept running from the pain and revulsion.

"You know what?" She asked, walking back to the sitting room, and joining Eric on the couch. "Let have a second look at what we already have"

"What?"

"You will have to go question Steven some more," she said.

"Yeah, I already thought so. Now that we know who he worked with, he should cooperate since there is no need to keep your fa…his accomplice in the dark," Eric said and Diane nodded, ignoring Eric's verbal slip.

Diane smiled at him. She was not going to keep recoiling from the fact that her father was a murdering bastard and he was alive. He was a monster who had made her mourn for nothing. She felt like he didn't care. If he did, he would have not made her feel like she was alone in the world all this time.

"Hey, we'll get him."

Diane nodded at Eric's words. She was not sure she wanted to see him. She didn't know what she would do if she saw him. Would she be able to kill him, or she would let him go? She was doubting her resolve and she hated it. It was like not trusting herself and she was supposed to be the one person she could trust in the whole world.

Rain began to hit her windows. She didn't feel like going to the bookstore and he didn't feel like leaving her house.

Eric's phone rang and he scooped it from the table. He had been expecting that call and he stood up to answer it, his face suddenly very serious. He spied at Diane and caught her looking at him intently.

"Talk to me, Stewart," Eric urged. He mouthed 'Results' to Diane and she nodded. The name had given it away. She had worked with Stewart a bit and it had been good. He was one of the good ones. She looked at the man as he paced up and down.

"So, you are telling me there are several prints?" Eric asked.

He nodded. They talked a bit more and then Eric thanked the man on the other side and ended the call. When he shook his head and sat next to her, Diane knew that whatever he was about to say wouldn't be good. There was a way Eric frowned when he had bad news that it was a giveaway. And he was now frowning that way.

"So?"

"They didn't get much except that Steven's prints were there and your fa…and Lamont's fingerprints were there." Diane nodded. She was not surprised but why did he look sad. "They discovered that she was alive when they buried her, and they found your fingerprints in the coffin"

His words hit her like bricks.

"So, I'm not in the clear. This is bullshit! I chose the casket, of course I touched it. And at the funeral I put his favorite photo of us in there so I left prints then too."

"Don't worry there are other prints too that must be from the funeral. It's not over. When is Vivian coming? We need to let her know."

"Later." Diane wished her friend was there now.

"I need to get to the office and get a handle on this," he said and stood, leaning back down to kiss her. Diane turned her head away and curled up and closed her eyes to sleep.

"Hey!" Someone tapped her. "Wake up, Diane," she heard someone say.

Diane opened her eyes and her heart dropped in shock and she fell off the couch. Her father was in front of her and he was smiling. He looked just as young as he had been the last night she saw him. His eyes were as green as she'd remembered, shining a familiar gleam. She didn't know whether to run away or hug him. When she stood up, she realized there was something on his pants.

"Dad?"

She should be holding her gun to him and telling him to get on his knees, but she wanted to know. She wanted to ask him why he did it, why kill? What happened to him? She walked to him slowly and that was when she realized what she had seen earlier was blood and the stain was spreading and she saw more on his pants. His sneakers were covered in blood and on her floor, near his feet was Catherine with her mouth open and empty eye sockets. Diane screamed and fell back.

"Isn't she beautiful, dear?" Lamont said to his daughter. Then he started walking toward her and Diane noticed there was a knife in his hands now and his smile was gone but he kept asking Diane if Catherine was beautiful.

Diane was in Eric's arms when she woke up. She was crying and sweaty. The day was gray already and going to get dark soon. Eric was smoothing her hair and telling her it was alright. Vivian was there too, but Diane had not yet seen her, she walked to sit down. They waited for Diane to calm down and then Eric gave her a glass of water to drink and she gulped it down like she had been walking the Sahara for days.

"I'm so sorry," Diane said.

"Stop that," Vivian answered.

"We have to talk," Eric said. "Steven said you would know where to find Lamont." Her face scrunched up in confusion. "He said only *you* know where to find him, you already know where he is."

Diane tried to think about it, but she drew up a blank. She looked from Vivian to Eric and back around and it suddenly seemed like the case was hinged on her remembering.

"This could all end in one day," Eric observed the obvious.

"How about you don't pressure her," Vivian snapped at him

"I know it can, but I don't know where he is, what place he could be hiding that I would know." Diane looked at Vivian imploring her to believe her.

"D, was there any place he used to take you? Anything special to him that we don't already know about?" Vivian asked. Diane nodded. They had gone to so many places together because it was just them after her mother died. There were so many places, but none seemed like a place that he would go to hole up after killing someone.

"I don't think anyth—" she stopped as something flashed into her mind. "I know where he is," she admitted as a memory flashed back into her mind.

It had been so long.

Chapter Twenty-Eight

The cabin was far from the town. They used to go there when she was done with school and that was one of the best times, she had with him. It was just them. They played games, fished and just… were. It was their getaway from life in the bustling city. It was like cutting off from the larger part of society and just enjoying the peace and quiet of life that the cabin gave them. It was surrounded by nothing but trees and the air there was so clear. The cabin was beautiful and warm.

Completely off any maps as her father had built the cabin himself with his father so no one knew about it. She slept like she had never slept before the first day they went there. She loved it because he was there, he was always there when she opened her eyes. He was always ready for them to do one thing or another and she felt like the luckiest kid in the world. And then they stopped going. It was sudden but then she got busy with boys and school.

He was fast to change the subject whenever she brought it up. He would say something about it being weathered and needing maintenance. He gave so many excuses that it soon dawned on her that they wouldn't be going there anytime soon and just like that it was forgotten. It became a memory at first, something to call up when she needed comforting, and then she grew up some more and the world offered more distractions and it was just gone. She could not remember the smell of the rooms, the way it stayed warm even in winter, or the way it seemed like a dream when her father sang as they sat near the fireplace.

"There was a cabin in the woods that he took me to when I was a child. He said he never took anyone there but me, not even my mother. Said his father and he built it. I spent many weekends there with him until one day we stopped going. It's not listed anywhere, but I remember where it is, I think." She saw Vivian smile a real smile since they started working the case together. It was real progress. With this, they could get her father in one swoop and that would be the end of it.

"I need to get back to the station and talk with the captain. We need a warrant." Eric shot up excitedly. "Vivian, will you stay with her?"

"Of course, go on cowboy save the day." Vivian smiled again and plopped down next to Diane.

"I'll call as soon as I have something. Diane send me the location of the cabin." Eric rushed out before Diane could hug or thank him.

Diane had not heard from Eric the night before, so Vivian had stayed over until the next afternoon before she had to run to work. Diane wasn't going to spend another day at home, so she went to work and worked on an ad for a new assistant. The sun outside was setting and even though the day was fading, there was still no word from Eric. He was not going to come over. He had told her that he would make sure he had the warrant before seeing her and that meant if she didn't hear or seen him, he had been unsuccessful and still trying.

Diane wasn't sure she could go through another day like that. The anticipation and fear were killing her. She wanted to go to the cabin and see him there. She could picture him having a bowl of cereal in the morning. He always did that even though he was a good cook. She could picture him being shocked by her entrance and then smiling that smile that she had always thought meant comfort until the dream of the other evening.

What would he do? Rush for a gun and try to shoot her? Try to speak to her? Make her understand that he had done everything under an influence? He was not the old man she knew so she didn't think he would smile at her and try to make her understand. If there was a bet, she would put her money on him getting a gun and blowing her to oblivion if she was slow.

Finally, after her open mic event was ending Eric was calling her phone. Diane quickly thanked everyone for coming out and those who braved the stage before rushing off herself to a quieter location.

"Did you get it?" She exhaled as she fumbled with the phone

"Diane, the place does not belong to your dad."

"What?"

"Yeah, I checked it out. It belongs to a Paula Andrews."

"Paula?" she asked, and her breath caught in her throat. He could hear the shift in tone and then she went silent.

"Yeah, why?"

"That was my mother's name."

"Well, I asked for the warrant and they wouldn't give it to me since we could not establish it's your father's cabin." His words were strained. "This could cause a problem since she's dead, the property is now yours. We need to get ahead of this. I can still try to get a warrant another way."

"Okay," she conceded.

"Okay?"

"Yeah, I know Larry wouldn't have made it easy." Diane leaned against a wall to keep herself from falling, focusing on her breathing. She still had a lot of customers around.

"Do you want me around tonight? I can come over once I get out of here," he said. "I can pick up some Chinese and we can watch a movie and figure things out tomorrow."

"That is sweet, but I think I will just sleep alone tonight" She didn't want him around. She needed time to contemplate her next steps.

"You sure, babe?"

She chuckled. "I'll be fine, Eric." She paused like she was going to ask something but thought better of it. "I'll see you tomorrow, Detective."

"Alright, tomorrow," he promised as the call clicked off.

She must have known that would happen. She didn't hope he would not be able to get the papers, but she felt just so. It took too long for him to call and his voice had been the first hint that things didn't go the way she had hoped that they would go. As she drove home, she wondered what she was going to do. Was she going to sit and wait for them to come at her like she was a killer when the killer was out there?

It was weird how life could turn around and things would go all wrong even with the light within reach. She could see how to solve this case and yet she was scared. She was scared it was going to be a setup. She had been thinking about it all day but then she wondered how Steven had known about the cabin, how was the cabin even in her mother's name when her mother said she never visited the place.

Smart criminals *did* avoid putting things in their name so things wouldn't easily track back to them. The more Diane found out the more she hated her father. She knew what to do and as she drove home, she decided she was going to do it. She was not going to let her father escape.

She was ready.

Chapter Twenty-Nine

It felt like a regular road trip. As if she were back in her father's car as they were going to the cabin, singing crappy eighties songs about love. She hated that the feeling was comforting. Diane looked at her phone and sighed. She didn't want to do this alone, but she knew what the other two would say even though they had a point. It was not as if she wanted to fall deeper into the net of the police. There were so many ways this could go wrong, and she would be hung dry as a psychopath.

As Diane drove the long way out of town she was plagued with memories and questions that more than twice she broke off the road and parked to scream because she had to let the frustration out somehow and she didn't want to plunge head-first into a passing car. When she got back in after the third time, she closed her eyes and let it all settle. If she was going to solve this case, she'd better accept the things she could not change.

The fact was that her father was a murderer and whatever conflict she had in her had to be cleansed and there needed to be a focus. She had to know that she was honoring not just Catherine now but all the other women that could just have been her. She was doing that for herself as well.

Turning on her car radio, she tried to lose herself to the music. A cursory glance at the gas meter made her sigh. She didn't buy gas before leaving since she was in such a hurry to put Eric and the rest of the town behind her. She didn't tell Eric she was putting the bookstore open today so he wouldn't go there.

Diane wanted to move things along before she had the chance to change her mind. She would have to buy gas at the next exit and be back on the highway before noon. Diane still had a while to go and wanted to arrive at the cabin before too dark. Winter made the sun go down faster than usual.

She stopped at the gas station and pulled the pump and plugged it into the car and when it was filled her stomach growled. Trying to ignore her hunger longer Diane grabbed a bottle of water from her console and drank until the ache went away. Still, hunger remained so she went inside the gas station. There was a young man behind the counter. His eyes looked down at a comic book not caring about a new customer walking in. His nose had a sprinkle of freckles on them which distracted her from her annoyance at not being swiftly serviced. Diane almost frowned when he finally looked up and smiled at her.

"Hi, Ma'am," he greeted her.

"Is there somewhere I can get something to eat?"

The kid nodded and Diane looked at the right breast side of his uniform, searching for his name. Tony. He smiled and told her to drive a bit down and she would find a quiet diner on the left side of the road.

She nodded in understanding. "Thanks, Tony."

Diane walked out to her car and followed Tony's instructions, hoping it would not make her get too far off course.

She got to the cabin some minutes past four, having gotten lost on the way up. Her car scrunched over the gravel until it came to rest in front of the cabin. It looked good as new despite the lack of attention to the road leading up to the cabin hadn't been worked on. An unmarked road especially needed someone to continue to keep it cleared for cars. She opened the glove compartment and retrieved the AMT Hardballer semi-automatic pistol she had owned for years. She checked to see it was properly loaded and then she got out.

The place looked different. It was a small place when she'd come all those years ago and yet as she looked at it, she felt it looked larger than life. The wood was shiny—polished. Someone had stayed there recently. The towering cabin in front of her, brought her fresh memories that made her stomach churn. One time when she was ten, she'd run to the stone grounds and then into the woods until the trees stole her away and her father chased after her. The lake was not very far from the house, just on the other side of the trees, it was where they raced to when the day was too hot or when they were bored and wouldn't mind a dip.

She teased her dad about his fish legs because he could swim like an athlete and he taught her to swim in that very lake. She shook her head slightly. She was not there to reminisce. She was here to catch a murderer. He was in there somewhere and she was not doing anything while standing out there. She slowly walked up the porch and then tried the door.

It was locked.

Diane knew that her father wouldn't have installed locks that would be easy to pick so she shot at the locks then she rammed her shoulders on the door and it gave way. It stung but she didn't want to focus on the pain. Once she was inside, she stood still scoping out what's in front of her with her gun pointed up. The sitting room was still the same. Nothing much had changed except the new TV which was not on. The house was clean. It was just how they had found Steven's house. Diane proceeded further inside.

She had forgotten how particular her father was about hygiene. Walking around the sitting room, she could tell someone had been there recently, but there was no sign of anyone being in the house at the moment. She walked to the bedroom her father used and as expected, the bed was made, and the room cleaned. There was a bag on the foot of the bed and there were clothes in it.

"Where the hell are you?" she whispered.

Diane turned the safety on her gun and tucked it in her waistband, walking to the bookshelves. She could remember them reading and then talking about the books they had read. She ran her fingers over the spines and she still got the feeling she got all those years ago. She walked to the living room and sat on one of the couches.

There didn't seem to be anybody in the house, but she realized she had not checked her room. It was different. The bed was bigger and the sheets on it were dark blue. She sat on it and turned to the window. It had a view of trees and nothing more. She had loved this place and now it carried this tainted feeling like she was never here at all.

Diane was about to walk out when she saw something it didn't use to be in the room. It didn't look like paint nor was it any kind of wood she had seen before. She walked to the wall near the bed and pushed the bed a bit until it touched the wall. The other side was hollow, but there was no knob so there should be some kind of hidden key or something. She was about to start looking for it when she remembered that it was just wood.

Diane walked to the kitchen and looked for the ax her father kept around for chopping up firewood. She saw it against the backdoor and took it into the room. She tore at the wood until she had torn open a space she could pass through comfortably. The other side was somewhat dark except the light pouring in from the place she had torn open. She used her hand to touch the right side of the wall on the inside and then the left wall until she found the switch and turned the light. What she saw was so shocking she jumped back and got scraped by jagged parts of the wood she had just bludgeoned.

"Shit!"

Slowly, Diane walked back to the body on the table. It was not the first time she was seeing her father's handiwork, but that time was different. She wondered who this was. The woman's face was stuck in a cry. It was not even a day old. Dry lines of tears were still visible. He had cut her up like he was doing an autopsy and beside her, he had placed the heart and her lungs. She saw the knife and gasped. She would know the knife anywhere and so would Eric. It was a knife from her kitchen, perfectly engraved and highly expensive. How did her father get her knife?

She looked at the woman on the table with her legs and hands spread and her hair spilling over the other side of the table, and there was just one thing on Diane's mind.

It was a question.

"Why?"

Chapter Thirty

Diane looked at the girl and wanted to pull her off the table or cover her with something, anything to show some kind of respect. She didn't know why her voice seemed to have disappeared. Her sobs were hollow, empty. She walked out to her room and bent over the bed. She could not stop seeing the woman and Catherine in her head.

Who was it? Why? Who? Why?

The questions where changing and so were the faces in her head.

Diane could not understand how he had stood in the same room with all the screaming. To brutally murder someone right behind the room she slept in as a child. She was not there, but she could imagine how much terror would be in the woman's eyes as her father tore through her.

Did he smile while she screamed? Did he plug something into her mouth, so he didn't hear her scream? Where did he get her from?

If he had gotten her yesterday, then he did it last night and left only this morning. That would explain the way she seemed fresh. Her father might not be far away. The cuts were still soft. The skin was cold though. The woman was gone—body, mind, and spirit.

She was dead and Diane could not help but wonder if she could have saved this woman by deciding yesterday to come to the cabin.

She realized something; she had not thought about it before. There had been something aside from the knife that was familiar. The clothes she had seen in the bag were hers and what was worse was that the dead woman on the table was wearing her clothes too. She realized immediately what this was. A trap.

She had been set up again. Her father was doing this intentionally. She could not understand why, but it seemed like her father had known she would come to the cabin alone. He had set all this up for her to take the fall for him. Diane looked around, there was nothing to do really. If she called the police, she would go to jail for sure. All the other deaths didn't have any forensic evidence on her, but now if a CSI team came in, they would have enough to throw her under a cell, the knife, the clothes, and she was sure her hair was on the clothes.

She took her knife and walked to the inner room. She was outside when she heard them, the sirens. She ran to her car and dumped the knife in the passenger seat. Now a new bout of questions was unloading in her head. How had they come so fast? Did Eric get the warrant or did her father call them? She reversed the car and sped off until she shot out of the dirt road and into the main road. She turned to her left and saw them coming.

She had to make a decision. She could stay and they would lock her up until things were cleared properly and they would see that she was not the one they should be running after or she could take the other road and run. She knew what her options were, and she made her choice. It was as easy as exhaling so she could live.

She ran.

There was no way Vivian could get her out of this, so there was no other option for her but to run.

It was like in the movies, but it wasn't one. It was real life. She had the adrenaline pump and she had the fear to keep her hands steady on the steering wheel. She could hear sirens blaring behind her. Their blue and red light whirling with the deafening sound. She could tell what was on their mind and knew it wasn't going to hear something she'd like. She could hear the accusations and the hate and the confusion. She was scared. She had never thought she would be in a situation like this, a place where she was either running or rotting in jail.

It was scary. In the movies, the thief would whoop and scream in delight like they were having the time of their life. It was as if they knew what was coming and they loved it still. She felt like the world was going to crash on her at any minute.

Diane took her eyes from the road for a second to look at the knife and then back. She wondered if they were all chasing her or if some had gone to the house. She looked at the rearview mirrors and cursed. They were not far behind and she was not sure she could outrun them. She was not going to stop. After this run, there was no way they were going to believe her or anything Eric said and that was if he was going to defend her after seeing that woman in there with Diane's clothes on.

Fuck. Fuck. Fuck you, dad.

She hated the spot she had found herself into. All she wanted was to honor Catherine's memory. To be the person she hadn't been for her friend when she was alive. What was wrong with that? She was not very religious, but she felt like she should pray.

Glancing at the rearview mirror she had some odd sense of relief they had not started shooting yet. Did they have a plan to get her? Diane didn't know where exactly she was driving to. She had cut off the road and was driving through the woods. She was sure she would end up at a dead-end very soon.

In all probability, she was screwed, and she knew it. She wished she had said her goodbyes properly because she was not sure she would be getting out of this intact. Following the next curve, she realized that it was a wrong turn.

"Shit," she cursed when she saw that there was nothing there, but a cliff.

She had not read the road properly, she had been too scared, too worried. She stopped.

They were behind her now, stopped some yards from her. She could hear them come out and then she heard that voice of Captain Larry. She looked at him through the rearview mirror. He wore black pants, a blue shirt, and a wide grin on his long face.

"Diane, this is where it ends," he said slowly over his bullhorn.

Diane thought of her father. The man she remembered, the man she had grown up loving all day and crying about all night when she thought he was murdered. She thought of Eric how it was so good to run her hands over his rough face in the night while he pretended to be asleep. About Vivian and Catherine, even her mother passed through her mind. It was so good to think about those people—the ones she had until that moment and the ones she had lost years ago. It was interesting how everything cleared out when things were about to end.

"You don't have to do this Diane," Larry said. His voice was careful. He was trying not to show that he didn't care.

Diane chuckled. She wouldn't be stupid enough to think that Larry would feel bad if she took a plunge into the lake belong at this moment. She laughed when she remembered how it was when they worked together when he was not yet a captain. Things happened so fast and you wonder where you were when time moved so fast. She slapped the steering wheel.

"We will check all the evidence and be sure, no one has made any conclusions yet. There wasn't a reason to run." Larry said.

He was trying to bait her. Although a dead criminal was a closed case as much as one behind bars, he would like to have her alive. It was not difficult to understand. He was a man with a very small mind. He didn't see far beyond his gratification. She had noticed it the other time when they worked together. She had seen how his ego floated in front of him that it blinded him. It was why she had disregarded him as much as she could and why he hated her that much. She didn't care though. But now, her life was hinged on him. The universe with its silly sense of humor.

"Look, I promise you'll be fine. Just get out of the car and let us take you in. Please, Diane"

If she had not worked with him before she would have fallen for it. If it had been Eric speaking, she would have believed him, but it was that blockhead and his little empty promises. She hissed and shook her head. She was tired and wanted to get out of this. She wished she could dream herself out of it. She looked at them and saw them as termites ready to encroach on her and eat her alive, and she wondered if they had ever thought that this could be all some kind of mistake.

Diane heard a voice over their radios talking about a body found then she saw officers reach for their guns. She made her decision. It was crazy, it was wild, but it was hers. Just as she had decided to run, she decided to drive and that was what she did. The car roared and as she drove over the cliff, she heard the captain scream.

Chapter Thirty-One

Eric was crying since the captain called. The sun was far gone but its heat lingered. Eric had thrown up twice because he could not stop thinking about how Diane drove off the cliff. He had imagined her dead so many times since he got the news that she drowned. He had thought about it over and over again until it felt like that was the only thing he was seeing.

That was why he had to drive off to collect himself. He sneezed and then tried to use his sleeve to clean his eyes. He needed to call Vivian and tell her the bad news, but he had to accept it himself first. How could he? He had held and kissed that woman, admitting to her that he loved her. He could not believe that it was the same person that was dead at the bottom of the lake. He would need to see for himself for him to believe that. He knew that it would take a miracle.

He blew his nose and then cleaned his hands on his pants and got in the car. His phone was ringing in the passenger seat. He checked and saw it was Captain Larry. He didn't feel like hearing the man's voice. He was not sure why, but he blamed the man. He blamed him just as much as he blamed himself. He could be wrong, but he believed his Captain was the main reason Diane took that option. Who in their right mind would drive over a cliff? Sighing, he picked up the phone.

"Where the fuck are you?"

"I didn't think I was needed, sir."

Eric wanted to say something else. Something that would probably cost him his job. But then how would he be able to help with the case if he was fired?

"Of course, you are needed here, Detective." Larry was angry, but he was biting it down, Eric could hear it in his voice. He didn't like people doing what they felt like.

"Come back, Eric. We are going to get the car from the lake."

Eric groaned. The more they spoke about it, the more it stung. The death made it seem like he had lost almost everything that he had ever had. He felt he had lost every opportunity to be happy and now he was left with nothing.

"Eric, I am sorry, but we have to do this. For her," Larry said in the phone and clicked off. Eric flung the phone at the windshield and banged at the steering like it was the enemy. He could not help it. The anger had poured out so fast and strong. He could not hold it.

For her? For her? What the fuck was he talking about? He could have…argh!

He screamed. If someone had heard him, they would have thought he was dying. They would be right. It was like every cell in his body was overheating and then he was crying again. Pain surged through like it had always been lurking in waiting. Suddenly, he felt spent, exhausted like the weight of the previous days had fallen heavily on him.

His eyes were red, and he felt many years older, but he turned his car around. He may have been cruel and self-centered and simple-minded, but the captain was right. He had to be there when they brought the car out. It was not for himself, but for her. It was the smallest thing he could do and even if it was going to kill him, he would do it.

As he drove, he tried not to cry. He was going to see her one more time and then he would do whatever he could until she got justice.

When he got there it was already dark, but lights were set up and they were already trying to get the car out. He could see the chopper and wondered why they were not done already. Headlights were put on to provide light. There were some people he knew and others he had no idea who they were. He got out of his car and was thankful for the cover of the night. The darkness helped him hide his red and swollen eyes. He stretched, looking at the patrol and private cars.

The captain walked toward him with a tired face. He looked at the man and his first urge were to punch him. That was going to be in the papers soon where Diane would be named and then she would be known as one of the many serial killers in the country.

Social media and bloggers were going to have their Christmas gifts early and the whole country would have one great orgasm over the demise of yet another wicked soul.

He spat.

The captain was close to him and he was raising a hand for a handshake. Eric took it and the captain smiled. It was supposed to be one of those reassuring smiles, but all Eric could see was victory written all over his face. He turned away and looked at the people walking around.

"They just came, they are trying to locate the car and hook it up."

Eric nodded and turned to the left where a couple of officers were looking at them. He sighed; he must have gotten a name for himself. It was sure to happen with the way he had almost broken down in front of them when he got the call and the way he drove off. They would soon start to call him the serial killer's boyfriend. He was that if he walked past them, he'd hear it.

"Don't mind them, Eric," Larry said. He had adjusted his shirt and he folded the sleeves up. He was looking at the chopper.

The wind the chopper had picked up died when it got higher and then the captain and Eric pulled off from the bonnet of the car they were resting on and walked forward. Both expecting something a bit different, but hopeful all the same.

It hit Eric that he had not called Vivian and then he brushed it off. If he was going to call her, he might as well just get all the details and tell her at once. The chopper went higher and the two men ran to the edge of the cliff to see the way the car was lifted from the water and then it hung above it for a while until the chopper went farther up and lifted the car with it until it was floating before them and then it pulled it over to the land.

Eric was the first to run to the car. It was still dripping water. A lot of flashlights were pointed at the car. Eric looked through the driver window and then at the passenger seats.

He turned to the captain. "It's empty!" Eric announced.

"What?" someone behind them asked.

They opened the door and the forensics team started their jobs. The Captain walked away from the car and Eric followed him. He was trying to be patient, but he was tired of holding things bottled up.

"We have to send people in," Eric said. The captain sighed and turned to him.

"I know, Detective."

Then Larry turned away and started walking to where another man was talking through a radio transmitter. Eric nodded and turned away. He had seen the knife the moment he opened the car door and he was sure the forensic guys would soon see it too. Whatever happened, he knew the truth. It was not difficult to see through whatever was going on.

He heard the captain talking to the man who he soon learned oversaw the divers. Eric was agitated. There were so many possibilities now. It was either she was dead, and the water had carried her under, or she had escaped. He wished it would be the latter, but no matter how he thought about it, he could not see her escaping the fall. His eyes drifted closed and he said a prayer for her. When he opened them again, he watched the captain shaking hands with the man, and then he returned to where he was standing.

"They will go look."

"What do you think?" Eric asked.

"I know what you are thinking, Eric. But it is not possible. The car was moving fast and even though she was lucky and didn't hit something on the way down, that was where her luck stopped."

Eric could see that the Captain had a point, but he refused to believe it. Diane was smart.

"I don't think so," Eric said.

The captain put his hands up in surrender and walked away. Eric turned around and put his hand in his pocket only to find it empty. He cursed. His phone was back in his car, probably broken.

He didn't know what had happened, but he was not ready to accept that she was dead. He knew what he was going to tell Vivian.

Diane was not dead, not until they found her body.